THE LAND OF LOST GIRLS

Jessica Milner

For my family, but especially Jenny, who read this first. For my niece Lyla, who wasn't here when I wrote it. For Aahminah, for reminding me. And for Bean, for everything else.

CONTENTS

THE LAND OF LOST GIRLS

The story goes that all children grow up, except one.

But that, dear reader, is simply not true.

There are many lonely children, lost children, who never find their way home, who never get to grow up.

It makes one wonder...where do they go?

1

Carrie, Clare and Columbus make three

No one had told her the house was alive.

Despite this startling discovery, Carrie was starting to like her Aunt Clare's house.

When she first arrived she had rather dramatically thought of it as her grand new prison– at least until school started again in a few months. She had walked up that gravel path on the first day, smelling the dirt and trees around her, foreign and damp and alive, and she had felt their cold strangeness seeping into her skin, as if she would never be warm again. She had put her hand out in front of her, shielding her eyes against the frigid winter sun, fractures of cold sunlight splintering through the gaps of her fingers as she squinted up at the old, Gothic house on the hill. She had imagined plucking it out of the landscape, like a god, and crumbling it to dust in her fist.

But now she felt she had come to an understanding with the house, which she had soon come to realize was an island unto itself. It was a house that switched the heating off when you accidentally spilt tea on the drawing room carpet, that banged pipes all night when you called it a ruin. Carrie might have been afraid if she didn't understand that the house was just temperamental, a little like her. Well, a lot like her. And the house did take care of them. It knew how to run a perfect bath when you were upset, clean itself of hard to reach cobwebs and almost always kept the temperature at the right level when it was in a good mood.

The understanding was this: If she didn't bother it, it didn't bother her.

The house seemed to actually like her Aunt Clare though, who clearly loved it in return. She spoke to it all the time – not with the hurried whispers of the mad, No, Clare spoke to the house in a gentle, respectful way, the way people spoke to Mother Nature, or wild animals.

Every place, Clare said, every house, had a story. It just so happened that part of this houses story was a little more magical than others.

Yes, despite the gloom and everything smelling perpetually of wood and floor polish, though no one actually seemed to do any floor polishing, Carrie was beginning to like it here, even if she didn't feel entirely at home yet.

She hadn't ever really felt at home anywhere. At seventeen, she had already lived in twelve countries and had barely had time to settle in any of them. Her parents were renowned literature professors, and though that might sound perfect to a girl who loved books and stories the way Carrie did but in reality, it was lonely and nomadic, with one sabbatical or teaching post or guest lecture after another. All that left little time to build a life anywhere. And now, they had dumped Carrie in the middle of nowhere with her estranged aunt and that had felt even worse. Of course, she loved her parents, but thinking about them always caused her a deep, visceral ache, hollowness inside her that she thought she might never fill.

There were things here though, that Carrie thought might soothe her in the tender, raw parts of her soul. Settle her, when her heart felt like it was jump-starting in her chest. Things like her and Clare drinking hot chocolate by the fire wearing oversized socks they couldn't walk in. Laughing together till their sides hurt. Sliding along the polished wood floors, the house making sure she never fell. Or things like Clare's cat, Columbus, who was probably about a hundred years old, probably remembered the house being built and whose fur was so haphazard he looked like he'd been put through the washing machine. Things like him, willingly approaching Carrie to go to sleep on her legs at night. This impressed Clare, because according to her Columbus didn't like anyone. Carrie did not tell her that it was probably due to the fact that she ignored him as much as he ignored her. They got along with a system of mutual avoidance, which suited them both.

Carrie liked her Aunt Clare too. In all honesty, she had not expected to – In fact; she had been very determined not to like her at all. But Clare placed a steaming hot cup of coffee in front of her almost every cold crisp morning. You just had to like people who do that.

Clare looked a lot like Carrie's mother – This was hardly surprising, since Clare was Aisling's younger sister. But she was entirely different as well. Yes, she had the same long dark hair, the same strong jaw - But Clare's irrefutable beauty served to make her face open, and kind. Carrie's mother was also very beautiful, but hers was like that of a Greek statue, magnificent, but cold. Especially when compared to the quick, easy smile of her aunt's. Where intelligence was primary and superior in the older sister, it was encouraging and enthusiastic in the other. They were separate countries on the same continent. Their borders travelled parallel to one another, only intersecting at pivotal stop points, like Carrie, or old photos, or drunken squabbles at family weddings.

But the best thing Clare had done – besides opening her home to her teenage niece who she hadn't seen in over a decade – was the library. Every wall was covered by a bookshelf with not a single empty face. There were also, big, inviting, leather armchairs, just waiting for Carrie to sink into. But the library was also messy, and extremely disorganized. At first she'd told Carrie she could sort it all out, as a kind of restoration project. But to Carrie it seemed perfect as it was. She liked not knowing what book her hand was going to land on next.

Carrie ended up spending most of her time in the library. It was like a warm animal den in the middle of the house, a comforting place for her to return to at the end of each day, before trudging through the corridors to her bed. Even though she knew she could not stay here forever, she sometimes tried to figure out how long it would take her to read all the books in this room.

It would take her longer than she could imagine, further into the future than she could see. She couldn't see herself at Clare's age, or her mother's age. She could only see shapes and colours, something possible but not guaranteed. So, she tried to read as many of the books as she could now, just in case. Sorted them out lovingly for hours, even though it made her back ache to sit and reach and push them back into the shelves.

She's doing this duty when she finds the first photograph.

2

Photographs of yesterday

Carrie remembered the day of the photo very clearly.

Sometimes, even in hindsight, it is difficult to pin point exactly the moment your life changed. Change can creep up on you. But Carrie would always know, would always be able to pull up that memory at will. She would always be able to see the library with its dark wood and its stories, and know that somehow it was where her story began too.

That morning she had walked. Walked for a long time, through vast fields and endless space. It was difficult and cold, but the sharpness of her breath and the exercise was exactly what she needed. She wanted to push and push her body until she couldn't any more. To feel every sharp edge of herself.

She stopped in a broad expanse of heather, a sea of sweet purple, and closed her eyes. She felt still, and peaceful. She felt free. Carrie understood then why she had come to love it here, on the moors. There was a timelessness here, and innate wilderness that would never be tamed. Carrie felt that wildness as the wind buffered her. She felt it tangling in her long blonde hair. She opened her arms wide to it with a wide, face aching smile. She felt ageless and clean.

By the time she got back to the house she was mud spattered, breathless and happy. For the first time since arriving a month ago, she was happy without reserve.

Carrie wished she could always stay here, not just for three months more.

She could help Clare fix up the house, which she'd apparently been doing for years. She could do her homework holed up in the library. She could have a real home. Her parents could visit whenever they had free time and she wouldn't have to go anywhere she didn't want to, not ever again.

Carrie felt a twinge of guilt at the idea of abandoning her parents to live with her aunt who she had basically only just met. But, she reasoned, a little petulantly, her parents had abandoned her first.

She shrugged these thoughts off as she reached the back of the house, where Clare kept her modest vegetable garden. Columbus sat cleaning himself and generally being unpleasant on the mismatched jutting stone wall. It was the kind of wall that looked like it might collapse underneath him – its old bricks sticking out like sharp teeth.

"Hello you." She called to him with a grin. Of course, he ignored her and proceeded to disappear into a bush, presumably to go and torment some unsuspecting birds. Carrie shook her head at him and continued inside.

Aunt Clare had been 'fixing the house up' for as long as she'd lived here. As far as Carrie could tell this mostly involved choosing between two identical paint colours, buying various tools that no one really knew the name or purpose of and drinking a lot of tea. But Clare seemed happy enough.

Just then she was in one of the back rooms. Carrie could hear her singing Scarborough fair in a soft, sweet voice.

"Are you going to Scarborough fair? Parsley, sage, rosemary and thyme..."

Carrie followed the sound of her voice, like following a willow-the-wisp. What she saw when she entered the room made her think, just for a moment that she really had stepped into a fever dream, a wash with colour and impossible things.

Clare stood by the back wall. Her hair was escaping her messy bun in long curls and her plaid shirtsleeves were rolled up, revealing green paint spattered arms, like she was growing out of the painting that stretched over the wall in front of her.

And it was a breath taking painting that Clare stood in front of. A mural covering almost the whole wall. Clare stood staring up at it, like she didn't believe she had painted it. Carrie saw little green paw prints littering the floorboards. Maybe Columbus painted it, she thought wryly.

The mural was a forest. Deep green, but somehow a hundred different colours too. It seemed to be bathed in an ethereal light, like it was glowing. It looked like you could step right into it. Carrie could almost smell the trees, the flowers, could almost feel the water droplets on the leaves as she came to stand next to her aunt, mirroring her posture to stare up with her.

"This is amazing Clare." She breathed genuinely.

Clare smiled, self-deprecatingly ducking her head. She crossed her arms and it looked like she was trying to guard herself against something invisible.

"I don't really know where it came from." She said quietly, "A dream, maybe." She sighed. "But it feels so real." She whispered, more to herself than to Carrie. She stared at her magnificent work for a moment more, as if she was trying to decipher something, some secret in its lines.

Then just like that the spell was broken. Clare grinned her mischievous grin and turned to her niece.

"Right then, Carys." She said brightly, a little too brightly, Carrie thought. "Sorry – Carrie." She amended, even though it was exactly the same number of syllables and Carrie didn't actually mind the use of her full name when it was Clare. She was more interested in the fact Clare was clearly unsettled by her own painting.

"Tea, I think." Clare chirped, turning and leaving the room like she couldn't get out of there quick enough.

Caffeinated beverages were Clare's answer to any and all problems.

Carrie was still thinking about it later, as she sat cross-legged on the library floor, her tea growing cold on the floor beside her. She knew this was a strange house. That was an understatement of epic proportions. But why would a burst of emotion frighten Clare so much?

The peaceful mood she had found on her walk was officially shattered.

Carrie sighed, frustrated, and reached up to tie her hair back. Her blonde hair was the only thing she had inherited solely from her father.

As she lifted her arm she knocked her elbow against the bookshelf with a sharp *thwack!*

“Bollocks-” She hissed in pain, cradling her elbow gently.

Just as she did she heard something. Something falling, to be exact. But there was no thud. It was a soft sound, like the scrap of paper.

Carrie ducked her head to peer into the bottom shelf. She groped around, dislodging a few books, until her fingers brushed something other than the leather bound covers, and pulled whatever it was out.

What it was, was a photo.

It was covered in dust, which Carrie carefully wiped off with her shirtsleeve. To Carrie, it looked like an old school photo. Rows of girls in matching white dresses, all bruised knees and gap toothed smiles...

And they were sat in front of the house. This house, hers and Clare's.

This photo had been taken a long time ago, but Clare had never said anything to Carrie about the house being a school. She supposed it was possible she didn't know. But Clare and this house were bound in some indefinable, deep way. She had to have known.

“Are you trying to tell me something?” Carrie asked out loud, raising her eyes to the ceiling. The house elected to ignore her.

Carrie looked at the photo again, and found herself slowly smiling. The girls, none of them older than her by the looks of them, looked happy. It was hard to imagine the house full with that much energy and noise.

One girl in particular caught Carrie's eye. She was sat at the end of the first row, right at the bottom of the frame. She was very pretty, with wide eyes and long dark curls. But it wasn't just that. It was that you could just tell that she was excited, vibrant with it. Not like those stern women you normally saw in old photographs, with too tight collars and sad eyes. The girl looked as if she had been mid laugh, and she was staring out of the photo, like Carrie was somehow part of the joke too. Clare had that ability – to make you feel included without even trying.

If this girl reminded her of Clare, then Carrie was the next girl along. The dark haired girl had her arms around another, like she was hugging her. The other girl could have been far less remarkable than her friend, if it weren't for her little sideways smirk, like she was trying not to laugh at her friend but couldn't help it.

Carrie flipped the photo over to see a long list of names written in elaborate cursive. She skipped to the bottom and found the last two names. The smirking girl was Anna Jones, and the laughing girl with the bright eyes was named Emmeline Scott.

There was no more information on the back of the photo. Carrie experienced a small pang of disappointment, as if she had expected the house to send her a flurry of words to sort through, the way she sorted through the books. It did make her wonder though, make her imagine who might have lived here before Clare, in a way she had not before. The house felt so alive, such like a friend, that she had almost forgotten to make room for the fact it's magic had been experienced by other people before her and Clare.

Somewhere, deep in the bowels of the house, Clare had started singing again.

"Remember me to one who lives there...He once was a true love of mine."

3

Lighthouses

This was a house of secrets.

All houses are alive, in their own way. They tick, and they creak and they breathe. And, most importantly, they are alive with memories.

Like that time you fell on the stairs when you were young and your mother made a fuss of you. The sofa you pulled the stuffing out of and the infinite number of hair ties that went missing, never to return.

All these things and more, all of your days, they live in the bricks, in the wood and the dust.

But this house, of course, was more alive than others. It wasn't memory that infused it with life, but something older, something unknown, some primal magic without a name.

Magic that had shown Carrie an old photograph. Clare had not seemed surprised. She had just let out a deep, sad sigh that seemed so unlike her that Carrie felt a pang of nervousness in her chest.

It had been getting to early evening when Clare had appeared in the library doorway. Carrie didn't know what her aunt had been doing all day, which wasn't that unusual, and she didn't ask, especially after the weirdness of the mural in the morning. For once, Carrie desperately wanted things to stay exactly as they were. And she knew, deeply, that there had been a distinct shift in them that day, and if she pressed any further, everything might very well change.

But she couldn't ignore the photo. She had become somewhat obsessed with it in those few short hours. She could hardly concentrate on anything. She wouldn't be able to settle to anything until she knew what happened to those girls, who they were.

And she was sure the house wanted her to know something, something vital – what with Clare's unearthly painting and finding the photo in quick succession. And when the house spoke, you listened.

So she had shown Clare the photo.

And Clare had shown her the room.

That was what Clare called it. 'The Room', like it was a separate country. It was up a flight of stairs and down towards the far end of the house that no one ever used. Because of this, Carrie expected it to be bare and empty, like all the other undecorated, unused rooms.

Clare had opened the door slowly, reverently, like they were entering a church. Carrie would learn that in one way, they were.

As far as Carrie was aware Clare had never mentioned this room in the month since her arrival. She couldn't have known if she had been up here, but she felt as if she probably hadn't.

But despite this, the room looked lived in. It was similar to the library, if the library was at the homely and inviting stage. Plush browns, warm reds and low lamplight made the room look close and cosy.

It had a lot of bookshelves in the corners and the same plush deep chairs from the library, but it looked...finished. Like it was just waiting for someone to occupy it. It looked too finished, too perfect, without a speck of dust in site. Carrie decided that it was most likely the house keeping it in impossibly pristine condition. Was it for Clare's benefit, or its own?

There was a desk by the window on the far wall with a various stacks of paper and handwritten notes. There was a framed picture on the desk but Carrie didn't quite dare to move anything in order to look at it. It felt like the room was stuck in time. Waiting for someone to resume.

She noticed another table then and couldn't help but move towards it, like she wasn't in control of her own body.

There were even more photo frames, crammed onto the table and crawling up the wall like a flood of faces. They all looked different but felt the same somehow. They were all like the one she'd found – all clearly former residents of the house. There were a few more of the schoolgirls. But there were also pictures featuring a cluster of nuns, a group of soldiers grinning and smoking, and a huddle of young women holding babies or with round swelling bellies. Had all these people really lived in the house? Suddenly Carrie was hit with some overwhelming emotion she couldn't explain. She felt she knew all of these people somehow. She felt connected to them, to the history and life of this house. The house was telling her its story. It was showing her its family.

She felt a deep love for the place that she would never be able to articulate.

She turned to Clare, who had watched her take in the room in silence.

"Please." She said in a whisper, tears pricking her eyes. "Tell me."

Clare had her arms folded tightly around herself, like she was trying to comfort herself. She moved her head like she was trying to compose herself before nodding toward the frame on the desk.

"There's one more photo." She said quietly.

Carrie advanced slowly, picking up the silver frame as gently as possible, like it was a new-born baby, or some kind of holy relic.

The photo in the frame showed Clare, maybe a few years younger, with a man Carrie had never seen before. They were smiling brightly and he had his arm around Clare, who was leaning into him. Carrie could see the house behind them.

The man reminded her a little of her father, strangely enough.

But whilst her father's light colouring made him look pale, his hair quickly greying, this man wasn't like that at all. This was... golden. That was the only way she could describe him. Bright sunlight hair and a wide sincere smile, the face hurting kind of smile that crinkled your eyes and warmed up your soul. His eyes were a sparkling electric blue. Together he and Clare looked like a couple from a fairy tale. Carrie looked up at Clare questioningly.

Clare moved up beside her, their shoulders pressing together.

Carrie was about to ask what happened to him. But it feels wrong somehow. There was a dreadful finality to that question that didn't belong in this room, that did not fit with this man.

She asked instead "Who was he?"

That is right, she felt it as soon as she asked. Someone Clare loved shouldn't have been defined by what took him away. He was a real person, with a life and people who cared about him.

Clare shrugged. It seemed sad and awkward and a little defeated.

"Would it be dramatic to say he was my soulmate? Well dramatic or not, that's who he was. Michael." Her eyes roam the photo and she softens instantly just looking at him.

"He had this great capacity for kindness. More so than anyone I'd ever known. He made it seem effortless, this...empathy. This natural understanding of people. In some ways it was, but not always. I actually asked him about it once, and he said that he desperately wanted to be a good person." she smiled like she still couldn't fathom something as wondrous as his words. Carrie wonders how long she had kept this stored up inside of her and how long she had waited to say it. "He had his moments when he wasn't that great, just like all of us. It wasn't like he was a saint or anything, I knew that. But he believed that if you really wanted to help, to be kind and you kept trying, well, it was the wanting that proved that you were already all of those things."

Carrie considers this for a moment. She very much wants it to be true. She hopes it is.

"He sounds like he was very wise." She said.

Clare let out a small chuckle.

"I suppose so. Well, I mean sometimes he was a bit of an idiot though. He was a man, remember." She nudges Carrie playfully. But then she lifts her hand as if she wants to touch the photo, her long fingers uncurling and shaking, before dropping them again.

"He died, you know." She said simply. "He always said he'd get rid of that stupid bloody motorbike once we, you know, grew up and everything. But he loved it so much I never had the heart to nag him about it. And there was the fact he looked very sexy on it."

If it had been anyone else at any other time these jokes would be in poor taste. A vain attempt to cover up all the morbidity and trauma. And it was in some way, but from Clare it didn't feel like that. Not entirely. Mostly it felt like a kind of permission. Permission to smile at his memory, permission to know him as a person, to know something of the entity that was Michael and Clare. This was a small part of them, a glimpse through the prism.

"But then he got knocked down by a car and that was that." Clare sounds as if she's thought this, felt this, every day. The words are clear and factual like she's been forcing herself to accept them as truth. Trying to make this horrific mess clean. But this was a stain on her life that could never be clean again.

Clare puts her hand on Carrie's shoulder, giving it a reassuring squeeze. Carrie felt a wash of guilt that heated her cheeks. Clare was reassuring her?

"We'd just bought this place."

Seeing Carrie still unable to speak, Clare leads back to the side table with all the other photos. She gently pries the frame out of Carrie's hands. When Carrie looked down she saw with detached feeling that she had red indents in her hands where she had been holding the frame too hard. Clare sets the frame down amongst the others. All of the houses other lost souls.

"It had been many things over the years, this house. And of

course Michael very much wanted a home for us – but he couldn't help wanting to do more. He was wealthy – he had a rich, snobby family that never liked me – or anyone, really – and he always felt very guilty about it. It ate at him, I think. He didn't think he deserved to have so much by accident of birth. It was deep, and hurtful and dark. But it did mean we could pay for the house in full straight away. He left a lot for me – you must have wondered why I don't really have a job."

Carrie had assumed that she simply did something dreadfully uninteresting, like typing business men's memo's, or something seasonal, like competitive ski jumping. Just another thing she hadn't bothered to investigate in the midst of her teenage angst. The guilt prickled under her skin again.

"Michael and I talked about opening the house up again. It was more than we needed, and once we saw what the house had once been we wanted to give the world a place like that. Make it a school again, or a foster home maybe. Some kind of refuge." Clare points to the photos of the schoolgirls. "This house has always attracted misfits. Strays. Lonely people. The outcasts. It's like a lighthouse, guiding people in the night...but...after Michael died...I just..."

She trailed off, finally out of words, out of jokes or stories. She didn't have to finish. When Michael had died she hadn't just lost him, she had lost a future with him. There had been dreams. There had been days never lived, children never born, arguments never erupted, stories never told.

Carrie didn't know why she didn't remember this. It had only been five years ago. She doesn't say anything though. She felt ignorant and stupid. She had never even thought to ask how Clare had come to be here by herself. She had felt as if Clare had always been here, a tree with her roots in this house. But she had a past just like anyone else. Carrie felt ashamed of herself. But it was often very hard to think of older people that way. It's easy to forget that people like your parents had lives before you got here. It frightened her. The idea that she could go on not knowing things like this about the people she loved. That there would be a time when she could no longer ask. She was sure there was a lot of small stuff too, that she'd never think to ask until it was too late.

“I'm sorry.” She whispers.

She isn't just saying it to Clare, but to Michael as well. To all the people in the pictures behind him. To the lonely people she would never know. To the house, for its losses.

She doesn't know if Clare heard her, but somehow that's OK. When she looks up at her Clare is smiling.

“You remind me of him sometimes.” she says. She doesn't sound sad now. She sounds more like her usual self. She had a natural gentility that coloured all of her words with intimacy and intention. “You're very understanding.”

Carrie let out a rather undignified snort, which rather removed some of the sobriety from the situation.

“I don't feel very understanding.” she sighed. “In fact I feel the opposite.”

Clare shrugs nonchalantly, like she knows the truth and that's enough. “I'm pretty sure you were twelve years old and living in china when this happened, so I wouldn't feel too bad about not knowing. I think your parents probably didn't want to upset you over someone you didn't even know.” Carrie thought Clare was the understanding one when she said this. “I think you're accepting.” Clare carries on. “Not many people would want to live with their aunt in a haunted house.”

“I didn't always.” Carrie admits. Clare made you feel like you could tell her all your secrets. She also feels that Clare is being much too kind to her.

“Well you might never have if you'd have known what they used to call this place. Lost girl house. They used to say the girls here told stories. Not just the usual – if you can call a living house usual – no. They had stories about...dreams, I guess. Visions. Some of them were convinced that the house allowed them to travel. They said they would leave for months, but when the sun rose on the night they would be in their bed like no time had passed."

Carrie raised her eyebrows. In this house she didn't think there was anything that was impossible. More just improbable. It was still quite strange though. She smiled then, despite herself. Maybe Clare was right. She had accepted the stories without batting an eye. She thinks it is because when you were in this house, you felt part of another world.

4

Following stars

That night as she lay in the darkness, Carrie clutched at her chest, trying to remove the empty ache inside her. It was not an unfamiliar feeling. It would come and go, leaving and staying for days at a time. She could never reason it out. You might have called it depression, or loneliness – but Carrie couldn't name it, or wouldn't, as if to name it was to bring it out into the daylight for everyone to see.

It was at once feeling hollow and too full up with an emotion she couldn't fully comprehend, even though it lived inside her like an animal. Sometimes she felt like her mind and body was a map of a country she didn't speak the language of, here be dragons written on the edges.

That night she felt very alone, and very ashamed of herself. She felt ashamed for not knowing the things that made up the house and her Aunt's occupation of it. For not understanding there was a secret adult world going on around her that she had shied away from. For retreating into her own hurts, her own problems, and closing her eyes against everything else.

There was a rational part of her mind that told her there wasn't anything to be ashamed of. That repeated Clare's words, that she was not to know the secrets of another person's life. But this was the kind of sadness that wasn't rational. It was the kind that just was. The kind that just lay dormant inside of you until it erupted without warning.

Perhaps erupted was the wrong word, at least for Carrie. For her it had crept up on her without her noticing, seeping into her like dirty water.

Her feet began to itch with the need to move. She needed to stop thinking. To do something. To prove she could choose and cope and control. She wants to be made up entirely of sharp edges, cutting through the haze of her mind, the tiredness. She wants to be a focused, fixed point.

She thinks about continuing to sort the library. But as she walks, she drifts past it, as if her feet have a will of their own. The house is taking extra care not to creak so Clare does not wake up.

Carrie eventually finds herself blinking back into reality in front of Clare's painting, in the back room. Impossibly, it looked in the moonlight as it too had changed with the sunset just like the world outside. Like Clare had not painted a forest in the day but at night. Carrie thought she could even see stars that had not been there this afternoon.

Clare, she thinks. What kind of world was it that would let someone like that suffer even a moment of sadness? And why had she never even thought about what had brought her aunt here? Did she assume that Clare and this house only existed for her, when she could see them? If a tree falls in a forest when no one is around, Carrie thinks wryly. Clare had forgiven her. She had been a child. She still was a child, even if she didn't always feel like one. But it meant she had a child's ignorance, without the innocence. She felt young and ancient at once. She felt like she didn't know who she was, like her heart was a tangled labyrinth she would never find the centre of.

She felt that everyone she knew was very far away from her. That she didn't really know any of them at all.

Who had she been kidding? She had imagined an idyll, a sanctuary. But she was not Clare's child, or her sister. And what would she even do, if she did stay here?

As always when she thought of the future it was nothing but a terrifying blankness. Carrie had no plan, and whilst she had things that she loved she did not feel that she had any particular skill set, unless reading a lot of books counted. Carrie was always afraid she would spend her whole life feeling adrift.

The sounds from outside seemed to fill up the room. She felt like she was stood in a real forest, the sounds were so loud, so real. A deep thrum of life in miniature, sneaking in, humming and building and surrounding her, deafening her.

She looked at the painting properly once more. It must have been the night, or the house or her own heart, but she swayed toward the painting like she was drunk. She was hearing it. Hearing the sounds of another place at once strange and hauntingly familiar. She raised her hand, leaving it hovering in the air, not quite being able to touch the wall. She feels like she's in a trance and her fingers are impossibly steady, like they know something she doesn't.

"Are you going to Scarborough fair?"

Carrie whipped around, her heart swooping with fear, Clare's voice whispering around her like a breeze, like a ghost, but she was alone. Clare's voice drifted past her impossibly, a sigh with no origin.

She turned back to the painting, the jolt making her lose her balance, pitching her forward like a ship in a storm, till her hands reached out in one last effort to steady herself, and she reached out to the painting, to the forest, to the world in the wall.

Everything seemed to slip into slow motion.

The planet fell from orbit, or maybe it was her, falling upwards like a discarded angel being recalled, a shooting star in reverse. She floated, adrift from the whole world for one brief single moment.

And then she was plunged into darkness, it was wrapping

around her like a blanket, her stomach swooping and her hair a bright halo all around her. She felt as if she was underwater and she could not find the surface. She was being torn from the world, bodily, physically pulled from existence.

She didn't know what was happening -

She was being sucked into a black hole -

She was disappearing-

She was -

The curtain fell.

Silence reigned...and then nothing.

5

A mighty creature

Carrie had always hated the phrase 'not like other girls'.

She thought that she probably was a lot like other girls.

She could be vain; despite the fact she couldn't be bothered doing her hair every day. She watched a lot of television. She had bigger thighs than she wanted but was too lazy to exercise. And she was also trying to be alright with that, though it was more easily said than done. She found painting her nails therapeutic. She listened to pop music and pretended she didn't sometimes. She took selfies, and wore leggings as trousers. All in all, with the exception of her nomadic existence and the whole staying in a magical house thing, she thought she was pretty normal.

She also felt she had a certain understanding of women, she felt that she both knew them and loved them. There was a secret world that existed, an unspoken code that existed between women that had always pulled at her. Ever since she was a child, she had never cared for princes. She had never been hyper aware of men, the way she was with women. She had never dreamed of men, the way she had with women. She had always sought to impress, to imitate, and to be at one with other girls, to be around them. It was not something new to her, and it was more than just feeling comfortable with other women. It was something deeper than that. She remembered watching actresses on the telly when she was little, no understanding why she cared about them so much more than the men that dominated the screens. Now she knew.

She'd been young when she'd heard someone at school call her a lesbian. She hadn't heard the word before, and she'd asked her parents when she'd got home what it meant. After a brief flash of surprise, her mother told her. It sounded familiar. It sounded right. The girl at school that had hurled the word across the playground had sounded so angry when she'd said it. Like it was a bad word, a dirty thing to be. But her mother had told her otherwise. Carrie thought about the word, nurtured it in secret for years afterwards. When she'd come back to her parents at fifteen and told them she was a lesbian, they had accepted it. Truthfully she knew her mother had guessed a long time ago. She'd been lucky with her parents, in that respect. Some people didn't get the acceptance she got. Even if she hated the being dragged around the world, she'd loved them for loving her just the same.

She thought of girls as magical. Not in the way the house was magical, though some of them probably were. But in the way that you thought about the summer before high school or having your first champagne. Girls were starbursts of imagination, of inspiration, of infinite kindness. They were caverns of gold, they were mermaids, they were impossible and the realest things Carrie had ever known. They were a dance, a song, a poem. They were dirty nails and blood. They were screaming at everything and laughing at nothing. Protective as mothers and cruel as animals. Bird bones and wishes.

As far as Carrie was concerned, to be a girl was to be a mighty creature.

And so, in short, she did not believe herself any more likely than any other girl to experience the extraordinary. Living house aside, of course.

But still.

Something extraordinary had happened.

Correction: was still happening.

Carrie blinked back to life.

The first thing she noticed was stars high above her. Twisting and burning very far away. She remembered the thing about stars, that they were already dead. That you were looking into the past when you looked into the sky.

Then she noticed the smell of wet earth, heady, cloying, and sweet.

She breathed in, trying to centre herself again – too afraid to move.

She was staring at the stars through the thick foliage of trees. She could see leaves of all different colours – burnt reds and pumpkin orange, yellows and greens. She remembers the barren branches of the trees that surrounded Clare's house. Where was she, where such life persisted against seasons, against time?

She tried moving experimentally. One tiny muscle at a time, one joint, one thought. Fingers first, then toes. Then, with herculean effort she spread her fingers out into the dirt, feeling it under her nails.

She pushed herself up, dreading what world she would see when she did.

She felt so scared she was almost calm. Past the point of fear, of urgency, into a strange numbness that meant she was able to take her surroundings in slowly, methodically.

She could have tried to explain it away. She might have said she had simply sleepwalked, out of the house, a somnambulist lost in the wilderness of her dreams. But she knew better.

Because she recognized this place. She was in Clare's painting. In the forest on the wall. She would know it anywhere. It was like no other.

Everything looked deeper and richer, like you were seeing colours for the first time, even at night. There was a hum, an energy, it was alive in the way the house was alive. Strange and old and amazing and real, real, real. More real than anything before.

That was when the noises began. At first they were far away, an echo from a far off time. Something that could have been a shout, or maybe just the wind. Carrie swallowed down her nervousness. She had no idea where she was or what she should do. Her heart started beating so fast it made her chest hurt.

People say that in extreme situations your instincts take over. Your panic turns to adrenaline inside you, to power, makes you able to do incredible things. Plumb the depths of yourself and find things you never thought yourself capable of.

But the noises were getting nearer and nothing was happening. No hidden superpowers emerging. She was frozen. She wished for a moment like none of this was really happening to her, screwing her eyes shut. Like Clare would be placing coffee in front of her any moment, telling her to wake up. It felt like if she stayed totally still, things might just carry on around her.

But life of course does not work that way, even if we wish it could. The things in the dark still find us. Thoughts still race and hearts keep beating. Time tick tocks.

And then the sounds were in the trees right next to her, her eyes flew open, and she understood somehow, intrinsically and on some deep level just what it was she had just fallen into.

She heard a shrill shriek that made her jump. It cut through the night, sharp and blinding.

The sounds Carrie was hearing were battle cries.

She had fallen into a war.

People shot out of the trees like stray bullets, ricocheting and screaming. One minute there was stillness, then the world was on fire.

Everything was glowing now, figures holding flaming torches – throwing them, burning anything, smoke rising up into the sky. Figures on either side of the forest, either side of her, hurtled toward each other. It was pandemonium, it was the picture of hell, and she was right in the middle of it.

Some kind of long dormant warning system shivered to life

inside her. She moved, finally, she moved. She managed to scramble back just an arrow flew past the place she'd been sat. She let out an involuntary gasp. She didn't want to die. She didn't want to die. She could die.

And then someone finally noticed her. Panting and ferocious, emerging from nowhere like a predator, there was a girl. One girl, stood still in a storm, a lighthouse in the dark.

This is it, Carrie thought. You're going to die, she told herself. You fell through a magical wall, proceeded to be completely useless and now *you are going to die.*

Clare, she thinks. She's going to lose you like she lost Michael. And your parents would never see you again.

She feels steel coat her heart at that. She couldn't let that happen. She would beg for her life in the dirt if it meant she got to keep it.

"Please." she manages. Her voice sounds breathy, ragged and desperate.

She wants to say more but nothing else comes out. There is nothing else. Just a word, a wish, to encompass everything. All the love and waning of her life went into that word.

And it worked.

Sometimes one word, the right word, is enough.

Something in her voice, her sincere eyes, made the girl stood in front of her give her a quick, stiff nod. A soldier's nod.

For one wild moment, looking up at her, Carrie thought – it's her. It's the girl from the photo in the library. The girl with the witch bright eyes.

Fire continued to flicker in the trees around them, torches and falling flames. Sparks like fireflies all around them. When the girl whips around at the sound of a fireball bursting on the ground, Carrie sees that of course it wasn't the girl from the photo. Emmeline Scott was probably ancient and forgotten by now.

This girl looked a lot like her though. In the light of the

destruction all around them, Carrie can see the same wild curls piled on her head like a lion's mane. Her hair was lighter though a rich chestnut colour that looked almost golden in the fire light. Her eyes were wide, wary and watchful and very pale blue.

"Fall back!" the girl yells. Carrie doesn't know who she's shouting to. Unknown watchers in the trees. "Fall back!"

"Come on." She yells to Carrie, sticking out her hand.

Carrie looks at it as if it is a foreign object.

"Do you want to live or not, Blondie?" The girl snaps.

Carrie looks at the fire, the smoke and heat stinging her eyes. Then she looks up at the girl, the lines on her palms covered in sweat and dirt. But its real and she's there and Carrie has no choice. She wants to fall into someone, someone who will make it safe again. She wants to give herself over to someone else, let them take care of her. She is more tired than she has ever been. She wants...to survive.

She takes the girls hand.

And they run.

They run into the dark of the forest, away from the fire, away from the danger. They run as fast as birds in the sky. They run until their lungs are knives in their chests. Carrie cannot keep going, and yet she does. She does not stop. She doesn't know where she's going but she lets the other girl pull her a long, into the unknown, down the rabbit hole, away, away, further and further into the nothing of the night. The only thing Carrie is sure of is the bark of trees under one hand and the warmth of the girl's fingers in the other.

6

Welcome to neverland bitch!

Carrie felt like her life was made up of darkness and waking, over and over, like the moon emerging every night.

Because she doesn't remember stopping. She wakes up, but she doesn't remember going to sleep.

She is covered by huge furs, like a medieval queen. She realizes she is in a rather spacious tent. She doesn't want to reach out and touch it though, because she has a strong suspicion it is made of something other than plastic. A part of her wants to burrow under these furs, like a small animal, hibernate until she emerged again at home. But she knows she can't. The only way to figure anything out would be to go outside. She can see sunlight streaming through the small gap of the tent entrance. It feels like a long time since she had seen the sun. She doesn't know if she's ready. She sighs, looking to the side, willing there to be a cup of Clare's coffee beside her.

There is not. Clare is not here to reassure her. Her mother was not here to tell her to get a hold of herself. Her father was not here to tell her some information from a book that would help her. The house was not here to protect her. She would have to find a way to protect herself. To somehow armour herself. But she had to know against what.

So she pushed off the covers and crawled, like a curious creature, to the tent flap. Lifting it slowly for her eyes to adjust, she stepped forward, into the light.

The camp was situated in a small clearing. It bordered the edge of the forest and a beach that stretched out away from them into infinite blue. It was a decent size, with several tents ranging in sizes and colours all in a circle, except one that stuck out like an odd thumb, several metres away from the others. The tent Carrie had been in was tall and made of dark brown leather. It was the biggest of all of them.

She tugged nervously at the shorts of her pyjamas as she crept through the camp, which seemed to be just stirring to life. A fire burned in a pit in the centre, cooking something that she assumed was meat. She did not ask what kind. In the distance she saw a figure wading in the sea with a net, catching fish. There were footprints in the sand all around her, evidence of life, of work and progress. It was a calm place, especially compared to the raging fire of the night she had fallen into.

“Sit down.” A voice said. It was not a bark or a shout, but it was an order.

Carrie recognized the voice as belonging to the girl who had saved her.

She's emerged from god knows where – the trees, it seemed, like she'd been a part of them, and stepped into the clearing; sitting down at the fire to tend to her food. She turned the pieces of meat over before apparently being satisfied and taking proceeding to expertly remove them from the spits. She offered one to Carrie.

“You wanna sit down and eat? Nothings gonna change, no matter how long you stand there looking at it.” The girl said dryly.

Carrie jerked awkwardly into a sitting position opposite her. She watched her in silence as the girl shoved the meat at her again. Carrie took it in both hands. It was too hot but she didn't complain. And she wasn't all that hungry. She felt too confused to be hungry and she had slept too long. She was very familiar with jet lag and that's how she felt now. Like time didn't mean the same thing as it had.

"Are you going to tell me what's happening?" Carrie asked simply. She was too tired for politeness. She bit into the unknown meat into her hand. It was good, whatever it was.

"Why don't you start?" The girl said. "Tell me how you got here."

"I don't know how I bloody got here," Carrie pointed out impatiently "That's why I asked what's going on."

The girl looked up at her intently. "Tell...me. Just...start at the beginning. It'll make it easier if you go through it." She explained slowly, quietly. Like she was trying to press knowledge into Carrie, like she was waiting for her to tell her something she already knew.

"I'm living with my aunt. Clare. This house that she lives in..." Carrie looked up from her food. The girl was no longer staring at her food, she was looking at her, listening to her. Unwavering and attentive. It encouraged Carrie. "Well it's sort of...alive. Anyway, I think it showed her this place. She painted it. She's very good at painting, she used to sometimes illustrate children's books, but that was before -"

"I don't care about that." the girl interrupted, forcing Carrie to swallow the rest of her sentence.

I care, Carrie wanted to say. It was something Clare had told her offhandedly, naturally. It was part of her, of her past, the one Carrie had known so little about. It was important.

She does not say this. She can feel herself getting defensive, and this girl might be the only thing that could get her home. She was also most likely the only thing standing between Carrie and imminent demise. So she decided it was probably best to not antagonize her. She seemed the antagonistic sort.

"Anyway." Carrie said curtly. "So she painted this forest. And I couldn't sleep, so I went to have a look at it and, well, I guess one minute I was by the painting and then I was here." Carrie finishes. She feels a little embarrassed at her vague explanation, but in fairness she had no idea how she had got here or why. She shifted uncomfortably at the silence.

The girl nods, thinking for a moment. "How did you feel? When you were looking at the painting?"

It makes Carrie feel even more awkward. They both knew the answer before the question was asked, that was obvious. She didn't like that. It made her feel wary, these people knowing more about her than she did, more about what was happening to her. Like she's part of something she didn't choose. She wanted some kind of control, but she felt it all slipping away from her second by second as she struggled to grasp what was happening.

So she does the only thing she can think to do. She lifts her chin haughtily and narrows her eyes.

"Sad." she said. "I felt sad."

It seemed the best choice of word for something she had never described. It was a very small word with a very big meaning. It encompassed a trauma with no name, all in just three letters.

The girl nods like this had been what she'd been expecting.

"Do you know what ley lines are?" She asked suddenly. Her voice is too steady as she waits for the answer.

Carrie did know what ley lines were. She had read a lot, remember. But she did not answer. She just stared petulantly, waiting for the girl to soliloquise since she clearly enjoyed being enigmatic and knowledgeable.

"There are currents of power that run all over this world, and through many others. Supernatural, some call them, or just energy, energy from the land and the old gods and nature. No one really knows for sure. But sometimes these lines intersect, like lines on a map. When this happens they create...hotspots. You would feel the power of the lines standing anywhere on them, if you were that way inclined, but on these hotspots that power is vastly increased."

The girl's voice was low and calm. It was soothing, like a bard of old telling tall tales. Her mouth curved around her vowels, the undercurrent of some accent or other. She sounds like she's done this speech a hundred times, but Carrie felt herself being drawn in anyway.

"For millions of years, people have felt the power of these places. They build there, they worship, they dance, they sacrifice. They harness that power. It has always been so."

And Carrie could see it, all of it. She heard the clang of swords, she heard the chanting of women, she smelled blood and incense. She sees that old world, and the new one. They were one in the same.

"Like Stonehenge?" Carrie asked.

The girl smiles a very small smile. "Like Stonehenge." She agrees. "This island is also one of those places, where the lines intersect, or so we believe; this story has been passed down by many who no longer live, you understand – we may never know if that's the truth. By the sounds of it, your house is on one of these hotspots too. Chances are they are connected by the same ley line."

Carrie took all of this in slowly, going over the words one at a time. Understanding, Clare had called her. She tried to be so now, and decided that that explanation made sense, especially since she had so far found no other to rival it. And she supposed this had been pieced together over some time, through many people's experiences

"But you don't actually know that's true. You don't understand the magic. And that doesn't explain why I'm here."

The girl's hard expression – which seemed to be her default face – softened again. Only this time she did not smile. This time she looked almost pitying. "No, but it isn't untrue either. We don't actually know how the magic works. But it's a theory, at least, which is better than nothing. We could just be experiencing magic with no explanation other than it's magic, but that doesn't make me feel any better about it."

"Well, what's your theory about the house then?" Carrie shrugged.

"The house felt your pain." She said seriously. "And so the island did too...That's how he finds you." Her voice was so strained and she looked so sorry all of a sudden, and Carrie came to understand in that moment that pain was in the blood of this place. It was in this girl, and it was in every grain of sand.

"Who's he?" she asked, not sure she even wanted to know any more.

The girl looked around, like a wary cat seeing something in the shadows, as if whoever he was might be listening to every word they were saying. It sent a shiver right down Carrie's spine.

"Pan." The girl whispered, like she could summon him just by speaking his name. "He's the boy that rules this island."

A boy, of course.

"He used to be kinder. Never truly kind, but kinder at least. This place was safe once, apparently. A dream place for all children to escape to. But he has ruled here too long."

"So what is it now?" Carrie was almost afraid to speak; the atmosphere had changed. It felt like they were telling ghost stories, not speaking of a child.

"You saw for yourself last night. This place is his game. We are all his toys, his pawns, his soldiers for his pretending. Only it isn't pretending, is it? It's fighting. Real fighting. This place...it's nothing but a graveyard."

Carrie felt a squeeze on her heart. Something that had once been needed, something good, had become tainted. She feels the quiet surrounding her, only the waves breaking and the crackling fire to make noise, and she wants to close her eyes and will herself away from here. She wants to feel safe. She wants to make herself still as a statue so nothing could touch her. But when she opens her eyes nothing has changed. The sun hurts her eyes.

"How do I get home?" she asked, her voice a little desperate. "I'm grateful for the food and the rest, and, like, the lifesaving and everything but I think I would really like to go home now." she nods, and she can feel panic rising in her chest and tears pricking her eyes.

"Honey, you ain't going home."

Carrie jumps as a pile of pungent fish is thrown onto the sand in front of her.

She lifts her hand to her nose and looks up to see another girl who's approach she had not even noticed. It was obviously the girl she had seen fishing in the distance when she'd first got up.

"This is Willow. She's American." The girl sat at the fire said, as if this explained her entire personality.

Willow was very American, the southern American that Carrie assumed only existed in cowboy films. She was also very tall. Her red mane of hair was plaited down her shoulder, matted to her with sea salt and sweat. Her skin was tinged pink from the sun, but otherwise she would have been very pale. She looked like what Carrie had imagined an amazon would look like, fierce and hearty and strong shouldered.

"Excuse me. Ma'am. Miss..." She shifted a little uncomfortably at the glares coming her way before grinning mischievously as if she were a child caught being naughty.

"What do you mean?" Carrie insisted. "I need to go home; I can't just stay here. I have a life." She cried. She was growing hysterical, her cheeks warming, but she didn't care.

"No one leaves. The only way you get to go is when the good lord takes you." Willow explained, like it was perfectly obvious. "Though some may say God has forsaken this place entirely."

"Welcome to Neverland, Blondie." the other girl finished, tearing off a hunk of meat with her teeth.

"My name is not Blondie." Carrie snapped, jumping up and beginning to pace.

She couldn't stay here, wherever here was, to die by herself.

"I can't believe this." She whispered, more to herself than either of the girls who were now staring at her like this was something they had seen a hundred times before.

"I'm not staying here. I am not going to stay here just to die in pyjamas with the cast of bloody Brigadoon!"

And with that she began to stamp away, toward the wood, toward anywhere but there. If she had been thinking clearly she might have thought it was stupid, since she didn't know where she was, but she wasn't thinking clearly. She was thinking like a girl whose entire life had been ripped away.

"Blondie, where are you going?"

Carrie ignored the calls, until she reached a large palm tree, which she then proceeded to kick. A lot. It felt good. She wanted to smash the entire world. She wanted to scream. Her breathing came out rough and painful until she couldn't bare it anymore, and she pressed her forehead against the rough bark of the tree.

"What's your name?"

The girl from the fire is beside her. Carrie can feel her standing close to her. The voice is gentle, like she's coaxing a wounded animal. In some ways she was.

"Carrie." She closed her eyes. Simple questions, things that she knew, that was what she could focus on, as she raked her nails into the tree. "Carys. It's welsh. It means love." she breathes this out, this thing she had known for as long as she could remember, and it calms her, just a little bit. She liked her name. She liked that it was chosen for her by people that cared about her. She liked that it belonged to her and it felt familiar on her tongue in an unfamiliar place. It placed her. It meant Carys Fairchild came back into being.

"Your parents must have loved you very much, to name you something so special."

Carrie had never thought about it that way. She lifts her head from the bark to squint at the girl, silhouetted against the sun.

"My name is Perdita." The girl smiled gently. "Perdy." She amends.

Carrie relaxes a little more, standing up properly. Perdy softens, seeing that she is no longer having a break down and harming the environment.

"Are you...are you being serious?" She asked quietly.

Perdita frowns, ready to be offended. "Yes, I'm very serious, thank you. I didn't actually choose it, you know." She shrugs her shoulders, setting her jaw.

Carrie shook her head. She puts up her hand until Perdy narrows her eyes at it. "It's not that. It's a lovely name. It's just, well the meaning. It's funny, when you think about it. Sorry, I have a thing about name meanings."

Perdy raised her eyebrows expectantly.

"Lost." Carrie supplied quickly, sensing growing impatience. "Perdita means lost."

She gestured around, to the island that belonged nowhere, to dream place, the place of lost things.

And they laughed.

Carrie couldn't help it. It burst out of her, half hysterical. It was all just so absurd and it came out of her in deep breaths and stomach twists instead of screams.

And then Perdy laughed too, shaking her head disbelieving.

Sometimes, that's all you can do. They laughed loudly and suddenly and inelegantly, and it felt better than any sleep, any food. It felt like it relaxed every muscle in their bodies, it felt warm and real and good. It was the first thing to do so in what felt like a very long time.

7

Clare

Clare had never been jealous of her sister growing up. Aisling, she had always felt, was simply beautiful in other ways. Intelligent in other ways. Whilst Clare drew, Aisling read. Whilst Clare sang, Aisling played the music, and so on. They did not compare themselves to one another. They simply complimented each other in the innocent way of children that knew no other way to be. Their roots were tangled and grown against each other. They were sisters and they loved one another in an intrinsic way that needed no explaining.

And they managed to stay that way for a long time. Until they didn't.

Aisling had always been a serious child and she had grown into a serious adult. One that you had to learn to navigate carefully. She was not cold, as some people thought, but rather a little melancholic, a little too introverted that it came across as mean spirited to people who did not know her the way Clare knew her. She was very smart, very much a devoted academic, but it made her a little awkward with other people. She would rather keep quiet than say anything wrong. Even when they were younger, Clare had not been this way. Clare was always saying the wrong thing at the wrong time, and everyone had always forgiven her for it. Aisling never took the same sort of risks.

Aisling eventually went off to a stuffy university full of equally awkward academics with a penchant for questionable knit wear, when she was eighteen and Clare was fifteen, leaving her sister behind for a world of old books.

She returned briefly to deal with the death of their parents, who had been involved in a sailing accident somewhere off the gulf coast. Clare had had no idea of what to do and no real desire to do it. She felt things very deeply, and she did not yet know how to be practical in the face of disaster. And so Aisling had returned and been a rock and an angel and mother all at once. She had sorted everything and asked for nothing from Clare. Clare would feel guilty about this eventually, but at the time she felt nothing but an overpowering sense of relief.

But still, through no real fault of her own, Aisling missed a solid chunk of Clare's most important years. There had been a flurry of plans and being solid and practical, then Aisling had flown away from her again.

Clare didn't hold this against her. She had had to lay the foundations of who she was, of the rest of her life, without her older sister's guidance and often she felt she hadn't managed as well as she thought. She'd muddled through her later teen years without her parents and without her sisters practical, sensible nature to comfort her and pressure her. And so, by the time Aisling graduated and finally did come back properly, it was really too late for her to do any kind of damage control. Clare was twenty, and therefore convinced she was fully formed. Like Athena springing from Zeus's head already covered in armour. She was wrong, of course, but she did not want to concede and so took next to no advice whatsoever from Aisling.

Clare had dropped out of art school in a fit of rebellion, declaring that it stifled her creativity and that the old still life teacher with the seventies shirts used to stare at her in class. To Aisling, who had always felt safer within the structure and confines of the school environment than anywhere else, this might as well have been the end of Clare's life. But Clare was a wild bird who was not to be caged. She wanted her freedom, even the freedom to make her own mistakes.

Clare realized soon that she did not truly know who she was.

She knew who she wanted to be however, and she spent a long time trying to become whoever that was before she realized that wasn't really how things worked.

By this time Aisling had met Jude Fairchild.

Jude was timid in a sweet kind of way, with boyish blonde hair and pink cheeks. He was unfailingly polite, or at least he tried to be, but his innate and crippling shyness caused him to come across as twitchy and a little too eager to please. Clare's sense of humour meant she leant towards teasing, but to do that to Jude would have been like kicking a puppy. Also, he always asked about her art and very clearly adored her sister.

Clare thought it was nice that the two had found each other, despite their equally quiet natures and the fact they both preferred books over people. It was around this time that Clare decided she did not think any such a connection would happen for her, despite the fact men fancied her a lot. It never went deeper than them staring at her on the bus.

She just didn't like the odds. There were a lot of people in the world, after all, and she decided it was very unlikely she was going to bump into her soul mate as she pondered different types of beans in the frozen food isle.

So she tried to be at peace with herself. She tried to settle into her skin, into the shape of her bones, into the body that contained her. She tried to ignore Aisling's good natured nagging.

She learnt to create. She used some of the money her parents had left her to travel. She felt foreign winds brush her skin. She got a tattoo she regretted and had a pregnancy scare after a brief but torrid affair with an Italian sculptor – this still beat her only other sexual encounter before that time, which was losing her virginity in art school to the unfortunately named Ralph, who listened to a lot of Oasis and wouldn't stop talking about capitalism. She slept on mattresses that lived on hard wood floors. She danced and drank and she met a lot of people – though she never found it easy to stay in touch with them. They were fleeting and more precious for it. She did have relationships, but they were the kind always meant to end. They were the relationships forged in sun and wine, ripened just right until they weren't. She learnt to open herself up to people, breaking open her ribcage to build homes for the pain of scruff bearded men with large hands and sad eyes. Until the wind came and blew them away again, like autumn leaves.

In short, she became OK with being Clare Collingwood, since as she crept through her twenties she began to realize she was never going to be anyone else.

Not long after they had met, Aisling and Jude had gotten married and had a baby girl.

Carys Elizabeth Fairchild came into being with fluffy white hair and a terrifyingly loud set of lungs, and they all loved her very dearly. Since her grandparents had passed away some years before her parents were determined to provide everything for her. This included opportunities most people never had, like travelling and experiencing other cultures, even if she couldn't actually appreciate them.

Clare had eventually returned to the mother land, and they had passed like ships in the night, leaving as she came, and so she only saw baby Carys a few times a year. This meant that she always felt a little sad, a little lost, since every time she saw her Carys had gotten a little bigger, a little more of a real tiny person, a little more of a stranger.

She had wanted to be the epitome of the cool aunt. She wanted her niece to have someone to turn to. But that was difficult when she was on the other side of the world. But Jude emailed her when he remembered, telling her little things like Carys finding a starfish on the beach or that she didn't like strawberry ice cream. Aisling took care of the practical side, sending pictures of a round faced toddler with unruly hair and a huge grin. She made sure Clare knew birthday presents to prevent clashes and when they would be in the same place next.

And so this was how they lived. Like the ebb of the tide, coming and going, back and forth, almost but not quite. And within a blink, ten years had gone by.

Clare had got a job illustrating some rather well known children's books. She got free copies when they were finished and always sent them off to Carys with handwritten notes and doodles inside. She would later wonder what became of all these. Perhaps the evidence was to be found in Carys' love of reading. Clare hoped so.

This was seven years ago now. Carys' tenth year in the world saw someone else enter Clare's world too. Seven years ago. A lifetime ago. He brought with him deep and irrevocable change.

Because that was the year Clare Collingwood finally met Michael Bellbrook.

8

Tip one: don't die

They say the definition of madness is doing the same thing over and over again, and expecting a different result. If so, Carrie must have been losing her mind. But sometimes it was all you could do. Sometimes, just waking up, again and again, was an achievement in itself.

Carrie pushed herself out of sleep, out of bed, every morning, because she didn't know how to do anything else. For five seconds every morning, the seconds before she opened her eyes, she would will herself to be back in the house. Considering how she had got here, it didn't seem to be such a strange strategy. She willed with everything in her, the strength of it straining against her skin.

But when she opened her eyes, she was not home. She could hear the sea, that constant reminder, and she would force herself not to cry.

It had been three days until the other girls go fed up with her doing nothing but "staring forlornly at the sea like something out of a Victorian poem" - Perdita's words, of course – and had taken her in hand.

Up until that point, Perdy had allowed Carrie to continue sleeping in her tent. Carrie had felt guilty, but she accepted the shelter as she was far too tired to object. But on the third day Perdy unceremoniously barged back in, the sun behind her like a halo, and declared she was going to help set Carrie up with her own tent. She pulled the covers from her and dragged her up, ignoring Carrie's hands batting her away.

As Perdy walked with her, helping her pick out a spot – which mostly consisted of thinking of contrived reasons as to why all of Carrie's choices weren't right – she explained a few things. First and most importantly, she explained 'the pile' – which to Carrie sounded like some kind of unfortunate haemorrhoid problem.

The pile was located in a safe, snug spot at the tree line of their camp. The girls hadn't been very imaginative with their title, since it was exactly what its name suggested. Not a haemorrhoid problem, of course. It was a pile of objects. The flotsam and jetsam of life.

People, it turned out, were not the only things to appear on this island. In fact new people had become something of a rarity. They had no real way of telling how much time had truly passed, since no one ever aged. They were caught in a hourglass that never ran out. But it had been a long time, since they had been so surprised to hear that it was actually 2016 back in the real world.

What had taken prominence were random objects from the real world, caught up in the islands unshakeable gravity. It didn't seem to have a lot of power for people sized hauls, but random useless objects? That it could do. Sometimes the girls found useful things – knives mostly, which according to the gospel of Perdy might as well have been holy relics. But there were also some less useful things. Like a lot of plastic bags, an old tire and for some reason, a broken microwave. What surprised Carrie is that none of the girls seemed to know what the microwave was for. She couldn't help but keep wondering how long they had been here, but she didn't dare to ask. She didn't need to hear that they had been here for a hundred years. She needed to believe she still has a chance of getting home, despite all evidence to the contrary.

That was why all of that morning sat sharp and mean within her. She knew Perdy was trying to help her – but picking a spot, building somewhere of her own – it felt like she was giving in and giving up. She had not even been there a week. She didn't plan on being there for a week. She should have been trying to get home, maybe finding the spot she had landed in, in the jungle forest (Carrie did not know the difference between a jungle and a rainforest). But she didn't know the first place to start, and it became clear that neither did any of the others.

One thing she was grateful for though was jeans. Thank god for whoever invented jeans. As they picked around the pile, Perdy presented her with an old, muddy worn down pair that looked a little too big for her and that no one else had wanted. She'd said if Carrie wanted them she would have to learn to clean them herself, and Carrie nodded, willing, as she hugged them to her chest gratefully. She'd been living in her pyjamas for days. Perdy nodded awkwardly at her over enthusiastic thanks. She didn't understand how precious something so familiar was just then.

Or maybe she did.

Perdy had been very kind to Carrie in those first few days. But it was a standoffish, practical kind of kindness that Carrie became increasingly grateful for. Perdy forced her to open her eyes. She arose some challenge within her, some spark. She would wordlessly help her with carrying water from the small collection buckets they kept by the tents. She would nudge her awake when she fell asleep at the campfire. Perdy always seemed very aware, like she was entirely in tune with the world around her, whilst Carrie was in a haze.

And Carrie soon became grateful for the forced activity. As much as she didn't want to commit to any kind of life here, as the days wore on and she gathered that no one knew how to get her home, the tasks Perdy set her became the only things she had to focus on. It made her feel almost real again. It distracted her. Even the frustration of when she could not take to something warmed her. And soon days turned into a week, and then another.

Carrie saw her pale skin tanning in the sun. She became used to the constant hum of the sea, the chirping of birds, the breeze cooling her when she lifted her matted hair from her neck. And she became used to her new friends, though they were something of an odd bunch.

Perdy was the clear leader. To Carrie she was also an impossible mass of contradictions. She would show emotions – pity, or trust or kindness, and soon as she did so she would shut down once more like she regretted it. She would insist she didn't want to hear about Carrie's life before, but she would save extra water for her after nights she'd spent crying about it, and never say a word about it. When Carrie would try to thank her she would become snappish and irritable – but there would be a slight blush on her cheeks that made Carrie smile to herself. Perdy was awkward, unable to handle displays of emotion. Carrie could be like that too sometimes, though she was always trying not to be. She tried to think of what Clare would do – Clare who was always eager and warm. She approached Perdy carefully, tried to sense her changes the way Clare would. Like approaching a wild animal. Carrie and Perdy slowly orbited one another in ever decreasing circles. They were hands and clear bell voices and driftwood in the same sea.

Willow was a loud, tactless and very loyal lieutenant. She did most of the hunting and the fishing – which she promised to teach Carrie, though seemed to regret it once she realized she'd underestimated how bad Carrie actually was at such a task. But if she was going to be stranded here, Carrie wanted to be useful, even if it did mean getting called and "Idjit" a lot. But Willow was funny and hearty, and it was hard to be offended by such unaffected honesty.

There were two other girls in their little tribe – they had found a way to exist with one another despite conflicting personalities, the way families did. And the girl with the most conflicting personality was most definitely Peaches.

Carrie had first spotted Peaches skulking about like a demon as she sat on a rock some ways up the beach with Perdy, who was attempting to teach her the correct way of holding a knife.

Staring at Peaches' steady progress into the camp, Carrie had been a little unnerved at the tiny creature, who moved as quick and efficiently as an animal.

She had a rat's nest tangle of dirty blonde hair and large wild cat eyes, wary and suspicious of everything around her. She was covered in dirt, despite the fact they lived within spitting distance of the sea. She looked like a rag doll and ate like a starving wild thing. And she did not speak.

They had named her Peaches because that was how they had found her. The girls had a steady supply of ripe, juicy peaches all year round, thanks to Pan controlling the seasons and causing a never ending summer. They had one favourite peach tree that grew by a waterfall just a few leagues into the jungle, and it was under this tree they had first found the girl Peaches. Tiny and swaddled in rags, she was curled up asleep, more bones than girl. She had hissed and bit at them like a wildcat when she'd woken up. Nala, who was the most diplomatic of all the girls, had lured her with the peaches that grew above her head. And since that day she had scurried among them, creeping and stalking, a silent sentinel that guarded her sisters. She'd never said a word but she seemed to understand the others well enough, though she preferred to live on the edges of things, in the trees, amongst the birds and the high safe places.

Nala was a doughy brown skinned girl with dimples in her round cheeks and rather unruly black eyebrows.

Like Peaches, she preferred to exist on the periphery, though for entirely different reasons. Whilst Peaches craved the safety of trees Nala simply craved peace.

Carrie first met her as she grunted and swore over a particularly large branch in the jungle.

She was trying to find appropriate tent building materials and Perdy kept announcing whatever she came back with to be wrong. She wouldn't have a shelter until she built her tent and to do that she had to know which trees would withstand weather changes, which would bend and brake. But she basically knew nothing about nature, which is what she was currently surrounded by. She was trying to heave the branch back with her to the beach, but she wasn't nearly strong enough. She was feeling very useless and very depressed, which wasn't necessarily new for her, but she didn't usually do it surrounded by this many bloody trees.

That was when Nala appeared, desert skinned and smiling, a rare vision. Her heavy black hair was covered with a make shift hijab, made from what looked like an old white shirt – but she'd sewn delicate pink threads into beautiful patterns, and decorated it with real wild flowers. It made her look like a wood nymph, or a fairy.

She laughed and beckoned and Carrie followed. Nala was sweetness itself, she was encouraging and kind as she talked to Carrie, showing her the henna patterns on her chubby hands.

Nala could make with those hands. She created. She sewed up their clothes, she made capes and furs from the animal skins Willow brought her. It was difficult for her, since she had to tan them herself so that she could handle them. She used an inky residue found in some of the trees. It was the same thing she used for the henna that wrapped around her hands like beautiful golden vines. Nala also was the best at stitching wounds. But she ducked her head as she mentioned this, and Carrie pushed the conversation on to something more pleasant. She told Nala about Clare's art and Nala seemed to relish asking questions about materials and what she preferred to draw. Carrie couldn't answer everything, but she tried. And in return Nala let her talk freely. She was very easy to talk to, even from a brief meeting. She had an innocent, childish face but her eyes had a spark in them. It spoke of cleverness, and she listened with patience to everything Carrie had to say. About her fears of staying here, about how she missed her family, about how Perdy was a slave driver and how her back hurt from hauling logs about all day. Nala smiled and continued painting Carrie's hands in intricate weaving patterns.

Nala heard her insecurities about her usefulness and nodded. She told her to keep trying, and the gentleness in her voice reminded Carrie of Clare. Of her telling her Michael's words, that it was the trying that was important. She locked that away within her heart, to nourish her and keep her.

And Nala gave her something else too. They were talking about cleaning – Perdy had done a favour for some of the mermaids a long time ago and in return they had given her a soft purple white powder that allowed clothes to be thoroughly cleaned with just the smallest pinch. It meant they could wash their rags – no tampons on an island run by little boys, apparently – and they would be as clean as if they had never been used. Whilst Carrie was sure she had a few weeks before she would have to put her personal store to use, she was glad of the information. And then Nala had said something that changed everything.

"You do have something important within you." She'd said, and Carrie had glowered at her disbelieving. "Some of the most important things. You have stories."

Carrie blinked. "Stories?"

"Yes." Nala said, as if it were obvious. "You have stories no one else on this island has heard. I assume they did not just stop making books because a few children disappeared?" She smiled her impish little smile. "And television?"

"Yes. We still have books and television." Carrie muttered.

"Well then. You say you like to read, tell us some stories, next time we all eat together. And there, you have one use."

Just one, Carrie thinks, would have to be enough for now.

And so Carrie became their bard. On the rare nights when all five of them gathered to eat at the same time – Nala and Peaches sticking mostly to fruit, unless they had fish or vegetables – well, mostly the one vegetable – palm heart, which was something they dug out of the palm trees that kind of looked like a leek –

Carrie would tell her stories.

She told them about a sad little boy who found out he was a wizard. She told them about a girl who fought in terrifying war games in order to save her sister – and smiled when Willow began wearing her hair in the same kind of braid that Carrie had described. Willow would hound her for the next part of the story until she gave in and told her whilst they were trying to fish the next day, which meant they barely caught anything since they were both so distracted.

It wasn't a lot, Carrie knew, but it was something. And she enjoyed it. It gave her something to think about and it reminded her of home.

Not the house, with Clare, but home with her parents, whose various houses had always been cluttered with books. For the first time in a long time, Carrie began to miss her parents exactly how they were. She began to regret being so angry with them. Maybe if she had appreciated them more, she might not have ended up here. She missed her mother's sensible nature, logical and efficient and good at problem solving. She missed her father's enthusiastic rants about crumbling old text books and the way he lost himself in his work. She wanted those things now.

Carrie had managed, with a little help from Perdy and absolutely none from Willow, to build herself a rather crude little tent. It was smaller than the others and a little pathetic looking, but it was hers. And she was secretly rather proud of it. She was also getting quite good at getting the palm heart out of the trees, and she could do her own laundry. She was beginning to feel quite self-sufficient, in truth, at least more so than she had ever been before.

She had been there for about three weeks, if her tally scratched into the boulder by her tent was correct. And she was beginning to settle. It was hard to remember that she did not belong here. It was hard to remember the battle that had raged when she had arrived.

But Perdy had scars on her shoulder and Willow had bad dreams. Underneath the sun and slowness there was some tension building once more within them. Carrie knew Pan would not go much longer without something else happening. That was how it worked here. They lived as well as they could, they existed and worked and made, until he got bored and waged another war. Then all the factions of the island would fight again, and hope they didn't die.

Carrie had not met anyone else other than the girls she now lived with. But there were mermaids somewhere – the ones who had given them their cleaning crystals. Carrie had wanted to cry at knowing mermaids existed. Then there were fairies, which were Pan's creatures, along with his lost boys.

There were the native people of this land, who lived far off in the mountains and who even Pan seemed a little respectful of. They were apparently ruled by a very beautiful princess who was a cruel as she was lovely. Her name was Wild Rose, and she took no part in Pan's games, but was a woman of little mercy. Carrie supposed you would have to be, to rule here.

And then, last but not least, there was the ones at the bottom of the barrel. The pirates. Carrie had sometimes thought she had seen a ship, a dark shape far off on the horizon, but she had never been sure and it had never come any closer. Whilst the lost girls of this tribe fought Pan on land, the pirates fought him on the seas. Everyone knew Pan hated the pirates and their captain most. But as long as he was hating them, he wasn't hating the girls quite so much. Who knew how long that would last.

Carrie was attempting to fish by herself. She had made little progress in her lessons with Willow, but she had made her own spear with Perdy and she thought she might as well practice.

It wasn't going well.

She had rolled up the ends of her baggy, but thankfully now clean, jeans, but it didn't matter since she'd already fallen over twice and got salt water in her eyes.

She stopped and stretched her aching back just as a shadow fell over her. Lifting a hand to shield her eyes, she saw Perdy stood smiling at her, the waves just hitting her bare feet.

"Come to laugh at how terrible I am?" Carrie called.

Perdy smirked and waded to meet her without hesitation, Moses parting the sea. When she stood next to her she motioned for the spear, which Carrie thrust at her.

Perdy tested it's weight for just a moment before spinning it in her hands, round and round her body, graceful as a dancer. It didn't touch the water once.

"Show off." Carrie muttered, though she was actually quite impressed.

Perdy shrugged as if it were nothing and held the spear back out for Carrie to take – but as her hands wrapped around it once more, Perdy shook her head.

"You're holding it wrong." she sighed. "Here, it'll be easier if I show you."

She stepped right up next to Carrie, gently taking the spear from her hands. The waves nudged them against each other, their bodies curving against one another just for a single earth shattering second each time. She moved behind Carrie, very close to her, and Carrie stood as still as she could as Perdy wrapped her arms around her. She could feel her soft breath on her shoulder, Perdy's wild curls stroking her skin. She wanted to sink back into her, her warmth.

Perdy pressed her fingers against Carrie's, moving them and placing them where they needed to be and Carrie felt a pleasant stirring inside of her, filling up her hollow places, sending heat coursing through her. She closed her eyes as they moved their arms, motion and skill and a beautiful girl stood right next to her. She couldn't focus when she could feel Perdy's lips brush her ear.

And all too soon, Perdy let go, continents shifted, stars fell, and they stood apart once more. Carrie blinked against the sun, and when she opened her eyes she started – there was a fish flapping about on the end of her spear.

"Ah!" She cried, swinging it around wildly without thinking, causing Perdy to jump out the way. "I did it!"

Perdy beamed as Carrie laughed loudly. Carrie didn't think she'd seen her smile like that before. It had her inexplicably happy. It was nice. She wanted to be that for someone. She might not be good at the day to day motions of this life just yet, but she could do that. She could make a sad girl smile. Her face looked even nicer when she smiled. Carrie saw that it made her nose crinkle, and she thought it was the best thing she'd ever seen.

"What do I do with it?" She asked wildly.

Perdy rolled her eyes, but not unkindly. They waded back to the beach together, and as Carrie watched Perdy in front of her, she knew that developing a crush on someone whilst you were trapped on a desert island probably was not the best idea. Especially since she wanted to get home as soon as possible and she was not that insta love girl. At least, she didn't think she was. She didn't think she would be giddy over the first girl that paid attention to her. But her life was full of surprises, it seemed.

And she couldn't help wishing, just for a moment, that this might last.

She tried to push the thought from her, since she knew it would not. Soon there would come drums from the dark horizon, soon there would be thunder in the mountains and the howls of fighting.

But right then, she let herself feel peace, since the first night she had arrived here, and she followed Perdy back to the safety of shore.

9

Firewood and fruit

Carrie and Perdy had embarked on one of their treks through the jungle for firewood and fruit.

Carrie was always struck at how beautiful it was. The greenest green leaves, the tallest trees. The sweetest smelling flowers all existed here. Pan was a cruel leader, but he had created parts of this. She didn't know which. It was strange to think of this cruelty belonging to the same person who had created all this beauty. But wasn't that the way the world went? Cruelty and beauty existing hand in hand, like good and bad? And there was a perfection to this place that spoke of delicate, focused precision. That had all the hallmarks of Pan's tunnel vision outlook on life.

Perdy stalked through the jungle, quiet as a cat on the hunt, spear at the ready. Always a warrior. Carrie wished she could be that effortlessly graceful, but she was still a little clumsy. She enjoyed walking and had done a lot of it, especially back at Clare's house. But this wasn't exercise, this wasn't that sweet sharpness of real hard work. This was careful and controlled and very, very slow. Carrie was none of those things when it came to walking. She wanted to experience what was around her, organically and truthfully, not through the eyes of a hunter.

So she stomped after Perdy and ignored her glares, just as Perdy ignored her inane chatter. This made Carrie want to talk even more. To fill the silence, though she didn't need to – their silences were never awkward – and so try and bring anything out from Perdy, any word, any clue. Until she met anyone else on this island, Carrie wasn't going to have anyone else to ask about getting home. She was also determined to remind them all that this was not her home. She needed to remind herself of that too, sometimes.

"I was thinking," Carrie breathed heavily. "Maybe some of the other tribes know how to get home. Maybe that's why Pan wants you all to fight. To distract you or something."

"Or maybe he's a child with psychotic tendencies." Perdy snapped back.

"Well I thought that if we got to him, or to some of the others, then I could ask them and I might be able to go home." Carrie ignored her and kept talking, tugging absent-mindedly at leaves as she passed them. "I mean, you got all those cleaning things from the mermaids because you helped them, right? So I could do something and get information in return."

She had been rambling, talking out loud more than to Perdy who she knew didn't want to hear it. "I don't know what I can do to help them, but I'm sure I'll think of something."

Perdy threw her arm down, her spear hanging limp at her side, her shoulders sagging. She stopped in her tracks and turned back to face Carrie, who had to stop suddenly to avoid walking into her.

"What exactly are you going to do for them? Tell them a story?" She threw her arms out wide.

Carrie blushed and shook her head. "I'm just saying-"

"Well don't!" Perdy cried. "Please just don't, because there is no way to get home. If you were going to get home, you would be there by now. That's how it works here! Pan isn't sending you back. He's never sending any of us back any more, so just stop talking about it. You're just making it harder for yourself!"

She breathed heavily when she'd finished, somewhere between angry and pleading. Carrie, for her part, was mostly just angry.

"Don't talk to me like that." She seethed. "I'm here and I'm trying.

I know I'm not as useful as all of you, but I'm doing my best. But that doesn't mean I'm just going to give up on going home. If he won't send me back, then I'll just have to god damn make him."

The low, volatile anger in her voice surprised her. But it was real. She saw Perdy shake her head but she didn't care. She had been letting herself get distracted, but she wouldn't now. She was sick of waiting for something bad to happen. She was sick of waiting for someone to tell her something. She had to take her fate in hand. She had to grab her fate by the hair and tell it to hurry the fuck up and do something useful. She had to try. She had to keep trying. If she didn't do that, she didn't have anything. She wasn't one of these girls, not yet, and she wasn't home. She belonged nowhere just then, and so she knew she had to carve out her place in the world. She had to do it all herself. She had to make them listen, make them help her. Somehow she would find a way.

But she didn't want to argue with Perdy, even if she was being a total idiot. She was still her friend.

"I know you've been here a long time. All of you, I mean. I know it's frightening to think about. But it wouldn't just be me leaving this place." Carrie licked her lips with nervousness, trying to think of how to phrase the thing she had been thinking about for days on end. "You could come too." She finishes, looking up at Perdy from underneath her eyelashes.

Perdy sags in defeat. "There is no home for us to go back to. Not anymore."

She turns back to start again. Carrie feels it like a blow to the chest.

Perdy inclines her head, not quite looking back. Then, wordlessly, she reaches her hand back. "Come on, Blondie. We've got things to do, haven't we?"

Carrie stands still for a moment, staring at the outstretched hand. This wasn't over, not by a long shot. But Perdy was offering an olive branch.

But Carrie stamped past her and carried on walking. She wasn't a child. She didn't need Perdy to tell her what to do. She already had parents for that. As she stamped her cheeks flushed with pain, annoyance, and sadness. She had to believe she could find someone to tell her the way home. The other girls kept their weapons sharp, ready for when the time came, for when Pan's terror emerged once more. She would keep her own weapons sharp, her mind, her heart and her hope.

They trekked for a long time, in the heat, humid and sticky and close and when they were done, they lay on the sand by the sea like driftwood washed up on the shore. Bleached and bones. Dead tired.

Carrie wanted to sleep and to forget. When she looked out at the water she thought about her parents staring at oceans together, her grandparents sinking to the bottom. She thought about Clare painting every shade of blue in the waves. She thought about Perdy seeing no world beyond it, and it made her terribly sad.

Without thinking, she shifted her arm to press it all the way down the length of Perdy's. She could feel the tiny hairs and bumps on her skin. She was soft and real, despite everything. Despite the arguments and the stubbornness and the armour she never took off. Right then she was an eighteen-year-old girl with sand in her hair, closing her eyes against the sun. Carrie thinks about what she'd said in the jungle. She'd wanted to give Perdy hope, but she had none. She was too scared to hope. Carrie didn't know how to tell her that she at least had to try.

They lay like that for a long time without saying anything.

"Did you ever learn Latin at school?" Perdy asks suddenly.

The sun had gone down and the world had become nothing but a cool breeze.

Carrie is momentarily taken aback. Perdy had always expressed utter disinterest in anything that had come before the island. Carrie had let her keep her secrets. She knew what it was to keep your past locked up inside of you, and she wasn't going to push Perdy. If she'd wanted her to know, she'd tell her. Perdy had been better at listening to Carrie, though not a lot. Whenever Carrie talked about her family, Perdy always changed the subject after a few minutes. If Carrie hadn't known better she would have sworn she looked sad. Carrie sighed. It was exhausting, trying to work someone out through layers of secrets. One minute Perdy was wrapping her arms around her in the sea and the next she was telling her to abandon all hope in the rudest way possible. It wasn't fair and it wasn't what she wanted. She thought these feelings were supposed to be easy, but they were proving to be anything but.

But Carrie smiles hesitantly at Perdy's question. "No. You had to be really good at French or Spanish or whatever before you could take Latin." she shrugs.

Perdy's brow creases slightly. Carrie recognized this face by now. The V between her brows, which meant she was thinking. The lines of this girl were becoming achingly familiar to her, like she had sketched her in her mind over and over.

"But you've lived everywhere. Aren't you meant to be good at languages?"

"Yes. I was very good at French since I did it in almost every school. But I never stayed long enough to progress. It was just easier to dump me in the French class."

Carrie kicked her feet self-consciously. It no longer bothered her the way it had for a long time. Increasingly, she had found since being here so long, things that had gnawed at her for years of her life were becoming more and more dulled, more and more things that had simply happened to her, things whose sharp teeth were falling out. She could feel parts of herself stitching back together again. A little mismatched, a few missed stitches, a few rough seams, but there.

But these things still bothered other people. She could tell from Perdy's sad smile, and it embarrassed her.

"Anyway." Perdy continued. Carrie was grateful for it.

Perdy was a good comrade in a storm. She knew how to carry on without ignoring what you'd said. She was a sailor who knew how to navigate. It had surprised Carrie to learn this, since she seemed too distant from her own emotions most of the time. Carrie thinks she is bringing this up for her benefit. It's an apology for before. It's a glimpse into something she had not allowed. It is a trust fall.

"I went to an all-girls catholic school." Perdy said, and Carrie noted that she didn't say when she'd done this. "We practically dreamt in Latin. The nuns saw to that, the old witches."

Then she sat up perfectly straight, pushing her chest out. She was trying to look matronly, but only succeeded in pushing her breasts out toward Carrie who felt a familiar swoop of desire in her navel. It was hard to look matronly whilst you were wearing black leather trousers. Carrie was distracted by the dips and hollows of her collarbones. The mountains and passages that made up her body.

"You girls!" Perdy boomed in a stuffy voice. She was attempting Irish, but it came off more as some bizarre mix of Indian and American. "The good lord did not sacrifice his only son so that you could be lazy lollygaggers! I despair of you all! You will learn your Latin verbs or so help me!" she wagged a threatening finger in Carrie's face, who slapped it away whilst she laughed.

This was new in Perdy. This was a lightness, this was a sunbeam fracturing out through her ribs and guard fences.

"Impressions are not your forte." Carrie grinned.

"How would you know? You never met Sister Bernadette – you should count yourself lucky for that."

"I take it you have a point?" Carrie asked dryly.

"Yes." Perdy settled back down. "Well as much as I hated the fire breather who taught it, I actually rather liked Latin." She became a little more serious again, a little more wistful. Full of the kind of nostalgia and remembering that was both good and bad. "I always thought it rather poetic. Learning a dead language."

Perdy stared straight ahead, out at the sea, like she was staring out into the past, the one she carried inside her and never spoke of.

"I felt as if we carried something ancient with us." She said. "Now I know those people are long dead and it made no difference, but at the time I felt, rather grandiosely, that it was some kind of homage. A remembrance, to speak a language of the past. To say to those people 'you were real. You existed. We haven't forgotten about you.'"

The words had a cruel irony to them. The sharpness slips between Carrie's ribs. She feels her heart strain. She wants to say all that to Perdy. She wants to tell she is more solid, more present, than anyone she'd ever known. But she bites her tongue.

"Transmarinus." Perdy whispers, the French in her voice makes it sound like a prayer, dark and low, makes it sound like a summons.

"What?"

Perdy is still staring ahead, like Prospero staring at a storm.

"That's Latin." She explains. "It means from beyond the sea." Finally, she turned to look at Carrie. "That's you." She adds, leaning toward her slightly. "A girl from beyond the sea. From very far away...from another time."

Perdy ducked her head and Carrie was sure she heard her voice quaver, just for a moment. She couldn't have said why. All she knew is that the whole of her wanted to envelope Perdy, wanted to be a balm, to soothe her, to lick her wounds. She wants to care for her and protect her, she wants it with a deepness that frightened her.

"I'm sorry about what I said." Perdy says quietly. "But I really was trying to help. It's been a long time since anyone here talked about getting home."

Perdy sighed deeply and shifted uncomfortably. Carrie was almost tempted to let her squirm. But Perdy was being honest with her, she was letting her guard down, and Carrie of all people knew how difficult that was.

“It's alright.” even if you're wrong, is what she didn't say.

Perdy's words echo back to her – no home to go back to.

God. How terrifying that must be – to think this place was the only one left to you. To not know what awaited you, if you could leave. She had not thought about that. But that didn't mean Carrie couldn't leave. If she could find a way to talk to some of the other tribes, then she had to do it. But she couldn't do it alone – she didn't know how to survive by herself yet, and she didn't even know how to find any of the other creatures that lived here. She had to be patient. She had to wait for someone to show her the way.

That opportunity would come sooner than she thought.

10

Lavender

When progress finally came, it smelled like lavender.

"I want to show you something." Perdy had said. They had dragged their tired bodies from the sand, as the sun set around them. Carrie followed Perdy into the forest. She was not scared, not for a single second. They existed then in a twilight entirely for them and no one else.

She took no notice of Willow's knowing grin. She gave a glance to the trees, seeing Peaches' feet disappearing into the foliage. Nala was humming somewhere, amongst the flowers. Perdy carried on walking, like nothing could reach her.

It was the most relaxed her shoulders had ever been. It was the slowest, the heaviest she'd ever walked. Her uncanny awareness meant that Carrie wasn't afraid to let her guard down either. She had no doubt that Perdy could switch back to being a soldier in an instant if she needed to. But right now, she didn't. She walked into the purple light all around them, steady and sure.

Carrie counted the steps they took away from the camp. It was the furthest out she had been. She had reached over a thousand by the time they stopped. It was easy, since they had no conversation to distract them. Somehow, they didn't need it. It was comfortable and safe, that silence.

But when they did stop...Carrie could only focus on what was in front of her.

A heady sea of purple, full and luscious and dark. Sweet and sharp scent filling her senses. She took a slow step toward it and Perdy hung back, watching her. She feels the way she did when she had seen Clare's painting. Reverent. Humble.

She smiled at the lavender brushed her fingertips and turned back to Perdy. Perdy was smiling too, but at her, not the lavender.

"This place is very special to me." Perdy stated. "He...doesn't know about it. As far as I'm aware."

Carrie whipped back round to stare at the lavender field. It was more of a meadow, really. A small grove of purple, untouched and undisturbed. She couldn't believe it. Pan didn't know about this? They always spoke of him like he was the one that decided when the sun would set. But this? This beautiful, secret place...was a crime. It was something he had not sanctioned...it was heresy. And she loved it.

And she understood, without being told, why Perdy had brought her here.

This was her secret place. This was her heart. This was...her hope. Hope she refused to admit to, out in the forest, at the camp. But it was there!

This was a reminder that Pan might hunt them, and kill them and hurt them, her and all of her sisters...but there was a small part, deep down, that he could never touch. No matter how many times Perdy insisted there was nowhere else to go, there was one tiny piece of determination that could never be extinguished.

And just like that, the familiar feeling of guilt returned to Carrie. She always felt guilty about something. She was exhausted with it. But she couldn't help it.

When she had set out here with Perdy she had counted. She had planned. She was using her to find her way through this jungle. She was using her to see if she could find anyone else on this island before the next war game, to find a way home. And Perdy was trusting her with a secret that could hurt them all.

She didn't want to feel guilty about wanting to go home. She didn't want to feel bad for missing her family. But Perdy...Perdy was important too. She was desperately important. And despite her bravado, she was delicate. Carrie knew that she had to consider that one day...she would have to hurt her. She would have to start really being selfish. She would have to choose between this tribe, and the one she had left behind.

She breathed in deeply. The lavender made her feel hazy. The day of the choice...was not today. Not right now.

Carrie opened her arms wide until she felt Perdy coming to stand beside her.

"The wind is just right." Perdy said. "Come further in."

They stood in the middle of the field, facing one another, holding hands. There was no ceremony. It felt natural. And then there was one small moment where nothing happened. Then the wind changed, and everything began to move.

It picked up the flower petals, lavender and blossoms from the surrounding trees and sent them flying all around them, tangling in their hair, landing on their noses. They laughed loudly, not letting go of each other's hands, lifting their faces to the whirlwind around them.

Perdy looked at her seriously as the wind finally died down.

"I don't know what it is about you." She shook her head. "I've never shown this place to anyone. Never believed there was anything but this...This fight. Then you fall from the sky and suddenly..." she shook her head. "Your stories, your optimism. You make me want to believe again."

Carrie ducked her head. She didn't know what to say. She didn't know if she should say anything, or if it would ruin everything. She didn't want to push too far too soon. Perdy sensed her hesitancy and smiled a little.

"Don't say anything. Not yet. I just thought I should tell you about...where I'm going."

Where she was going may not be the same place that Carrie

planned on going. No matter what, even if Perdy agreed to come home with her, they would still have to find out how. And that meant finding a way around this island, and Pan. Perdy might be feeling feelings for the first time in a bazillion years, but that didn't mean she was ready to die for them.

"Come on." Carrie smiled. "I wanna see the rest of this island." she nodded upwards, up toward a small mountain not too far away. She had to get her bearings. Being here with Perdy, hearing those words, cracked open a place in her heart that had never been opened before. But there were other people already in there. Other people who already needed her. Things she needed to do for herself. If she was ever going to get home, she had to stop trying to be kind, like Clare. She saw now that she would have to learn to be brutal. It scared her, the fact she was ready to do just that. Some dark, primitive thing swimming about inside of her started to come to the surface.

Perdy nodded. "Alright. Let's go see the island."

The top of the mountain was still. There was a light breeze, but not the wind Carrie had expected. It meant she could stand still, really look, really remember what she was seeing.

What she saw was that never land was very beautiful, and much bigger than their tiny patch of beach.

She saw a plume of blue grey smoke, high in the rocks and the mountains where the native people lived, secret and far away. Lush green trees blanketed the earth as far as she could see.

The tallest, widest tree, the giant tree, the one in the distance covered in golden flowers and apples that rested in its leaves – this she knew was the realm of the fairies. They lived in the surrounding trees and hollows too, but that great tree was their high place, their heart, their church and senate.

But the most beautiful part of the island – that belonged to the mermaids. A lagoon, purple pink and blue, heavy with white lilies and fleshy pink starfish. Pregnant with life and beauty, their pools and hair and bodies were littered with shimmering pearls, like tiny white teeth. Salt and sand and seaweed, the mermaids were fiercely lovely and very deadly, as all beautiful things were, in some small way.

The small pool she saw glinting through the foliage was their home during the calm seasons. They stayed there to birth their children, until the children were old enough to brave the seas themselves.

Pan's hideout was nowhere to be seen. The fairies, his loyal subjects, had taught him to disguise his home well. It was somewhere out there though, a wolf blinking out of the trees. It was a chilling thought, amongst the beauty of the place.

And there was of course the pirate ship, off in the distance. It seemed to endlessly circle the island, unable to leave, waiting, waiting forever for the war to start again.

Last but not least, Carrie smiled to see, was their tiny patch of beach. She saw Perdy's impressive dark leather tent like a beacon. She remembers the furs that covered the inside, warm and inviting and familiar. Then there was Willow's tent, simple and effective, and Carrie's ramshackle tent, a much smaller spot off to the side. Peaches and Nala were not in evidence on the beach to those who did not see the signs of their guardianship, their food and footsteps.

The island was every colour you could imagine, and some you could not. It was bright and impossible. But there was a wildness to this place, a danger she could never allow herself to forget, no matter how easy that was becoming.

Carrie shook her head. She wondered what damage Pan would reap here and when. Whenever it would be, she planned on not being here. But none of the girls knew the way home, short of asking Pan very nicely. The fairies wouldn't help her even if they could. So that left the native tribes, the mermaids and the pirates. She had no way of getting to the pirates until they came closer to the shore. If she remembered the way here she might be able to track their progress, though it would most likely take them few weeks yet. So the mermaids and the natives were left.

Neither of them took too kindly to trespassers, but she didn't see that she had any other choice. She was going to have to kamikaze her way through this and hope she didn't die. So pretty much the thing she'd been doing since she'd got here.

She had almost forgotten Perdy was there until she nudged her.

"Your staring at the mermaids." Perdy gave her a lopsided grin. Carrie blushed, readying herself for a lie.

But Perdy, who was a lot more relaxed than usual, tucked her hand behind her back and swayed on her tiptoes excitedly.

"Do you want to go see them?" She asked.

Carrie blanched. She hadn't expected things to fall into place so quickly. If Perdy took her to the mermaids, she could find her way there herself.

Oh so familiar guilt prickled under her skin. It seemed like that was all she ever felt recently. Perdy, normally so silent and stoic, was acting like an honest to god teenager again. She was trusting her. And Carrie was using her in return, planning to leave her. She bit her lip as she ducked her head. Hadn't she felt so cruel, so bad, when Clare had revealed her pain to her? Wasn't she fighting to be a good person? Wasn't she always trying to be a little better, like Michael? The kind of trying that you couldn't stop?

And where had it got him? She thinks this savagely, it rips at her. She hadn't ever met him, but she knew him. She felt the same as him. And he had died at thirty-three. They had made a martyr of him. Canonized a normal man. He wasn't just him, he had been pulled apart and shared out until he didn't exist, only his ideas and his wants and his goodness. That's where it had got him, she thinks as tension builds in her temples. Where would it get her? Dead at seventeen?

"What's wrong?" Perdy's voice sounds very far away for a moment. "You've been obsessing about those mermaids since you got here. You're really going to turn me down?"

She had a point.

Why, even here, high above everything and everyone, did Carrie have to overthink everything? Couldn't she enjoy herself at all? She wants to be free. She wants to be weightless. She wants to see some mermaids.

"Alright." She nodded, almost frantically, forcing all the other bad thoughts down into her stomach, standing and stamping on them. "Alright. As far as first dates go, seeing real life mermaids pretty much wins the lot."

"Uh, excuse me." Perdy retorts. "Our first date was me saving your life. Didn't you know? And here I thought you were so smart." She joked, raising her eyebrows.

"Well, mermaids are more fun than imminent death."

"Oh, I wouldn't rule out the possibility of imminent death when dealing with mermaids." Perdy said, turning to start back down the hill. She turned and held her hand out to help Carrie down. Just like that first time, Carrie took it.

"If we're on our second date already, I should probably know some more about you." She starts hesitantly, not looking at Perdy, knowing she could shut down at those words.

"You know what you need to know." Perdy shrugs, feigning nonchalance.

"What, that your name is Perdita and you live on a magical island? That's not exactly a lot. I don't even know your last name!" Carrie shook their entwined hands imploringly. Perdy glared but didn't let go.

"Fine. My last name is Scott. Happy now?" She answered in clipped tones.

Carrie couldn't help the beaming smile that spread across her face. She nodded.

Perdita Scott carried on walking, but she pressed her lips together as if fighting a smile.

Carrie liked her name. It sounded familiar. It niggled at her slightly, it scratched at the back of her mind just for a moment. She had heard it, she knew it, but she couldn't remember why.

When she tried to think back the thoughts ran away from her. It was so easy for her mind to become clouded the more time she spent here. She reasoned that it would come to her, if it was important. Important things always come back, in their time.

Mermaids, Carrie thought. Just think about mermaids instead. Don't think about how you're basically using the best girl you've ever met to get home to a place you don't know if you even fit in. Think about mermaids.

"Oh my god...I think I might cry." Carrie whimpered.

"Jesus, Mary and Joseph – please try to control yourself."

They were crouched behind a convenient cluster of boulders and plant life some way from the lagoon but close enough to see without being spotted. Perdy was poised as always, balancing easily on one knee. Carrie was wobbling about uncertainly with what felt like the worlds hardest log digging into her leg.

But it was so worth it.

Because, you'll be happy to know, that all the stories are true.

Mermaids are just as miraculous as you imagine, and more.

They were lazing happily in the gold of the setting sun. Carrie could see two mermaid quite close. One was braiding flowers into the others bright blue hair. Their dark brown skin glistened, like their whole bodies were covered in light. Like they were made of stardust.

All the mermaids had varying tones of dark skin. It made their tales and hair all the more vibrant. Pinks and blues and greens, every colour there could be. Some had dark black hair, some had big curls, some had shaved heads. They were all beautiful and none were the same.

Carrie felt a little awkward, then. They were living people and she and Perdy were watching them like they were zoo exhibits. She flushed in shame and turned away. She was glad she had seen the mermaids, but perhaps it wasn't the best way of doing so. She was aware of her own paleness, her own legs, she was aware just then of the voyeurism, and it sat uncomfortably in her stomach.

Perdy seemed to sense the same thing, and they silently began to make their way back to their camp.

Carrie is still thinking of mermaids all the way. They were miraculous. They were also very different from the way the movies always made them seem.

"Why were none of them wearing bras?" she asked suddenly, as she tugged at the grass that rose up to their thighs.

"What?"

"You know." Carrie said innocently. "In the movies. The mermaids always wear, like, little bras. Made of clamshells and stuff." She shrugged. "They always looked kind of nice."

Perdy shook her head, utter confusion on her face.

"First of all," she intoned in a serious voice "why would anyone voluntarily wear a bra when they literally have no reason to?"

"Very fair point."

"And second, if they were going to follow the human centric societal norms and force themselves into the god awful things – "

"Still very fair."

"Then why-" Perdy's voice rose over Carrie's interruptions "for the love of all the saints, would they make them out clamshells? That's just about the most uncomfortable thing I can think of. And the smallest."

Carrie raised her eyebrows as Perdy finished. "Remind me not to ask questions in the future."

As their camp came into view, with the smoke from the fire drifting on the breeze, Carrie thought again about her plan. The reason she had wanted to see where the mermaids lived. Second date over, she thought bitterly.

Time go get back to work.

Carrie could remember a lot of useless information. For

example, she could swear in six languages (though this could come in very useful, depending on the situation) and she could tell you that snails can sleep for three years without eating.

And so this came in handy and meant she could pretty much remember her whole way to the lavender fields, and then to the mermaids. She did it by remembering the little things, like that tree stump that looked like a small green dog, or that one purple flower in a sea of white ones.

She had had to be stealthy. She was not a naturally stealthy person because she got far too impatient for covert operations. But one of the unwritten rules for survival on the island was that you didn't leave the camp alone unless you had to (she thinks this is just a rule for her though, since she knew the others did it all the time.) and especially don't be stupid enough to do it at night. Which is exactly what she was doing.

But it wasn't like she had a lot of choice. It was the only time no one would notice she was gone. She was also, still and despite her best efforts, a late riser, and she hoped this meant no one would think to check on her before she managed to sneak back into the camp in a few hours' time.

She'd managed, with a lot of swearing under her breath, to make her first pitch torch to take with her. Peaches was on watch tonight and Carrie just had to assume she was not being followed by the tiny girl. She'd waited at the edge of camp, counting the seconds until someone woke up and came to drag her back by her hair. But no such thing had happened, and she knew absolutely that this was nothing more than sheer dumb luck.

She was hoping for a little more luck as she headed into the darkness of the forest.

Forests are, by their very natures, liminal spaces. They existed outside of time and place. There is a reason all the fairy tales take place in forests, you know.

And this forest was no exception. This forest was probably the reason for all those fairy tales. This forest had eyes and ears. Carrie's heart was in her throat as she slowly and carefully made her way deeper, knowing the many dangers she was opening herself up to. This was, she knew, the part of the horror movie where you wanted to grab the main character and shake them, yelling "what the fuck are you doing?!" But sometimes you had to do something undeniably stupid if you wanted things to change.

She knew also that her presence, for what little it contributed during the day, would be missed. But she could think of no other way to get answers. And frankly, after weeks of sunburn, blisters and obscene amounts of fish, she didn't think she had a lot to lose.

To distract herself from the creeping, night time noises all around her, Carrie let her mind wander. Or as much as she could without losing her sense of direction. She started to think of everything she missed.

Not the big things, the things that had been nipping at her heels since she got here. She thought about the little things. Things like her phone. You don't realise how boring life is without stupid candy games and a good wifi signal – she also wanted to look up the difference between a jungle and a rainforest. She missed chocolate. She missed her makeup. These things, she supposed, didn't matter in the grand scheme of things, but she couldn't help it. These were the odds and ends that made up her life. She had taken it all for granted. Now what she wouldn't give for a hot shower. A cup of tea. Some tweezers for her eyebrows. Small things.

There was a part of her that felt a little bad about wanting these things back so badly, since they did not compare to the enormity of being stranded on a near deserted magical island. An even louder part of her thought "fuck that". She was perfectly entitled to miss whatever she missed. It wasn't making her weaker, she thought, squaring her shoulders. Perdy would say something stupid like that. But for Carrie it was making her stronger. It was making her even more determined, and that was exactly what she needed right now.

Unfortunately, this meant barging into someone else's house in the middle of the night and announcing herself, like that worlds worst criminal.

At first she didn't see any of the mermaids. The lagoon was so still it looked like one of Clare's paintings.

As Carrie approached the edge carefully, she placed her burning torch as far away from the water as possible.

Out here in the circle of the lagoon the moon shone down, bright and clear in the sky, its full round twin sitting perfectly mirrored on the surface of the water.

Carrie held her hand less than an inch above the water, she could feel the rocks beneath her digging into her knees.

"Hello?" she asked quietly, into the silence.

With a sudden *whoosh!* Of water a slimy hand shot out of the lagoon, grabbing her arm painfully and tugging her down.

Carrie let out a yelp and tried to wrench herself free but the thing – no – the mermaid – gripping her was too strong.

The mermaid thrashed wildly in the water, trying to pull Carrie further and further toward the edge. Carrie twisted awkwardly onto her side, kicking out blindly, trying to dislodge her attacker. She felt like she managed to get one good blow, but then another pair of hands managed to grab her feet, pinning them together. She hit out with her one remaining hand but it was of little use.

Carrie tried to hold onto something, anything, but the rock around her was now too slippery with the water whipped up by the struggle. Her fingernails clawed, bleeding now, against stone.

She barely had time to take in a huge gulp of air before the hands pulled her over the edge and into oblivion.

Whoever said drowning was a peaceful death was a bloody liar. And obviously had never drowned.

Carrie thrashed around blindly as everything became nothing but a sharp, painful blackness.

Air – bright, cutting air like a knife – just for a second before she was under once more. She kicked and span and moved – she knew that she couldn't stop if she had any hope of dislodging the hands that held her under water. The hands that were killing her.

Then, quick and blinding as thunder, something bright flashed across her vision. She thought she might have been hallucinating until one of the mermaids hurting her let go, smashing her against the rocks at the edge of the lagoon, pushing Carrie's shoulder underneath her. Carrie seized the moment and kicked of the wall, right into the second mermaid, who let go in surprise. Then she kicked upwards, or what she thought was upwards, against the weight of her own body, her own exhaustion, toward the surface.

Her head throbbed and she lost focus quickly. She saw a trickle of blood floating out in front of her like a plume of red smoke.

She saw three mermaid tails before her body took over, fighting even when her mind couldn't, to save her. Her legs kicked. She swam. Her body doing its duty, speeding her toward air, toward life.

She gasped back to life in a storm of hot tears and blood.

Looking around wildly, breathing huge, aching breaths, she saw she was just an arm's length from the rocks, and with herculean effort and shaking hands she grasped and clawed her war out of the water before flopping face down onto the wet rocks and closing her eyes.

At first she heard strange sounds.

Glugging and guttural, like someone trying to speak underwater. But more than voice replied to the sound. They were talking. This was their language. She couldn't understand the mermaids, but she understood the tone of their conversation. Anger.

Carrie opened one eye experimentally. So, she wasn't dead, she guessed. She managed to turn over and push herself up onto her elbows. Her whole body felt impossibly heavy. From exhaustion, yes, but also from the water now clogging her clothes. She could only hope she did not die from hypothermia after everything else.

She peered into the lagoon when she could concentrate a little better. She kept her eyes on the three bright heads, the mermaids still arguing in the water, the water spilling around their shoulders.

Carrie looked back and saw that somehow, against all odds, her torch was still burning, having been far enough away to escape the splashing of the water. She tried to scoot closer toward it. It wasn't much but she hoped it might at least warm her hands, or dry her hair.

She guessed the two mermaids being dictated to were the ones who had tried to drown her. That meant the other must have helped her break free from them, since she knew that was the only way she had escaped them.

Her saviour saw her watching them then, and swam gracefully toward her like the water was no barrier for her. Her long green hair, decorated with pearls and pinkish crystals, floated behind her like light following a shooting star.

When she reached the edge she pulled her top half up, using her arms to rest against the rocks, her tail moving gently in the water behind her. The other two mermaids hung back now, glowering but staying silent.

"I must apologize." The green mermaid spoke. Her voice was low and rich. She inclined her head as Carrie watched her warily. "We do not harm those of the girl clan." She looked back over her shoulder to glare pointedly at the others – one blue and one pink. "At least, not usually."

"Well," Carrie squeaked in a high pitched, shaking voice. "I'm feeling pretty bloody harmed!"

The green mermaid's expression did not change save for her arching one perfectly shaped brow.

"Though you did enter our home without permission." She pointed out. Then seeing the guilty look on Carrie's face, she sighed. "They acted in defence of their people, as I'm sure you would have done. Because of my trust for Perdita I give you one chance, and one chance only, to explain."

"We don't have time for this Selene!" the blue mermaid snapped, though she looked pointedly at Carrie. Knowing they had another language, Carrie realised she was speaking English only to direct it at her. "You know what is coming."

Selene looked down and nodded gravely.

"Just kill her and be done with it." This was the third mermaid, the pink one.

Carrie opened her mouth in outrage as Selene hissed, causing the others to shrink away from her.

Selene turned back to Carrie. "Portia is right. We do not have time, on tonight of all nights."

"Please, don't kill me." Carrie said quickly. "I wasn't going to hurt anyone, I swear." The blue mermaid, Portia, looked at the pink one who was smirking at the idea Carrie could hurt any of them. "I just need to know how -."

Selene held her hand up. "I didn't mean that, child. I meant the summons have finally arrived once more."

Carrie shook her head. The way Selene had spoken, it made it sound as if what she meant was obvious. Selene's perfect face fell when she saw Carrie's confusion.

"Which is not why you came. Well, whatever the reason, you picked the worst night possible."

"The reason is answers, ok, please I need to know ho-"

"I am being merciful!" Selene cut her off loudly. "By not killing you for your trespass, since I have rather more important things to do tonight. Portia will fetch a salve for your head wound. This will be continued the next time we meet."

"There isn't going to be a next time, I need you to answer me." Carrie spat, getting angry. She was scared and confused and annoyed.

"Girl, take mercy when it is offered." The pink mermaid drawled.

Portia swam up and gave her, rather unceremoniously, a clamshell containing a greenish grey paste, rotten sweet. So this was the dirt she was supposed to smother all over her open wound. She hugged it close to her anyway. She would take it, especially if it did its job half as well as the cleaning crystals did. She tried to smile graciously, but it hurt her head and probably looked more like a grimace.

"Thank you…and I'm really sorry." She whispered, a little brokenly.

Selene pushed away from the edge. "I cannot say when we will meet again, girl child. Since the summons came tonight, we are relocating until it's all over."

Carrie sat up again in panic. "You're moving? But – I almost drowned to talk to you!"

Selene was moving to the middle of the lagoon. Why were none of them listening to her? Portia and her pink friend disappeared under the water.

"The summons." Carrie said quietly to herself. The fear, the panic, finally clicking into place. "You mean – Pan? Is he starting his games again?!"

Selene nodded solemnly. "Go back to your sisters. What is coming will not be pretty."

And she disappeared also, leaving Carrie in silence once more.

11

The ballad of Clare and Michael

When Clare thought about meeting Michael for the first time, she thought of sunshine, and the smell of books.

It might not actually have been all that sunny. Isn't it funny, how memory works? A day can be perfectly average, but then when you look back, it's impossibly beautiful. It's never raining, in the past. Everything becomes lens flare on the camera in your mind. Nothing but blue skies, in nostalgia land.

But it definitely smelt of books. That much she knew she had right.

That's because she met him, of all places, in a bookshop.

Not in a romantic, both reaching for the same obscure 19th century novel kind of way.

No. More in a bored stiff, can't wait to go home and drink wine alone kind of way.

She'd been invited to a gathering at a local book store. There were a few authors there, and her, with her hateful cutesy drawings of rabbits, that littered the probably now spit and crayon covered pages of a beloved children's book series. She figured that she was mostly there to make up the numbers, seen as most people became quickly disinterested in her when they realized she wasn't actually the author, nor did she know the author particularly well.

So she'd been sat for hours, with the occasional child coming up to examine the example drawings she had around her, like an embarrassing halo of paper and failure. She squirmed under the scrutiny of their mothers, who shot her a sympathetic smile before shuffling off somewhere a little more interesting. God, she thought. Even the guy who wrote the book about how dinosaurs were actually aliens had more people coming over to him than she did.

She'd been there for hours and she wanted to go home. She wasn't trying to be ungrateful. She was glad she was in work and could draw for a living. She was glad they were giving her a complimentary lunch for being here – though unfortunately it was alcohol free. She just wasn't glad of the sticky pressure of scrutiny and examination. She wanted the comforts of her messy flat, with the wobbly table and its mismatched cutlery.

As she pondered this, she was staring off a little grumpily at the nearby bookshelves (she was stuck in front of the self-help section. Which would have been fine, if she actually wanted to read think yourself thin! Or new dimensions: your step by step guide to self-actualization and success. Which she categorically did not.) She was snapped out of her reverie suddenly, as a small child bounded up to her and she was forced to grab hold of the little table as he all but launched himself over it.

"Henry! Bloody hell, where are you? I swear to god, you're a ninja..." a disembodied voice called from somewhere in the mass of people crowding the store.

"Hello." She said quietly, guessing that the boy in front of her was master ninja Henry.

Henry was a gangly looking boy with sandy brown hair and large glasses that kept slipping down his nose and that made his eyes look freakishly big. His elbow, she noticed, was plastered with a lurid purple monster plaster and he had a rather prominent gap tooth.

The man that came looking for him however, was a different matter entirely.

He was tall, he was blonde, he was undeniably gorgeous, and his hair was sticking up everywhere as he pushed his way frantically through the crowd, looking completely petrified.

"Henry, what have I told you about running off?" He puffed as he reached them. He crouched down, turning Henry to face him by gently taking hold of his shoulders.

Henry rolled his eyes. "Don't run off unless something is chasing you or..." he intoned monotonously as if this was a ritual he had to repeat every day – Clare suspected it probably was.

"Or you see Angelina Jolie looking to lower her standards with your uncle." The man finished with a curt nod, before straightening up.

Clare couldn't help but grin at the exchange, seen as it was the most entertaining thing to happen since she'd got there.

Then the man finally turned to look at her.

And he froze.

Or maybe the whole world did. That's what it felt like, just for a second.

His eyes, heaven blue, seemed to widen, almost glazing over slightly. "Holy shit." He whispered, breaking into a small, hesitant smile.

And those were the first words Michael ever said to her. They were actually rather fitting, all things considered.

Here's a tip, dear readers: marry someone who's first thought upon seeing you is that you're so earth shatteringly beautiful that only profanities in front of a minor can accurately sum it up.

Clare raised her eyebrows expectantly.

"You're not allowed to swear in front of me." Henry piped up, and they both looked down at him, as if only just remembering he was there. "Mummy said that I have to tell her whenever you swear or when you fall asleep on the train, so she knows when you're making me vulnerable to kidnapping."

Clare narrowed her eyes in confusion, wondering if this was a regular occurrence, as Michael lifted a fist in pretend threat, shaking it like a cartoon villain. He caught Clare's eye and smiled sheepishly.

"Don't worry. That plaster is from falling off of a giant plastic spoon trying to pass itself off as actual art. Not from any child abuse."

Clare sighed. "You're talking to an artist about pretend art and child abuse...in a room full of her art and children."

Michael glanced around him, as if only just seeing everyone else. "All of these are your children?"

Clare let her eyes close in annoyance.

"He doesn't hit me." Henry supplied.

"Or anyone, for that matter." He looked down at his nephew. "Uncle Michael doesn't hit people. Hitting people is wrong."

He looked at Clare pointedly when he said uncle, as if trying to impress upon Clare the fact he was not father to this child and therefore probably did not have a desperately miserable housewife waiting for him at home. As if that made this current conversation any better.

"But mummy said that you hit Uncle George when the tennis was on for being racist toward the Italians."

Michael sighed dejectedly. "Fine." He conceded. "Sometimes hitting is OK, if your cousin is being an idiot."

Henry nodded, seemingly satisfied, turning to smile at Clare as if waiting for her also to accept this bizarre pronouncement. "I don't have any cousins." He said simply.

"I'm sorry." She said, shaking her head. "Much as I enjoy listening to such wise life lessons, is there something I can actually do for you?"

"Oh – I just go where my fearless leader tells me. Isn't that right, O captain, my captain?" Michael asked jovially, placing a loving hand on Henry's shoulder, who nodded with a grin.

OK, so this guy was mildly charming. In an annoying, smarmy sort of way. And he definitely cared about this kid, she could tell as he looked down at him. And plus, you'd have to care a lot to come here voluntarily, she figured.

Then Henry thrust the book he was holding out to her and she was confronted with one of her drawings. If she never saw another cartoon rabbit for as long as she lived...

"Why are the rabbits wearing clothes?"

If she was lost before, she was lost now. She looked down at the drawing, a fluffy rabbit in a blue jumper. The simple answer was that the people who published these books decided it would be massively inappropriate, for some reason, to show naked rabbits. But she didn't feel like that was the answer the boy was looking for, she opted instead for a rather unintelligent 'uuuuh' sound.

"Real rabbits don't wear clothes. Humans do."

Clare, who had basically no experience talking to children, looked up at Michael for guidance. He was watching her with his arms crossed, looking thoroughly amused and entirely unhelpful.

"Do you think they're jealous of humans? Are they trying to copy us?" Henry got a far off look in his eyes as he thought about this. Michael raised his eyebrows mockingly, as if he was also very interested in her answer.

Before Clare could actually engage in an existential discussion on the mind set of sentient humanoid rabbits, Henry spotted something in the distance and ran off again.

"Jesus, Henry, can we not do this again, please?" Michael called plaintively and Clare ducked her head to cover a smile. Clearly this was something of a habit with his nephew.

To put him out of his misery, she stood up to peer around a cluster of people currently blocking their view.

"He's alright. He's listening to a talk by the dinosaurs-are-actually-aliens guy."

"Can you see him?"

Michael moved around her little table to stand right next to her. He sighed audibly once he saw Henry safe not far away from them, but he didn't move back. He simply but his hands in his pockets, settling into position.

“Sorry about...” He gestured vaguely to himself. “You're probably sick of bored parents and snotty children. Not that I'm either of those things, but I'm coming off just as bad, I imagine.”

Clare shrugged. “You're somewhere between the two.”

“Ah, so I have a little bit of snot leeway. Good to know.” He nodded and she let out an undignified scoff, which made him smile happily. Not at her, never at her. He was smiling like everything she did was some kind of new and exciting experience to him. “You're not...one of the bored parents, are you?” He asked, attempting and failing at casual.

“Well that was not subtle at all.” She rebuked. “But no. Single and only mildly expensive.”

Michael shook his head. “You'll have to forgive me. Again. I suppose...” His voice became lower as he leaned in closer to her. “I get a bit nervous when talking to an exceptionally beautiful woman.” he stared down at her seriously. Some might say devastatingly.

“Smoother.” Clare breathed. His gaze slowly went down to her lips and lingered there for a purposefully long moment. “I have a question.” she whispered, and he leaned closer still. “Does this ever actually work?”

Michael chuckled and nodded. He shrugged, unaffected, and moved back around the other side of the table. Clare found herself digging her nails into the wood of her chair.

“I've had no complaints yet.”

Clare twisted her mouth to the side, narrowing her eyes whilst she considered him and what she was doing with him. What she was thinking of doing with him. Sure, they only just met about three minutes ago. But it’s not like she was blind.

“I find that very doubtful.” She said, even though she didn't mean it. “But perhaps you haven't tried chatting up a very tired woman whilst she's surrounded by the Kate bush style wailings of an army seven year olds...have you?” She quipped.

"First of all, don't talk shit about Kate Bush."

She held her hands up in surrender. So, he was disgustingly handsome, charming, willingly accompanied his nephew to god awful things like this and he appeared to have an above average taste in music.

"And that is true. Normally these things are full of the dinosaurs-are-aliens type of guys. And no offence, but he isn't really my type. Too much beard. But I am sorry to inform you that the Michael Bellbrook related complaints desk is currently closed for maintenance."

"Ah." Clare nodded knowingly. "Well, I knew there had to be a flaw somewhere."

He grinned – it was a large grin that some might have said ruined the overall Adonis thing he had going on. But to Clare it didn't do that. It made him...real, more human. It made him look a bit silly really, a bit goofy, since it made his mouth look a little wonky. She sighed. It suited him. The bastard.

"I better quit whilst I'm ahead then." Michael said.

"Were you ever ahead?" She frowned.

"Ooh!" Michael mimed a shot to the heart, clutching his heart. He stepped away, edging toward the direction Henry was last seen in and she laughed.

"Till next time..." He looked down at the card with her name printed on it. He smiled again. "Clare." He nodded, like he was sounding it out, like he enjoyed the feel of the word in his mouth. Like it was the most important word in the world.

"Next time? How do you know there will be a next time? You don't even know me."

"That's true. But I'm fairly sure the pretty children's book illustrator is not, in fact, an axe wielding serial killer. And even if you were, with a face like that, I'm willing to take my chances."

Then he disappeared into the crowd for some quality Henry-wrangling-time. Which she also got her first traumatic experience of later that day, when they met again outside and without preamble, fell into step beside one another and carried on walking all day. He raised his eyebrows impishly at her when the three of them were mistaken for a family. He picked Henry up and swung him around wildly, and Clare shrieked as he threatened to do the same to her. They both stopped Henry climbing over public property. He said her name a lot.

It would not be the last time he said her name. It would not be the last time he was struck to incoherency upon seeing her. It would not be the last time she fell head over heels for that stupid smile. But all of that was yet to come. All of that would happen. And it would be amazing. They would go on crappy dates, they would stay home for days on end, they would get covered in paint, they would get a cat and a house. They would have mind blowing sex. And arguments. And they would be very very happy. They would forget what it was like to be alone. It would be good.

But not for always, and not for long.

12

A show of strength

It had not been for nothing, Carrie thought sullenly.

It had not been for nothing, it had not been for nothing, it had not been for nothing.

She had not almost died for nothing.

The sun was peeking through the foliage as she finally glimpses of the camp. She had been walking for hours. Thankfully the humidity had risen and dried her out – mostly. She did not think she was about to die from some Victorian brain fever from all the cold, so that was a plus.

But she hadn't even had chance to ask about getting home. She tried not to cry. Her heart squeezed in her chest at her own foolishness.

But tone thing had come out of that night, she supposed.

She knew, without a doubt, that she did not want to die.

She had been trying to survive for almost a month now. She had been saved by Perdy the first night she got here. But that had not been for her as much as it had been for her family. She hadn't thought about herself, she realised, as she had thought about that night so often as she fell asleep. She had thought about Clare alone in her ghost house. She'd thought about how she was no longer on the same world as her parents. This was not their sky. She hadn't thought about if she wanted to survive simply because she wanted to.

Sometimes surviving felt a little pointless here.

There had been some nights, secret nights, sad nights, when she had wondered why she was even bothering. It had not been the first time she had felt this in her life, and she had always found a way to push herself through it. But the thought was there. It was not something that scratched at her every day. It was just a dull kind of pounding, a heavy sludge of knowledge that death was, factually speaking, a possibility.

But now she felt clear and focused. She was sad that she had not got the information she had wanted. But still, she felt like a knife. Sharp and ready and violent. She wanted to fight for her life with a frightening ferocity. She wanted to hit something, she was suddenly full of energy, quick and smashing against the air in front of her like glass.

When she finally emerged back into the camp she stopped suddenly. Everyone was there. Everyone, all her girls, stood around, waiting.

Of course, she thinks. They were worried about Pan's summons.

Nala was chewing her thumb nail, her round shoulders curled in, making her for once look smaller and younger, like the teenager she was.

Peaches was smashing two rocks together noisily, startling like a cat at the smallest noise.

Willow was pacing – stamping really. She occasionally let out a frustrated grunt.

And Perdy. Perdy was the only one who was still. She was staring into the unlit fire pit the girls crowded around, as if she could see answers in the ashes there.

When she heard Carrie coming through the trees, her head snapped up.

"Where the hell have you been?" she snapped, standing up quickly. "We've been waiting for you."

"I..." Carrie gestured vaguely behind her. "I got lost." She said lamely. Suddenly being brought back to the present, she felt out of it.

The girls however, did not seem to really care about her answer. They carried on in their own personal turmoil.

Perdy moved towards her. She raised her hand, her fingers hovering around the cut on Carrie's head.

"You're hurt." Her wide, blazing eyes roamed Carrie's face.

"I'm ok. It's really not as bad as it looks. My head hurts, but only like I've had too many vodka red bulls the night before." Carrie tries to joke but her voice comes out flat.

Perdy doesn't look convinced and Carrie knows she didn't understand what she meant, but for once she doesn't press the issue, just nods instead, keeping a wary eye on Carrie.

"Well, as long as your eyes still work."

Carrie raised her eyebrows in question as Perdy moved to Nala, taking a small white scrap of parchment from her, which she held out to Carrie.

"We waited for you." Nala cried suddenly, like she'd been holding it in. "You - You are our bard." She added quietly, nodding to the paper now clutched in Carrie's hand.

All the girls moved in around her. Carrie suddenly thought about all those old fashioned radio broadcasts. Declarations of war. Those clipped, smooth voices, so calm, decimating everything around them. Knowing that they had to tell people their lives were about to change and not being able to do a thing about it. She felt like that now. She almost wished she could tear the paper up and forget all about it, that they could carry on living peacefully like before. She knew that the other girls had gone through something like this many times, when Pan decided to launch a fresh attack. They lived on a knife edge, but it had been so long this time. He had let them feel safe, and now he was ripping it away from them again. She hates him. She hates him so much she wants to scream. Seeing these brave, bright girls quaking caused icy fear to seep into Carrie.

She began to read in a shaking voice.

"To all the factions of my island."

The writing was clumsy and childish, littered with mistakes

and inkblots. She wondered if Pan had written this himself, his summons, as the mermaid queen had called them. Whoever's handwriting this was, it belonged to a child. It somehow served to make the words even more frightening.

"I have found out that my trusted second, my Tinkerbell, has been stolen." All of Pan's second in commands were called Tinkerbell. For the fairies the name had become a title, an honour.

"Return her to me, or all shall be punished. You shall know no rest. No freedom, no peace. I am all powerful on this island, and I will let you know it until my fairy is released. Your leader, Pan."

There was a pause. A single beat of silence.

"What does that mean-"

"They're gonna come for us, we gotta get ready, we can't let em-"

"Who's been stupid enough to take that fairy? Can't they see what they have done?-"

And the girls all talked over one another in loud voices. The rising panic was only broken not by a word but by a horrific snarl from Peaches.

They all turned to look at the tiny girl, who looked for all the world like she was about to give an impassioned speech, or pounce on them all.

Perdy was the first to recover. She inclined her head respectfully. "Go on Peaches."

Carrie moved forward to stand next to Perdy balling the paper up in her fist.

Peaches bounded over to her left and pointed up into the mountains. Then she pointed to the sea and then to the darkening clouds now just visible on the horizon.

Carrie didn't want to interrupt Peaches, since this was the longest thing she's ever said, so she tried to listen and look at the things she didn't understand.

The mountains meant the native people. That they had taken the fairy? Or had she just wandered into their territory? It seemed highly strange if she had. It seemed reckless for the native people to risk Pan's wrath like this.

She looked out to the sea. That much of Peaches' speech was clear at least. A storm was coming. Dark clouds, like smoke, travelled towards them. The pirates would be in for one hell of a night, that much was for sure.

"You don't know that the natives took her." Nala pointed out. "It could all be a trick to turn us all against each other."

"We're already all against each other." Willow pointed out.

"Well it wasn't the mermaids who took her." Carrie blurted out without thinking.

Perdy looked at her sharply, suspicion clouding her face, but she nodded. "The mermaids are in the middle of breeding season. Selene wouldn't risk the babies, even if Satan himself wandered into their patch."

Carrie exhaled softly in relief.

"The pirates are the only ones left then." Willow looked out at their ship far in the distance. "And that would mean Tink flying out to 'em, since we haven't seen their boat anywhere near the shore for weeks."

Peaches moved her arm in a low circle.

"No, you're right Peaches. It wasn't us, obviously." Perdy sighed, squinting up at the mountains. Carrie could tell that none of them wanted her to be right. "I think it might have been them, for whatever reason."

"But you said they never took part in the fighting if they could help it." Carrie pointed out. She watched Peaches jump down from her boulder to come and listen to the others properly. "So why start something like this now?"

"Their chief kicked the bucket not so long back. Daughter became the leader."

"Have some respect Willow." Nala snapped, making Willow blush at her own bluntness.

"Didn't mean nothing by it." She grumbled in a small voice.

She scuffed at the sand with her foot. Her old west accent was becoming more pronounced the more agitated she became, as was her gruffness of manner.

"Wild Rose." Carrie remembered hearing the name of the native leader.

"Indeed." Perdy sighed as they both stared up at the mountains, like Wild Rose was just going to appear on the edge for them to see. "Her father was a peaceful man. They defend their borders, naturally. Some of their younger boys like to run off and play at taking Pan down, but it's cockiness. It's bluster. In general, the understanding was that they and Pan tried to leave each other alone. Even Pan knows they have forgotten more about this island than he could ever hope to know."

"I take it Wild Rose is a different beast altogether."

“She has the anger of youth on her side, like you." Nala smiled at Carrie kindly. "She hasn't done anything like this until now, but I'm sure she would not sit back and let liberties be taken, if one of Pan's creatures came into their territory. If she thought Pan had sent a spy, if she thought he saw her as weak now that her father has died, perhaps she's trying to make a point."

"A show of strength." Perdy finishes, nodding again, thinking her way through Nala's words. They made sense.

And she'd dragged everyone else into it too, Carrie thinks bitterly.

The storms raged for three days and nights. They were horrific. Biblical.

Pan was true to his word. He punished them mercilessly. Their supplies got ravaged by a herd of boar driven in from the jungle and they could only salvage what was left after they managed to get them off the beach without being gored by a tusk.

They tried their best to cover their food stores and belongings with branches and leaves, holding them down with rocks. But it took hours to drag the rocks to the camp and their fingers bled, since it was raining the whole time, and the rocks got slippery as well as the ground underneath their feet.

The pile of precious items found on the island, where Carrie had got her jeans, had its own handmade leather cover for situations like this - though they wasn't sure how long it would last. The wind and rain had never been so strong.

Their tents had been made just in case of storms too, but that didn't mean it wasn't difficult. Carrie had images of their tents simply collapsing in on top of them whenever she was in there.

The thing that changed most was the sleeping arrangements. Since it was too cold and dangerous for Nala and Peaches to stay by themselves in the woods, everyone decided to move into one tent. They told themselves it was for warmth, piling their furs and leathers into Perdy's big dark tent. But it was a comfort, too, to all be together.

They piled in on each other like puppies as the rain lashed down and the wind howled. Even Peaches, wild untameable Peaches, curled in on herself and slept soundly between her sisters. She smiled as Nala teased her and braided their hair together.

The heavy, unrelenting rain scared all the fish to calmer waters, the animals to their hideouts. It was smart. It was guerrilla warfare. He wasn't attacking them like they had all thought. He was driving them to the edge and pushing them off.

Carrie could just about squint through the rain to the dark shape bobbing around like a bottle top on the ocean. She wondered how the pirates were holding up. She hadn't met them, and Perdy insisted they were all a bunch of brutes, but that ship. It didn't look sturdy enough for this onslaught.

She wondered what they were doing for rations, if they were eating nothing but palm hearts and peaches, like the girls. Whilst Carrie was glad she was in no danger of getting scurvy, the constant bloating and cramps from eating too much of the stuff made them all irritable and uncomfortable.

The forced inactivity did not help. Nala could always find ways of making it all seem like an adventure but even she became dispirited as the storms continued into the week.

Peaches and Willow hated being cooped up. Peaches tried to bite them all several times and they often had to stop her from tearing huge holes in the tent with her teeth.

Willow complained. All the time.

Only Perdy and Carrie managed to resign themselves to it, though in different ways. Perdy's stoicism and natural wariness meant she could make herself still for long periods of time, like she was still keeping watch through the rainfall.

For Carrie, she joked that it was that she had always been lazy. But deep down she knew it wasn't that. She could sleep and sleep herself into a kind of sluggish apathy. She could sleep for long periods of time - sometimes it didn't feel as if any time had passed at all though.

On the days she could not do this she continued to tell the girls stories. Sometimes she didn't want to, felt to tired or her head hurt from too much sleeping. But she tried, mostly. She was glad she had read so many books.

One day they all watched as Willow, ignoring all their attempts to persuade her not to, dashed out of the tent flap and out into the rain. It was the heavy, cold kind of rain that hurt like pins.

Then she began to scream. She howled and raged at the sky, like Odysseus cursing Poseidon. Kicking at the debris and driftwood the storm had washed up on the sand.

Then of course, quick as a flash, Peaches scrambled out after her where Perdy was still holding the tent flap open. If Carrie didn't know her too well she would have looked like any other little girl playing in puddles.

"They're never going to get dry." Nala shook her head like a resigned mother. "What if they get sick?"

Carrie smiled at her lovingly and wrapped an arm around her.

"At least we'll never run out of water. All we'll have to do is ring them out over a bucket."

They both laughed, but they both looked up when Perdy stood. She let the tent flap close behind her, but she kept turning back to look up at it, thinking.

"Not you too!" Nala whined.

"Oh come on." Carrie said, dragging her heavy limbs up to stand by Perdy. She held her hand out for Nala. "We haven't got anything else to do."

Nala bit her lip. Then she determinedly tucked her headscarf into her tunic and threw a heavy fur cloak over her shoulders. "Not for long."

She let Carrie drag her up and all three of them followed the others out into the rain. They ran around, and laughed and screamed and tried to catch droplets on their tongue. Peaches scrambled up on Perdita's back for a piggy back ride, and Carrie whooped in surprise as Willow scooped her up too. They raced around and fell in the sand.

Later, when they had all gotten too cold to carry on, they'd packed back into the tent, shivering and grinning like fools. They didn't have a fire, but Nala gave them all cloth to wrap their hair in and the covers were warm and dry.

Nala, Willow and Peaches all curled up in a corner together, playing some kind of hand slapping game that Peaches was obviously winning.

Carrie sat next to Perdy, feeling like a pair of marshmallows in all the fur cloaks they had piled around them. Perdy's nose was pink and she wouldn't stop sniffing, but she insisted she was fine. Carrie thought it was exceptionally adorable. So she was human, after all. Perdy's wild curly hair got even crazier after the rain and she kept trying to smooth it down, but nothing seemed to be working.

"Today was a good day." Carrie sighed. She felt peaceful. It was a rare feeling.

"There might not be another." Perdy scooped her mass of hair away from her face as Carrie rolled her eyes. "We'll go crazy if this goes on any longer."

"What are you thinking?" Carrie asked the question knowing she wasn't going to like the answer.

"That I'm going to get that fucking fairy back."

13

Crocodile

Carrie knew without thought that she wasn't going to let Perdy wander off into the wilderness alone. Even if she couldn't protect her, she could at least distract the monsters out there till she got away.

She knew she wouldn't be any better at surviving out there, but she knew she would go spare worrying back at camp. It was a selfish decision in one way. But really, she wanted only to know Perdy was safe. Why would they let her go alone? Safety in numbers, they stuck together, always. They were part of the same tribe. Not sisters, like the others. Something else. Carrie was going to stand at her side.

Willow, as second in command, was to stay behind and protect the others. She itched for a fight, but she didn't complain like Carrie would have. She knew that this was the most important task, and that Perdy was trusting her. Nala wanted all of them to go together, if they were going to get Tinkerbell back. But Perdy insisted that for her skills in medicine and Peaches light foot and hawkeyed gaze, they were too integral to the continued survival of the tribe to risk on a fool's errand.

"You don't think it, but you're the most important of us all. Anyone can fight. You keep us alive."

She was about to insist Carrie stay behind too - Carrie didn't know what excuse she would think of, since she didn't think she was as important to survival as the others. She didn't wait to find out what Perdy would have said. She beat her to the punch, pointing out that she did not in fact bring any practical knowledge to the group whatsoever.

"So why not let me come with you?" Carrie shrugged nonchalantly, knowing the challenge in the question.

Perdy squared her shoulders and jutted her chin. "You have just as much value as the rest of us. Stop being self-pitying. You are important...to the team."

Perdy didn't look at her until she finished, and Carrie raised her eyebrows with a smirk.

"I'll not ask-"

"I'm not asking either." Carrie said, cutting her off. "I won't let you go alone. None of us want you to go off alone. You stop being a martyr." She held Perdy's gaze until she saw the ghost of a smile tugging at her lips.

Perdy inclined her head, finally relenting.

Nala unexpectedly flung her arms around Carrie, since they had been sat next to each other. Perdy had gathered them all up into a circle to explain the barely formed plan she had made. It mostly consisted of looking for the fairy and hoping they didn't die.

Carrie laughed and held onto Nala's arms. She looked back at Perdy, who really was smiling at her now.

The other girls gathered together, since it was going to be their job to protect the camp. With their numbers lessened, there was a risk of them being attacked whilst Perdy and Carrie was gone. They could hold their own though. Boys always did have a habit of underestimating girls, especially small ones, quiet ones, homely ones.

Perdy took Carrie's hand and moved her closer to her. Carrie thought it was going to be last minute don't die in the jungle advice, until Perdy put her hand gently on Carrie's arm.

"I know what you're going to say." Carrie said in a rush. "And it's ok. I'll do everything you tell me. I won't get in the way."

Perdy stiffened in surprise and raised an eyebrow. "Well, good.

But that wasn't what I was going to say."

"No?"

Perdy smiled softly. "No." She said gently. Her eyes roamed Carrie's face and she raised a hand to brush a stray hair from the cheek. "I was going to say-" She swallowed. "I meant what I said. You are valued, very much. If anything were to happen to you..."

"You would be?..." Carrie raised her eyebrows expectantly. She'd never seen Perdy so unsure. "Upset? Mildly inconvenienced? Totally devastated and heartbroken?" She gave her a playful nudge with her arm.

"Yes." Perdy stammered quickly. When she spoke again however, her voice was soft and serious. She looked right into Carrie's eyes, her own almond eyes crinkling at the corners. "The last one."

Carrie was surprised that she felt calm. Well, not calm. But she wasn't shocked, or nervous. She was happy. She felt the same. It didn't feel complicated.

She stepped closer to Perdy, who crossed her arms and held tightly onto her elbows. Now she would barely meet Carrie's eye. "Nothing's going to happen."

Perdy nodded, clearly only half convinced. She gave her a small smile, which Carrie returned. She hoped that Perdy knew how much she trusted her.

As Perdy left the tent, braving the rain still pelting down to go and retrieve some more weapons and food, Carrie was struck suddenly, like a slap in the face, by a memory. The single image of Michael and Clare in the room, the picture from all those years ago, smiling happily with no idea their lives were supposed to end.

The jungle was humid, but fortunately the mass of leaves above them kept most of the rain away. They were travelling further in than Carrie had ever been before. She was struck by the denseness, like this small island managed to stretch on forever with no end. It was sticky and warm and close, and it made her want to cry and go to sleep. She almost didn't know which was worse - this, or the rain.

The jungle was also shockingly, dizzyingly green. She'd never seen green like it. Elf green, emerald green, feeling healthier just by looking at it green. The kind of green you didn't see anymore, in the real world. Pure and untouched by human hands. Old green. Gaia green.

Occasionally bursts of colour punched through in the form of fruit and flowers. Pulpy, juicy mangos, round as fat as the sun. Perdy and Carrie laughed as their fingers were covered in mango juice. Bruise purple plums, sticking out like wounds. Bright pink flowers, their orange and red sisters vying for supremacy next to them.

She didn't know how long they had been walking. Just like when they had gone to the lavender field together, their conversation had eventually drifted into an easy silence broken only by Carrie pointing out weird jungle stuff she saw.

It was when she was looking at the ground, the pungent dirt squelching under her soft leather boots, that Carrie stopped.

Because in a single step, the sound of the rain stopped. The ground was dry, no sneaky water droplets managed to drum their way through the leaves above.

The rain stopped.

Carrie froze in confusion. Turning to look behind her she saw some rain fall managing to get through the trees. In front of her - nothing. You didn't need to be an expert to know rain didn't work like that - especially supernatural rain controlled by a child that had been specifically directed at you.

"What are you doing? We have to hurry if we're going to get there before dark!"

Carrie held up her hand and took an experimental step backwards.

Rain fell on her hair. She stepped forward again. No rain.

Was it possible Pan was doing this deliberately? But why? It didn't seem like something that would concern him. He had sent the rains in order to spur them into action - Why was he going to make their job any easier now?

"Where are we right now?" She called to Perdy, who was tapping her foot impatiently.

Perdy glowered and rolled her tongue into her cheek in impatience. She crossed her arms petulantly, but seemed to realise Carrie wasn't going to move until she answered her, and looked around her.

"I can see the roots of the great oak." She said, nodding to something Carrie couldn't tell apart from any other the other tree roots she could see. "The tree is so big that they spread out for miles across here. They use the roots to mark a border between Pan's territory and the natives."

Carrie laughed as some kind of understanding tickled at the back of her mind.

"Do you think...maybe he can't reach this far?" She hissed in a stage whisper.

Perdy considered it for a moment, realization dawning on her at the same time. "But...He can still reach the other side of the island - it's why the mermaids relocate all the time, instead of staying in one place all year round."

Perdy motioned her forward and continued walking. Carrie followed, but she was no longer focused on everything around her. There had to be a reason the rain had not followed them this far. It wasn't just respect for the borders. More and more she felt as if Pan was just a ghost story. It had been hard to be scared of someone you had never seen. But when the storms had come she had understood a little better the volatile and cruel nature of the boy. But that was all he was, wasn't it? What if he was not nearly as powerful as everyone else seemed to think?

Sometime later, as the sun began to set, suffusing everything in a deep orange glow, they came to a river that cut through the ground like a knife wound.

Perdy squatted down by its edge, poking a stick in to test its depth.

Remembering her encounter with the mermaids just a week before, Carrie stayed as far back as she could from the water. An icy fear filled up her stomach and she made herself stay still, as if the panic that gripped her would make her do something reckless if she moved. Like the running water could see her and was waiting for her to throw herself in.

"I-" Her voice came out suddenly, high pitched and breathless as Perdy looked at her.

"I don't want to go in the water." She managed, though her voice still sounded meek and a blush grew on her cheeks.

Perdy rose slowly, like she was trying not to frighten her. She nodded and looked around as a familiar frown of concentration fell on her face.

"It would take hours to go around it. We don't have enough daylight for that. We can't wade through or we'll be soaked. And there aren't any rocks in the water for us to step across."

"Well, we could just put rocks in there ourselves. I'm sure I saw some earlier, not too far back."

Perdy nodded with a smile. "They would have to be big enough to stick above the surface. How would we lift them?"

She asks this slowly, as if she's waiting for Carrie to work out the answer for herself. It's calming her down, and she suspects that this is the idea. All she knows for sure is that she'd do just about anything to avoid going into the water. She'd been having that very nightmare ever since she'd almost drowned. She felt as if she still had that water in her lungs even now. But Perdy was urging her to think, and she did. She would let her fear of the water help her come up with a solution to avoid it.

"We're in the middle of the jungle." She said slowly, thinking as she talked. "All we would need would be some logs, some sticks, to roll the boulders onto. Then we can roll them as far as we like."

And so that is what they did. Carrie almost enjoyed it, working with Perdy. The steady rhythm of activity, of having something to focus on. But she knew every second brought her closer to the water, and that terrified her.

Ever since the mermaids she had been feeling worse and worse. Worse than she had since she got here, and that was saying something.

Normally she was gripped by a gnawing, raw sadness. Tender and saw and with no obvious cause. A sluggish sort of heaviness. Over the last few years she had learnt to carry that sadness around with her like a lead weight. A huffing, pawing animal that had made its den inside her belly. This she was used to. This she could almost handle.

What had come upon her after the mermaids was different.

She'd been having panic attacks. The first time it happened she hadn't known how to anticipate it, she'd not understood fully what was happening at first, only knowing that she was scared. She'd thought she was having a heart attack. The other times she had felt them coming, like hearing a great train blaring and chugging and bearing down on you from a distance, unstoppable. She had hid in the jungle until they had passed.

When the storms came their confinement made it difficult. She'd become snappish and withdrawn so that the others would stop asking if she was alright. She appreciated that they cared, and she did feel bad, but she didn't want to give them even more reason to see her as the useless one of the group. Plus it would mean explaining about the mermaids and why she had gone there.

Her forced confinement had also meant a lot of sleeping. Sleep punctured with nightmares of being underwater. Most of the time the other girls didn't wake up from their sleep, but there had been one time when a hand had silently taken hers in the darkness. She couldn't be sure, but judging from the size, she had a suspicion it might have been Peaches, who had never touched her before or since.

And so, as she and Perdy pushed the last of the rocks into the river, Carrie's stomach twisted painfully with remembrance.

"I'll go first, so you know where to step." Perdy tried to catch her eye, but Carrie couldn't take her eyes off the water. "The rocks might be slippery, so be careful."

Carrie nodded, swallowing, cotton buds in her mouth, her palms sweating and itching, as she watched Perdy's careful step onto the first of the boulders.

Carrie watched Perdy with her heart in her throat, feeling too warm, like she was going to faint. Thankfully she didn't.

Perdy managed the first two rocks fairly easily.

It was on the third one that all hell broke loose.

Several things happened all at once - the way these things always do.

First Perdy flung her arms about and did an overdramatic wobble - But as Carrie stepped forward in panic Perdy turned and grinned at her, standing perfectly poised and balanced on the rock.

Until she wasn't.

Carrie barely had time to react before a dark heavy shape crashed through their make shift damn and sent Perdy splashing into the murky water.

"No!" Carrie yelled, flinging herself forward.

The thing that emerged from the water covered in dark scales, sharp teeth snapping at the air.

A crocodile.

Its mouth emitted a strange croaking noise, stopping and starting, like it had something stuck in its throat, like it was ticking an irregular beat.

It flopped its huge weight down, splashing as Perdy yelped -

Her leg was caught underneath it from where she had fallen backwards, and she couldn't twist round to reach any of her weapons. She and the crocodile thrashed together in the water as Carrie watched feeling helpless.

She was going to die, she thought. Perdy was going to die.

That just could not happen. The idea was impossible to her, simple as that. It could not and would not happen.

Carrie's fear of the water had rooted her to the spot. It might have been a second or a hundred years before she heard Perdy let out another frustrated cry.

Do something, she told herself. Do anything, try anything, to let her live.

She stopped thinking about anything but Perdy. She let the idea of her fill her up, like Perdy's spirit was ghosting through her. Finally she moved with it.

Without stopping to hesitate, Carrie grabbed the knife that had been nestled safely in her boot and one of the thinner sticks they had used to move the rocks. She let out a howl, a terrified animal noise, and leapt into the water.

Swampy green things clung to her, slimy and oozing it seemed to her, but she ignored it all. She struck out haphazardly at first, hitting the crocodile on its hard shell like scales, crying loudly the whole time.

The crocodile turned and snapped its massive jaws at her and she saw its fleshy pink tongue. She hit it in the mouth with the stick, aiming for that softness. Carrie felt a movement beside her. Distracting the crocodile meant Perdy had been able to shift from under its weight. The crocodile's attention was shifting between them. It was snapping at them but not approaching anymore.

For one brief moment, as they panted and heaved, their shoulders bumping clumsily against one another, they thought they might have won.

Until the crocodile lashed out once more, its massive tail

smashing into the rocks they had moved so laboriously into the water like they were nothing but pebbles. Its huge mouth grabbed and snapped Carrie's stick in two like it was a twig. The force of it being ripped from her clutches left dark red marks on her hands.

"Your knife!" Perdy yelled to her, reaching for her own.

Carrie had been holding the stick in one hand and her knife in the other, but somewhere after she had jumped into the water she had ended up clutching them both between her hands like instruments of prayer. Thankfully, she had managed to keep hold of her knife. Gutting fish with it was one thing however. A crocodile was something else altogether.

She flexed her fingers, which felt numb with cold and trying to keep hold of the knife.

Perdy she suddenly noticed, was pawing at her clothes frantically. She had no knife in her hand. Panic swept over her face. Her knife must have gotten lost somewhere in the murky water swishing round their legs.

"Give me your-"

Perdy didn't have time to finish her sentence. The crocodile snapped at them quickly and Perdy jumped out the way, slamming into Carrie and forcing them both back and into the water. Carrie saw Perdy kicking frantically at the snapping jaws of the creature. She knew the soft leather of those boots would offer no protection from those sharp teeth. Luckily the crocodile was distracted. Not so luckily she was making it angry. Perdy had a habit of riling people up at the wrong time, and it seemed this was not limited to humans. Carrie could sense their window of opportunity closing.

Her hands with wet with scummy river water, but she adjusted her grip on her knife and plunged forward.

It wasn't graceful - It wasn't even skilled. It was survival. Blindly, Carrie moved her hand under the water until she met the fleshy belly of the crocodile. Then she pushed her knife forward. She didn't know if she stabbed it or if she just grazed it, but it let out a strange choked sound. The two girls watched, breathless, as its green bulk vanished under the water and away.

"Oh my god." Perdy shook her head in disbelief, and crossed herself as a thousand watt smile lit up her face.

Carrie pushed herself up from where they were both still sat in the water, staring after the creature in horror. She thrust her knife at Perdy.

"Take it off me, I don't want it. Can you literally just take it from me, please?"

Perdy took the knife, though she didn't bother disguising her confusion.

"You ok there?" She asked almost patronizingly.

"Did I kill it?" Carrie asked her desperately.

Perdy's shoulders soften, though her tone does not. "No, Carrie, you didn't kill it. You just scared it."

Carrie nods and lets herself believe this. She didn't want to have killed it, even it was going to kill them. The thought made her skin crawl. She could kill fish for food, and she didn't question it when Willow brought back a speared boar for dinner. But there was something different about this, about inflicting pain on purpose.

"Sometimes it's kill or be killed, Blondie."

She knew that, but it didn't make her any happier about it. She wonders how Perdy felt the first time she hurt a person, if it was anything like this. It was probably worse. How long would it take for Carrie not to care? Everything here seemed stained with violence of some kind. Would this place chip away at her slowly, the way it had done everyone else?

"Come on." Perdy said gruffly, getting up to slosh through the water and climb out. Carrie followed her and climbed out after her as she said "We still have a long way to go to find the natives."

"Not unless we find you first." A deep voice growled.

The girls whipped round and watched two men melt into

view as if from nowhere. They'd probably been watching them struggle with the crocodile the whole time.

"We know why you are here. We've been sent by our princess to collect you." Said the man on the right. He had long dark hair twined through with braids and an angry red scar on his arm.

The two native men were tall, dark brown skin stretched taut over muscles honed from a lifetime navigating this jungle. They held two spears, which they pointed directly at Carrie and Perdita.

"I think this is the part where you surrender." The one on the left smiled cockily. This one had a single plait threaded through with feathers.

Perdy took a step back in indignation at being caught so easily. But the way Carrie saw it, they were getting a free escort to where they needed to go. Even if they were at risk of being impaled.

She rolled her eyes and stepped in front of Perdy, putting her wrists out.

"Take me to your leader."

14

Wild Rose, Tiger Lily

Wild Rose was a ferocious woman.

Just like her name she was sharp and beautiful.

Like Willow she was very tall. If Willow was an amazon, Wild Rose was the queen of them. But whereas it looked a little awkward on Willow, who slouched to hide her height, on Wild Rose it served to make her look lithe and lean. She had perfectly controlled movements. She was not traditionally beautiful. Her nose was slightly too big, adorned with rather distracting gold rings and her full mouth was constantly turned down. Her cheekbones were high and sharp as knives. Sharp enough to kill someone.

There was also the scars. They started just under jaw on her left side, gleaming scratches on her skin and travelled down to her shoulder. But she didn't hide them. She squared her scarred shoulders and held her head high. They seemed to make her even more enigmatic.

Her skin was a dark warm brown, her hair long and jet-black. But she had light hazel eyes, slightly pointed, like a cat. Her left arm was covered in tattoos. Inky black vines and flowers adorned her skin, from the top of her shoulder just under her scar, twisting all the way to her fingertips, which jangled with many rings.

She wore a simple brown dress. Carrie thought she knew why. This was a princess who needed no adornments, no crown. You could tell she had an innate sense of power just by looking at her.

She crossed her legs gracefully in front of them, examining them thoughtfully where they sat, their arms tied behind their backs. Carrie wondered exactly what she saw.

"Look to your right." Wild Rose said, in a deep slow purr of a voice.

Carrie did. All she saw was a leathery faced man, crinkles and long silver hair.

"There's...uh...an elderly gentleman?" Carrie raised her eyebrows questioningly. She felt Perdy stiffen beside her. But she didn't know what else she was supposed to say.

Wild Rose nodded. "Look around." She gestured to the tribe around her. Then, looking at the sea of faces, Carrie understood what she was supposed to see. There was a tableau of life all around her. Laughing children with their parents, and grandparents. People of all ages.

"You age." She said in shock. "Your tribe can age."

Perdy seemed to wake up then, twisting around awkwardly to peer at the people around her in awe.

"How is that possible?" She breathed, whilst Carrie couldn't stop smiling.

"There are many religions, many gods, who only exist because people believe in them. So it is with this island, and its power. This tribe has lived on this island since it was born. Our blood, our sweat, our mothers milk runs through this land. Who is Pan, to us? Some white invader, a child. Pan has no power over us. He is nothing to do with this people. No power in our territory." she waved her hand as if flicking away a pesky fly. "We do not believe he has power over us or the land we inhabit, as so, he does not." she shrugged.

Carrie frowned. "Is it really that simple?"

Wild Rose smiled, a little smugly. "Belief, faith, imagination. These are powerful magical forces, no? Are you saying you have experienced no such thing here?"

The smell of lavender pricked at Carrie, in the back of her mind.

"Yes." Carrie said slowly. Thoughts flickered quickly through her mind. "I think we have." she thinks about the lavender field. Perdy's secret place. She had not given it to Pan. Not in her heart. And so he had never seen it, he could not touch it. It didn't belong to him. It belonged to a place inside Perdy.

"I think..." Carrie said slowly as she thought it through in her mind. Wild Rose watched her patiently. "I think there are still places here that he is blind too, even now. He can't hear us now, can he? And there are other places too, not many, but they are there. If we keep parts of ourselves back, certain thoughts, if we don't surrender ourselves to him...then he can't sense them."

Wild Rose nodded quickly, almost proudly, like Carrie had been a child sounding out the alphabet for the first time. "I see you are different from your sisters." She cooed with a grin. "You are new here still, yes?"

Carrie nodded, not daring to look at Perdy to see what she thought of this pronouncement. Besides, Perdy was biding her time. Keeping silent and letting Carrie wade in clumsily. Let her step back then. Carrie finally felt like she was making some kind of progress, finding something out about this place after being in the dark for so long.

"I see it in you." Wild Rose continued, staring at her intently. Carrie stared back, which seemed to impress the princess. "You are not his creature, not yet. Not like this one." She jutted her chin rudely at Perdy, who glowered back at her from underneath her eyelashes. Perdy's jaw twitched as she bit back a retort.

"Haven't you ever wondered why you still get your woman's blood every month?"

Carrie had wondered this, actually. They didn't age, outside of native territory and yet they still experienced bodily functions and changes. How did their body understand that a month had passed, even though they did not age? They still experienced time in some form, clearly. Peaches would forever be too young, to ever experience her period. But for the older girls it was still a fact of life.

"Little boys like Pan, they do not understand these things." Wild Rose pursed her plump lips. "And so he cannot control it. Everything else, yes. But not things belonging to the realm of the feminine."

Carrie's mind was whirling. It seemed so deceptively simple. Too simple. There had to be a catch. It couldn't be so easy as just willing it so. Life didn't work like that, did it?

"That's why he has only just found you. He did not sense you because you cling to the life you have left behind. You have one foot there even now, I think. Now you have been here longer, he sees you. Unfortunate, but none of us can hide forever."

Perdy shifted and shook her head. Carrie knew how she felt. She'd fought against Pan for so long, and was now learning that there was something else she could have been doing the whole time.

"You're just saying we have to believe he doesn't have power over us?" Perdy sneered.

"Yes. But one person, that won't be enough for any wider change. Our belief has sustained us for longer than you could imagine. We are generations upon generations, which is why Pan has no power here. That is why he sends you, and doesn't come here himself, with his boys. It will help you, though."

Carrie nodded, taking the gift of this information. At last, she did not feel entirely helpless. "Thank you." She breathed. "You're right. I'm...I'm not like the others – my sisters. At least...I don't want any part in Pan's games."

"Well, you're still here, aren't you?" Perdy hissed angrily. Carrie blushed.

Wild Rose stood abruptly. She barked something in her native language to the two men who had been standing guard behind them the whole time.

"If you just got us killed, I'm going to will you back to life and kill you again." Perdy muttered to her as they were dragged up and began marching after the princess as she walked away.

Hoping that she wasn't in fact walking to her execution, Carrie though about what she had learned. There are chinks in Pan's armour. That meant that maybe he wasn't the only way home. She felt validated. And, well, a little smug. She had known, known she shouldn't stop hoping. She had done that before, and it had brought her here. She wouldn't do it again. Wouldn't do that to herself again. Not like everyone else in this bloody place.

Wild Rose lead them to a small opening in the rock face that guarded the tribe's camp. With a snap, Carrie and Perdy's ropes were cut and they found themselves alone with her as they rubbed their sore wrists.

Before they had disappeared silently, one of the guards had given Wild Rose a flaming torch. This is what they followed as Wild Rose disappeared into the gaping mouth of the cave.

When Carrie's eyes adjusted enough to see in the flickering light, she saw pictures. She felt Perdy come stand beside her. She was still being sullenly silent. But they stood staring up at the walls together as Wild Rose's deep voice curled around them, like smoke and incense. Her words told the story of the pictures painted on the walls.

"There is a legend, amongst my people. That many moons ago, before the memory of any now living, there was another princess born to this tribe. My ancestor. She was the kindest member of this tribe, the wisest, even in childhood that much was clear. Her name...was Tiger Lily."

Carrie's eyes traced the drawings. A young girl with pink cheeks and a mischievous smile.

"She was prophesied. To bring peace back to this land. To be a true leader. But she was taken from us, before she could fulfil her sacred purpose."

The pictures changed. The girl stopped smiling, caught in shadows. Feral little hands grabbing at her from the darkness swirling around her.

"Pan stole her from her people, in order to provoke us into his games. He took her to his skull cave. He placed her in the water, separating her bodily from the land of her people. I doubt even he knew the consequences of his childish actions."

Carrie closed her eyes at the next drawing. Tiger Lily stared out at them from behind a blue window. Drowning, she was drowning. Her eyes looked desperate. This was so long ago, centuries ago, but Carrie felt a sharp tug on her heart, for a girl dying, alone, because of a boy.

"The water rose too quickly for anyone to get to her." Wild Rose's voice quavered for the first time, with pure and unadulterated anger. "She sang to the earth mother, sang herself into death. Her voice was swallowed by the sea and carried back to the shore. Now, her spirit lives on in this land. In the rocks and the trees and the ground. In the hearts of my people, and in the wind, she sings still. And she waits...waits for the day she is born again, so her spirit can reside in her body once more. That's why our tribe is one who wishes desperately for girls, and why princess is our highest title. Only then, when that child is born, the one with the true spirit of Tiger Lily...then, and only then, will her land be free from Pan once more."

Carrie's eyes pricked with hot tears. She saw Clare's painting in her mind, the deep beauty and magic of this place, being tainted by one boy and his need for power. There was power here, and life, that he could not even contemplate. If these people could let the death of their girls make them stronger, she could be strong too. She would drag herself home through the dirt if she had to.

Perdy cleared her throat and when Carrie looked at her, she could see the emotions roiling within her. Carrie took her hand. Perdy blanched as if being brought back to reality, and she squeezed Carrie's fingers back.

"Our souls do not belong to Pan." Carrie said to Wild Rose, her voice clear and strong, surprising even her. "This land does not belong to him, or to us. We will not come here without permission again."

Wild Rose gave one slow nod, leader to leader. "And your girl tribe will have an ally with our people. We will never take part in Pan's games. But you may have your prize, on the condition we may call on you, if needed."

Carrie blinked in shock. She'd almost forgotten why they had come here.

"Tinkerbell." She reminded Perdy.

"She is yours to return to the boy."

Wild Rose stepped closer to them. She placed the torch down by a boulder where it continued to flicker and burn. She took Carrie and Perdy's hands in her own large ones and smiled down at them both, as they stood in a circle.

"You don't know how to leave this place, do you?"

They were trudging back to the camp sometime later. Perdy was marching ahead of Carrie and Wild Rose, who walked side by side. Carrie got the impression that Perdy was trying to feel in charge again. Carrie smiled and let her get on with it.

Wild Rose shook her head pityingly at Carrie's question. "This is my land; I know no other. But I believe you will find your way home."

"It's hard." Carrie sighed. "No one so far seems to know anything. Even if they did, I think they're all too scared of Pan to say anything."

"You cannot blame them too much." Wild Rose looked ahead at Perdy. "They have lost much to him. You must be patient, as we all must. But do not give up hope, Carrie of the girl tribe. I sense a shift in this place. Things are beginning to change, I think. Most people, when they come here, they want something new. You, I do not think that's why you came here. Maybe you don't know why you are here, but when you find out, everything will be different."

She hoped the princess was right.

15

Death on a 1967 Harley

People said death rode a pale white horse. For Clare it rode a black 1967 Harley Davidson.

For Clare death came on machines. It had gears and cogs. First a boat, then a bike. It always travelled and moved to seek her out. For Clare death came with a low rumble, the kind you feel deep in your bones. The kind so low and dark you got past the point of hearing it, as you feel it down somewhere in your sticky red core.

It had been a blinding hot day in July, when Michael Bellbrook died. The kind of day that suffocates you in flower sweet air. The pavements and roads too hot, hot enough to burn your bare feet pink, heat sizzling and shimmering in the air.

Clare had managed to wrangle her unruly mess of hair into something resembling a top knot, piled precariously on top of her head where it can get even more tangled together. The heat always made it expand into a huge mess of tangles. But at least it wasn't cooking her neck like a lid on top of a pan. And she couldn't wait for Michael to come home and take it all down. She trailed her fingers up her neck, feeling the arch and curves of her bones, pushing them into the base of her hair. She imagined it was Michael, his long rough fingers, calloused from fixing his bikes up. His hands Strong and impossibly gentle. She imagines him holding her face the way he always did.

She loved the way he did that. There was always a few seconds of time, before or after kissing (something she also very much enjoyed) when his fingers would press lightly into her skin and he would hold her still, there in front of him, and he would just...look at her. Like he couldn't believe she existed. Like her knew her down to her bones. Like he couldn't work her out. Like he was a lost puppy. Like she was the single fixed point in his life. She thinks she likes this even more than the kissing part. As for the parts that came after kissing, well that was another ball park all together.

She realised, that for the first time in a long time, she was OK with having nothing to do. Most of the time she felt twitchy and useless when she wasn't busy, but not right then. She was sat in a white shift nightdress, fresh and clean and soft against her skin. A breeze, smelling of jasmine plants, was coming in from the wide open window of her beautiful, huge, mortgage free magic house. She was waiting for someone she loved to come home and kiss her senseless – and screw her senseless – and she didn't have anything else to do. And that was good. She was...happy. That was it. Clare was peacefully, blissfully, lazily happy. She didn't even have to think about it, and that was a new kind of happiness, the best kind. Happiness that just is.

Michael Bellbrook could switch between extremes quicker than anyone he knew, and navigate them better too.

He wasn't violent, or anything like that, before you go there. Of course he and Clare were very loud, passionate and very, very stubborn, so there had been a few rigorous shouting matches over the years. But they were always good to clear the cobwebs away and always left the pair of them feeling very satisfied and happy.

No, these were more nuanced extremes, but extremes none the less. For example - at least in his more hedonistic days – which he was actually still in the middle of, though he liked to pretend to be a grownup – he could be found dancing on a table with no shirt on, smoke in one hand and vodka in the other whilst Clare threw monopoly money at him. Then a short while later with very little ceremony, they would be tucked peacefully in bed together, him smoothing Clare's hair softly from her face, his arm going numb beneath her so he didn't wake her up.

He could be effortlessly, annoyingly charming, to the point where even the obvious insincerity of it was part of the charm. But then he could feel things very deeply, and be honest and unashamed about them.

He knew people who, from the outside, seemed to exist solely in one state. Permanently stoic or cripplingly shy, too obnoxious and just plain bonkers. He had known many people. But this meant he knew that people were not just one thing, one feeling. People were oceans with ever changing currents. He liked to think he embraced this, and always tried to remember it.

He thinks maybe this is why people seem to like him so much. He was the kind of person who tried very hard, for example, not to get annoyed at particularly rude waiters. He reasoned that they probably didn't go around everyday scowling or spilling soup on your new trousers. They might be having the worst day of their lives. It had always been important to him to try and really understand people, and that's what he always tried to do. Some of his less likeable family members used to call him Saint Michael, barely disguising the insult in their joking tones. He didn't care. He tried not to care.

Besides, being Saint Michael was infinitely better than being anything like his cousin George, who was pretty awful even by Michael's standards. Since Michael and George were the fourth generation of a well to do lot – old money and even older ideals – they had always had money. Even inheritances shared out between them and Michael's younger sister Emily, still amounted to more than others had in their whole lives. They didn't have to work, and whilst Michael didn't exactly go in for the nine to five, he had at least learned some basic skills and did the obligatory, if very brief, stint in retail in his teens. He still did a few odd jobs here and there, mostly fixing up bikes and other engines. Both he and Clare were very good with their hands (her favourite joke, when it came to them. Very good, she would laugh, and they wouldn't emerge from the bedroom for a good long while.) Cousin George on the other hand had chosen what many disgustingly wealthy people chose to do and had not worked a day in his life. This wouldn't have been so bad, since he did have the means and no one knew what they would choose were their lives switched, only George had not the personality to redeem him. Michael suspected he'd also never said anything decent to anyone in his life either. George was the type of man who believed that having money meant he didn't have to care.

It had disgusted Michael, growing up. Seeing the way George ordered the staff around. His casual cruelty towards those he considered inferior. Back then Michael had been a child. He hadn't exactly understood his privilege and what it meant, not yet. Back then all he knew is that he felt very sad, very guilty and very helpless. He did not want to be a bully, like his cousin. He didn't understand things like his nanny, tugging him away from beggars in the street, him feeling pound coins rattling in the pockets of his school shorts. He didn't understand why his family had so much money when other people didn't have any.

And so he had grown up with a heaving, itching sense of desperation inside of him. He thought it might choke him, some nights. At first he had been resentful. He'd tried to act like he didn't have any money. He'd drank a lot. But that was self-indulgent and it wasn't fair either, since there was no point in wasting what he was lucky enough to have. So he had started to give. Give money and bits of him as much as he could. He tried very hard to be kind.

Clare had calmed him down, eventually. He didn't think she knew just how much. His own guilt had hung around his neck like an albatross, for as long as he could remember. But she had steered him right and brought him home. She had brought a balance to his life he had never managed to find by himself.

They still gave, a lot. After they had bought the house, they still had more money than the two of them needed. They gave as much as they could, but not so much, that it would bankrupt them also. They worked – Clare had always worked, scrimping and saving and drawing to fund her travels, and she still had some of her share of her parent's life insurance. But they still worked. Not all the time, and free-lance, painting and fixing, but still. He was not idle. He was...comfortable. He had been riots and chaos, and Clare had calmed him, shown him how to live with the tumult inside of him. He had done the same for her, she would say. He was still unerringly himself, he still yearned to help, but he didn't kill himself trying to do it. Clare had travelled through his wilderness and found who he had always been, even when he didn't know it. He was happy to discover that he was a good person, capable of loving and worthy of being loved, by a very, very good woman.

And he never talked to boorish cousin George. Things were the best they had been in a long while.

He felt happy that he could buy a house for Clare. And what a god damn beauty of a house. It groaned and creaked in reply to them. They felt it as soon as they got there, that the house was listening to them, and they felt it love them and warm them. Clare had already started talking to it, and whilst it had taken him a while to stop replying, thinking she was talking to him, he was starting to get used to it. And he found himself talking to the place too. He told it to take care of her, whenever he left her there. It was a habit now, even after just over a month. Even popping out for milk, he'd say, see you later. Look after Clare. Or, hey I'm going out on my bike for a bit, back soon and look after Clare. And he trusted the house to do so.

They even had a cat. He was a dog person, an all animal's kind of person really, but Clare was a crazy cat lady down to her core and she had been more than happy to adopt the thing. Well, he adopted them, the way cats do. The cat had wandered in one day when Clare had left the back door open in a rush to get to the loo. His fur was stuck up like he'd been electrocuted and it never changed. And so Columbus, as he'd named him, had settled into life at the house nicely. Mostly by acting like he had always been there, which maybe he had.

So Michael had a girl, a house, a cat, and a bike. Everything he could ever need. He smiled. He felt the ragged edges of his soul begin to soften. He began to accept that he also deserved to be happy. And he was. He was.

He gripped the handles of his bike a little harder in anticipation. He felt his t shirt, sweat stuck to his back, lift slightly in the breeze. Delicious green fields surrounded the country road on either side of him, a soft blanket to protect them and their home forever. He grinned his wide grin – the one Clare always said made him look goofy. His goofy toothy grin, that he loved because Clare loved it.

He was riding home to her. He liked to say that they had travelled for so long because they had been looking for one another, following the heart strings that bound them. Feeling one another existing worlds away. And now they never had to go anywhere again, if they didn't want to, though he suspected they would. They had found their place. It comforted him, more than he ever thought it would. He thought he was a nomad, a wandering soul. But he had been wandering to here, and to her.

He pressed his bike to go just that little bit faster. Clare always admonished him for things like that. He barely ever took her out on the bike, mostly because of the second date throwing up on the hard shoulder situation, but also because he was well aware of the risks. But he had been riding solo for years. He was experienced, and he loved feeling like he was flying.

And he was careful, like Clare told him. He always found it faintly amusing that the least careful person he'd ever met told him always to go at a snail's pace. But it was done with love. Just like when he swore loudly upon tripping over jars of dirty paint water she'd left on the floor for no discernible reason.

Yes, he was riding home to her. She wouldn't mind him going a little faster, on a deserted road like this one. Not when he was coming home to her.

It was too bloody warm. Sweat got in his eyes.

Clare would have her hair up. He would take it down. He'd pull it gently as they made love on the floor. It was too hot for clothes.

Sometimes he couldn't believe he had found someone like her. Sometimes it feels like it was always going to happen. When he held her against him, her skin and bones and sweat and taste, that was home.

Too bright. Blinding bright.

He's thinking about Clare underneath him when a white hot sun flare hits his bright blue eyes and he jerks instinctively away.

He hears the squeal of tires. Someone else speeding home to their girl, maybe.

He isn't angry with them, in those eternal seconds as he understood, somewhere primal and animal within him stirring, as he knew he was going to die. That person in the car might be having the worst day of their life. Michael was, until then, having one of his best. He had a girl, a house, a cat and a bike. Arguably a good a time to die as any.

Michael had just enough time to conjure an image of Clare in his mind. If he's going to bloody get killed, he's going to at least think about something nice whilst it happens, thank you very much. He thinks about her laughing, Cheshire cat smile, her long hair falling around her shoulders. Pressing her fingers into his face to feel the shape of his goofy grin. She smells like paint and jasmine.

And that, as they say, was that.

16

The bad kind

In films, when people die, they always find time to say something important. Or maybe their widow finds a letter about how much her husband really loved her and then she moves on with her life, complete with montage and emotional music.

That doesn't happen in real life.

And it doesn't happen to Clare.

Because you never think you're actually going to die, do you? Sure, it'll happen one day. Probably. But you never think of it just...happening. You never think you're going to pop out for milk one day and never come back.

When her parents had left for their sailing trip they had said "be a good girl, Clare bear. Take care of yourself. Call Aisling if anything happens. You can call us anytime if you need to, and we'll come right back, alright darling? Oh – and remember to water the plants."

Michael hadn't said anything, as far as she knew. She'd been asleep when he left. He might have kissed her, or she might have dreamt that. She didn't know.

She had not followed her parent's advice. She had not been taking care of herself. She can't remember stopping. It wasn't a decision as such, just a slowing. A forgetting. A drifting. Everything had just become a little blurry for a long time.

It wasn't like she cried herself to sleep every night. At least, not anymore. She read books, she paid her bills on time, she tended her garden and did her art. She fed her cat. She drank hot tea.

But when she thought about it she wasn't sure what else she'd been doing for years.

Sometimes the time before, with Michael, felt like a hundred years ago. Like he never existed. Sometimes he felt like yesterday.

She knew he'd be annoyed at her. But she told herself she didn't care because he wasn't here.

Clare used to have a lot of friends. Or rather she and Michael had had a lot of friends. Mostly couple friends who drank a lot of wine and tried to find out each other's secrets. Michael could be friends with just about anyone, if they weren't terrifically awful. Even though Clare was intuitive, even though she could draw people into her and understand them, even though she had that effortless warmth, she found it difficult to really call them her friends. She was always gripped by the idea that no matter how safe they felt with her, how much she knew them, they didn't seem to really know her. They all seemed to exist in a giant conglomerate of couple problems and mutual need. Their own tiny society, with their own politics. Michael said she was too serious about it, that it wasn't like her. But she had been alone for a long time. She could get along without the constant undercurrent of passive aggressive jealousies and lusts. And the endless supply of cheese and wine nights.

It had been easier when she was younger. In your twenties being an artist is romantic, its important. Once you get older, it stops being a proper job. Your friends see you as nothing more than a kept woman without a degree, especially when your boyfriend happened to have a lot of money. This was only partly true and it made her feel itchy and sick. Michael made jokes about being her sugar daddy and she tried to throw dirty paint water at him. Then he put a frame over the stain it had made on the wall and called it art. He'd made her laugh and she'd carried on her work, made her own money. Later she would have no choice but to do that.

It had always seemed enough, the two of them. Their shared

history that only they knew – but their personal histories, only shared with the other. How Clare had felt so abandoned by her family, how Michael had hated himself for as long as he could remember. It was enough that it had all been told once. They would never have to repeat those things out loud again. Someone knew. Once Michael was gone she had never had the will or the energy to teach her history to another person.

After the funeral she had stopped talking to their friends.

Michael's family sort of took over, even though this time she had actually wanted to plan things for him. She got to at least pick out some of the songs – she had disregarded Michael's insistence that he wanted highway to hell playing as he was cremated. She'd picked let it be, and that was something she was still trying to do.

His family had let her grieve with them, but it had lacked sincerity whether they knew it or not. She wasn't part of their family, at least Michael's mother, the real head of the house, had always made her feel that way. His sister, Emily Jane, mother of Henry, had been naïve and sweet and silly. She was lost without her big brother and so she let her mother guide her. There seemed no real point in trying to get to one another, now the thread that linked them no longer existed. At the wake, she'd hid under the table with Henry, eating ham sandwiches in silence. She'd waved to him as she'd left and had not seen Michael's nephew again.

She had been worried that they would try and take the house. But she had dug in her claws, her hooks and her heels. She'd promised she'd do something with it. A lie, even then, but she'd almost believed that she would.

Michael had left her some money – more than she needed. He'd left some of it for charities of her choosing, and the house was already paid off and given to her in its entirety. The rest of his money went to Henry. At that point, Henry Bellbrooke Winters became set to inherit the entire Bellbrooke fortune as well as the money his father's family brought in. That was until his little sister was born a year later. They named her Michaela, for the uncle she would never meet.

Would he forgive Clare now? For not taking care of Henry? For letting him enter those teenage years with only his strange family for guidance? The years that had haunted Michael until his death, the years at boarding school and the years of sticky tar darkness that never came out – had she abandoned his nephew to that wilderness? She didn't know. He would be fifteen now. She tried to imagine the small bespectacled boy in the bookshop, all grown up and finds she cannot. She wonders if he's still covered in plasters, if he's still asking questions.

One by one the flowers and the food had stopped arriving on the doorstep. She'd never answered the knocks and so it appeared, like it had been left by fairies.

Aisling came back for a while but did not bring Carys. She'd held her all night and stroked her hair. But soon she had to go too, back to her life, her husband, her child and her love.

People stopped calling. The sun continued to rise and set. Her friends stopped trying to be understanding and got irritated. She was wallowing. Michael wouldn't want this. We all loved him, but you have to move on. Stop being so unreasonable. Stop being selfish. We're only trying to help you, you just don't appreciate it. Clare soon stopped listening to the answerphone messages. She who had been strong and bold and brutally alive became a modern day Mrs Havisham.

If sadness - we are calling it sadness, because there are many words for it, and none. So if sadness - the bad kind - in her niece was roiling and churning, dark and pulpy offal that stuck to her guts - then for Clare it was a void. An absence. She was as empty as this house. She had rooms in her no one would ever enter again. She felt the world falling in on her, as if she didn't fit in it anymore. As if the things that made up everyday reality were clothes that she had outgrown.

One day, after many years and no time at all, Aisling's child came and rang the doorbell. The bell that peeled through the house was a signal, a call to prayer and a warning all at once. A warning of unstoppable change. Like the clocks starting once more. If Clare and Michael had met a little earlier, if many things had been different, if it had been raining that day and he had stayed home and she'd gotten pregnant on top of the red Moroccan rug – if they had had their life and a child – that child might have looked a lot like Carys. But she wasn't theirs. She had a perfect smile and not a lopsided one. Her parents had raised her and she did not even know how much she echoed them in everything.

Some memory had finally stirred its dust in Clare. Of company and kindness, animals snuffling nervously round her heart once more. It had been strange, and good and sad, and nice. She had thought of Michael as more than something she had lost. It felt ok to do that.

Carys had reminded her that time had been passing and that somewhere along the way the pain had dulled without her knowing. She felt ashamed at the neglect of herself. The world had not been fair to her and in return she had stopped being fair to herself. In trying to take care of her niece – who had sad eyes and sharp claws – she had begun to inadvertently take care of herself as well. She wanted to. She wanted to smile. She was tired. She wanted to never sleep again. She had wanted to see foreign skies again and to stop being scared. She wanted to try for all that, at least.

But, as always, she had lost that too. Carys was now gone. Everyone was always gone. Clare felt as if she was always being forced to rebuild herself. To remake herself, from orphan, to widow to whatever she was now. But she was always losing.

She wanted to go to sleep and not have to think about any of them ever again. None of them had ever been hers. Not even Michael, a man from another world. She feels selfish and sad. Her own self-pity slips around in her belly, a wet slapping organ moving around inside her and she cannot seem to get rid of it.

Clare floats through the house that she did not buy, feeling as if she was just a caretaker in it until its real occupant arrived. She loved the place and she thought it loved her – but maybe her sadness simply gave it a purpose. They took care of one another. But was the house tired of her yet? Would the spirit that made it real and alive leave her in its skeleton one day?

She presses her head against a window. She's high up in the house, in the dark parts no one ever explored. The house, like any human body, had its useless bits. That room is an appendix, that bit a tailbone. The cool glass is wet with condensation against her forehead. The coldness starts to hurt and she welcomes its painful clarity before moving on.

She finds herself in the room with the painting on the wall. Columbus runs out as she enters, like he'd been doing something wrong just by being in here or like she'd scared him. Even though she knows full well that he's a skittish little shit, it sort of makes her want to cry.

She stares at the painting she had made with phantom hands. She hears its flat green leaves rustle. She hates it. She really bloody hates it. She knows in her bones this was somehow the cause of her current situation. It had cleft a chunk from her life. She wants to hiss at it.

Instead, she crumbles before it, like being felled by an angry god. Clare clutches her stomach and wails. She thinks she might be sick. Spittle and tears make her face wet. She feels the floor rise up to meet her knees. She puts her head against the wood of the floor. It's the only thing she can concentrate on. She feels drunk.

Then there is a fracture of light.

"Well, this is very depressing." On overly cheerful voice says.

An impossible voice, a dead voice, a gone away not here anymore voice. A such a waste voice. A sorry for your loss voice.

Michael blinks into existence, appearing through wet stuck together eyelashes, blurred at the edges. Jeans, first. She sees his knees in front of her own as she lifts her head. Skin poking through holes ripped in them. They had been the height of fashion and she'd hated them. Then legs, belt with ironic dollar sign buckle. She'd bought it him as a joke after their third date and he'd worn it ever since. Plain black shirt, because he was very cool like that and didn't even need to make an effort.

Then there he is. Sun through clouds. Sickeningly beautiful, hers and not hers. There and not there, dead and sat in front of her, smiling.

"This floor doesn't look very clean, Clare. Look – god, it's covered in paint. Why are you lying down like this anyway? You look like a sad...wet...log." Michael raised his eyebrows as she stares at him. He puts his hand to his ear mockingly. "What's that? Gosh Mikey, I think you're right! I'm being totally pathetic right now and not like me at all. Golly, I think I better get up off the floor and have a nice hot drink. Thanks Michael! Your welcome Clare bear!"

She rocks back on her heels like an animal, springing away like he'd jumped at her.

"What...what the fuck is happening?...What is this?"

She sinks back in front of him, examining him like he's a newly discovered species.

He smiles her favourite stupid looking smile and tears blind her. Her cheeks feel raw and tender as they fall.

"You look as if you've seen a ghost." He says softly. He's trying to be kind. He's doing what she always did for other people. It was actually rather annoying. "Don't make me give you my best Aisling scowl." He says. She thinks the movement of his face is the hand of god in motion.

"Is this real?" Clare whispers. "Are you a ghost?"

"How the hell should I know?" Michael shrugs. "Though if I am a ghost, shouldn't I be wearing a long dark sheet and jumping out of cupboards?"

"This isn't funny." She swats his shoulder. He's solid. She half expected her hand to go right through him.

"It's a little bit funny. Oh darling, you used to have a sense of humour."

"And you used to be alive!" She snapped.

Michael just smiled sympathetically and nodded.

Clare closed her eyes and lowered her head back down to the floor. She felt too heavy.

"Please." She sniffed. "Please just stop whatever this is. I can't do it. I'm too tired. My head hurts too much." She doesn't know if she's talking to Michael or the house.

She feels a strong grip on her shoulders as he lifts her back up from the floor.

"That's because..." Michael brushed her long hair back over her shoulders. "You've been crying too much. And I'm sorry, I'm so sorry Clare bear. But you have to stop now."

Clare's shoulders sagged in defeat where he held them. "I'm trying."

It was meant to be easier than this, wasn't it? Giving up. Standing still.

"No Clare, I don't mean like that. Love, you have to stop...stop this. All this. This...I hate to say it, this wallowing."

"I'm not wallowing!" she cried, offended.

"You're literally lying on the floor!" Michael closed his eyes for a brief moment. "I don't mean it like that. I just mean...I know you're depressed. I know you want to stop everything, but you can't. You just can't."

She threw his hands off her. "Oh, why the hell not?"

"Because Carys is out there somewhere, in danger, and she needs you!"

Clare opens her mouth to protest but nothing comes out. A guilty blush creeps up her cheeks.

"I might have done the same, if it had been me and I'd lost you. In fact I would have been the same. I would have drunk and drunk until I died, probably. But I'd like to think that if Henry needed me, I'd stagger around enough that I could do something for him." Michael moves his face even closer to hers, willing her to feel his sincerity. "And I hope that no matter how much I loved you, so much that it hurts to look at you, I wouldn't put your memory above the safety of a child. And she is a child, Clare. Carys is Aisling's child."

Clare felt a fissure run through her heart at the mention of her sister. She could imagine Aisling's face, her fury, her despair. She couldn't cause that. She could not betray her sister. Her blood would not let her.

"Oh!" she gasped, lifting her hands to her mouth. "Aisling. She loves her so much and I..."

"That's why she sent her here to you." Michael jumped on her moment of understanding, staring at her intently.

Clare nodded. "They saw how unhappy she was. She told them she didn't want to move around all the time. They didn't know what to do with her. They thought she'd be happier staying in one place. Aisling said she was like me, that they trusted me. They didn't want to be apart from her, but they did it for her. They always did everything for her."

"Did you did tell her that?" Michael sounds like he's really trying to work it out with her.

"Well, I assumed she knew. She's clever. She's really clever."

"Well, how would she? Aisling and Jude, god love them, wouldn't know the words to tell her. Not really."

He was right, he was absolutely right. It shot through her like a dart. You could be as clever as anything, but that didn't mean you didn't get tricked by your emotions. Didn't mean you always knew the way to say things.

"Right now, for as long as she lives with you, she's your responsibility. You have to help her."

Clare shook her head in a sudden panic. "There's so much death in my life." The words came out without thought, like they had been living inside her, waiting for a voice. "Maybe she's just safer away from me!"

Michael shook his head, trying to shush her and calm her. "Hon, you know that's not how it works. You can't control death. I couldn't control it when it came for me. But you can control this, I swear to god you can. You're sick of losing people? You don't have to lose this one. This is it baby. This is it! This is the thing you get to control. This is the thing you get to keep."

He always knew what to say to her. She'd missed that. She had given up on everything because it had seemed easier that way. She'd wrapped herself in her loneliness here, like a shield from all hurt. But Carys had come and she'd dropped the shield, just a little bit. And she wanted that, wanted a family again. One good thing. And if she lost again at least she would have tried for it. She'd been standing still for so long. She had to move again.

"I don't know how. Michael, I have no idea how to get to her."

Michael smiled in relief, he looked like he might be crying. "That's ok! That's ok." He urged. "Look, if there's a way for her to go somewhere, there's a way for you to go there too. Try anything, everything. You were always stronger than you knew. You find a way, you hear me? You just find one." Michael jabbed a finger at her painting on the wall. He was a little breathless. "All you have to do is be brave, and get that kid back home."

He holds her face in both his hands. It had always fit, his fingers were so long. He turns her face with his to stare at the painting.

"Bring her back home."

The light comes back, it hurts her eyes. She's trying to see if his face had changed, screaming inside, willing him to stay. He drops his hands to his knees again.

"Is this a dream?" she whines, not wanting to know, needing to know.

"No darling. It's not a dream." He lifts his fingers. There's oil on them. He must have just come from fixing his bike outside. He's gone before he can touch her face again.

17

Clare calls in Claudette, a clairvoyant.

Clare never had visitors to the house. Even the post was left in a little box at the end of the long path that was her driveway, her groceries left in boxes on agreed days. No one wandered up that path by chance. She was like a wicked witch in a fairy story. Alone in a deep dark place.

So when the doorbell rang - for the first time since Carrie's arrival two months ago at least - Clare just about jumped out of her skin.

She was early! Clare thinks. She wasn't meant to get here till - She glanced at the clock on her bedside table. Oh. One in the afternoon.

How had she slept so long?

Clare jumped clumsily out of bed, trying to move past the dizziness that made her stumble.

She'd fallen asleep in her clothes last night. After scouring the internet and placing the most awkward answerphone message known to man she'd felt drained, until the phone had rang and she'd decided one o clock would give her enough time to tidy up. So much for that plan.

Michael had not appeared to her again. The bastard.

She'd been terrified to go to sleep in case she missed him. When he hadn't returned to the room with the painting, she had set about trying to do as he said and put a vague plan in motion. After that she had wandered round the house to look for him, Columbus following her on her patrol. But nothing else had happened. The house began to dim the lights to signal her to go to bed. She'd fallen onto the bed with the cat curled up next to her and slept the whole night and day.

She had no time to change her clothes now. She sprayed some deodorant on herself and threw it on the floor as she haphazardly fought her way to the door through mounds of clothes and the other junk that littered her floor. On the way she heard a loud clank!

She swore loudly as her foot began to throb and looked down. Her bare foot had collided with a large and varied array of mugs that seemed to be colonizing her floor. Most of them seemed to be half full of cold tea.

She was always making cups of tea and forgetting about them, or leaving them in odd places and making some more. Aisling had once said it was more than likely it was her alone keeping the tea bag industry alive.

Clare wiped the cold tea from her foot onto the carpet and ran from the room. As she made it to the stairs the doorbell rang once more. She just about managed to avoid tumbling to her death as Columbus shot out in front of her and ran down the stairs ahead of her.

Remembering the messiness of her appearance, Clare scooped her long hair up from her neck - but realized she didn't have a bobble to tie it up with.

So in last nights crumpled clothes, the ankle of her jeans soaked in tea, face still puffy from all the crying the day before and her hair flying wildly about her face, Clare finally wrenched the door open.

Claudette was a large woman. Beautiful, in a homely sort of way. She reminded Clare of lullabies on a stormy night. Her hair, wrapped in a bright blue turban with big yellow flowers on it, smelled like coconut oil. The large multi coloured beads she wore round her neck jangled loudly as she walked. She had dark brown skin and almost shaped eyes that surveyed everything around her.

"Yes, yes." Claudette said slowly, in a thick Caribbean accent. "There is certainly something strange about this house."

Clare had scoured the internet for hours looking through all manner of spiritualists, psychics, even a priest offering buy one get one free exorcisms. She knew that wherever Carys was, it wasn't as simple as walking to the front door and asking for her. She needed help.

"Oh, I already know that bit. Weird magic house? Check! We're fine on that end. That isn't really why I called you."

She was nodding eagerly to Claudette, who was stood staring at her like she just said she went round licking the windows. Clare suddenly dashed forward and grabbed hold of Columbus, who was prowling around to make himself known and dangerously close to knocking several things off the kitchen table. He also had an unfortunate habit of darting out from nowhere like a hell demon, and she decided she couldn't afford a lawsuit should the clairvoyant in her kitchen trip over him.

Claudette rolled her eyes. "You can put your cat down. We ain't gonna bother each other."

"Well, he's a bit manic-" Clare sputtered as Columbus decided the best way to wriggle free was to attack her hair with gusto.

"Put the ugly thing down. He's just acting up. Animals, especially cats, feel the shifts within the spirit world much more than humans do."

Clare released the offended cat and he ran off with one long glare at them both. Clare is sure she's going to find a puddle of revenge vomit somewhere in the next few hours.

"So, let me get this right. You're telling me that you are in fact fully aware that your house either is in some way alive with a kind of spiritual power?"

"Yes."

"And you're not bothered about that?"

"No. Not really."

Claudette rolled her eyes again and cocked her hip. "White people."

"Well, I say not really. I am more concerned about what it's done with my niece. It's sort of a long story. Why don't I make us some tea?"

Neither of them mentioned that during this entire conversation, Claudette's accent had gone from Caribbean to very clearly east London.

Clare does not tell her about Michael. She doesn't want Claudette to tell her she was more than likely slap bang in the middle of a nervous breakdown. She wanted to cling to the idea that whatever she had seen, it had been real. She wanted to dig her claws into that idea and never let it go. Clare knew it had made her stronger. The idea that Michael had crawled his way back from death just to talk to her. To help her to do this. She felt so scared, so alone. If she lost that conviction, she had nothing.

But she'd told her the rest. Not that there was a lot to tell, in the end. Not so much of a long story, since Clare didn't really know the details. She did know that Carys wasn't just a teenage runaway. She was somewhere...other. And she had known that something was wrong with the painting ever since it had come to her, fully formed.

"You have to show me this painting." Claudette announced with no preamble when Clare was finished. She wanted to cry with relief. She wanted to hand over the reins, just for a little while. She knew it couldn't be forever though. She'd always had other people to take care of her. Her parents, Aisling, Michael. Sometimes it hurt her head to think about everything she knew had still to happen.

Claudette's hand was covered in rings. Shining green and deep purple. They hover, gleaming on her pudgy fingers, over the painting, blending with the colours but never touching the paint.

"When I was young, I knew I was different. My parents had it hard enough being the only black family on the estate, at least at that time. I didn't want to bother them with what I knew I was. It was clear to me from a young age that I was in tune with something that most people were not. My parents were good people. They wanted to protect me, in their own way. They didn't want to give the world another reason to hate me. I'm black, and I'm a woman. Being in touch with a supernatural energy would have made me a triple threat." She raised her eyebrows at Clare who nodded sagely.

"So my parents decided the best way to protect me was for me to deny that part of myself. We stopped talking of it. My intuition, I called it. But not speaking of it didn't make a difference. It was still there. I felt the energy of people, of places, everywhere. The more I tried to ignore it the worse it got, until it got too overwhelming for me to even leave the house. Like you."

Claudette had been pacing slowly in front of the painting as she talked, but she glared at Clare, hearing her scoff at that last part.

"I leave my house." Clare laughed unconvincingly. Claudette just stared at her, eyes made of iron.

"Going into your garden doesn't count."

Clare opened her mouth, and closed it again. She crossed her arms grumpily.

"I'm going to carry on now." Claudette said. "I became very isolated. Very alone. And that is when I began to feel it. A dark energy. A place apart from this world. It called to me. But I knew, I knew deep down that this was a bad place. A place for people to pour all their hurt and anger into." She hissed.

Clare shivered at her tone.

"But I did not let it take me." Claudette pointed at the painting.

Clare stood up from where she had been leaning against the wall, moving swiftly to Claudette. "And you think this bad place has my niece?"

"I'm saying that-" Claudette pointed at the wall again. "Is what has your niece."

"But you think it's the same place?"

Claudette sucked on her teeth and nodded grimly. "It's likely. It feels the same. It's been a long time, but you don't forget that kind of darkness."

Claudette turned to her with a face full of pity, and Clare felt her stomach drop. "So...what do we do?"

"I'm going to need everything you know about this house."

The fire was blazing in The room. It had not burned since Michael had occupied this room. But now it crackled in the low lamp light, warming the room, making it feel close. Clare listened to the wood popping in the quiet as she waited for Claudette to speak.

To an outsider it probably looked like they were holding a séance, the way they were sat right across the desk from each other. That or the world's weirdest job interview.

Claudette had cleared Michael's desk for all the files about the house. She'd ask if she could move the laptop, the picture of them, the lamp that he'd stolen from a library when he was at uni. Clare had nodded numbly, not knowing how to object. Claudette had been very gentle with it all, leading Clare to suspect she knew exactly what she was doing and why. Clare forced herself to watch. Those things hadn't moved since Michael had put them there and since she and Carys had looked at that picture. When it was done she sat in his chair with shaking limbs.

Clare had told her everything she knew about the house. They read the reports, the articles, everything that had ever been collected about the house. They had school records, medical records, bibles, army ranks. Death certificates. But overall it was nice to read about the house. About the sense of safety all of its occupants had felt here. They would never truly know why the house was the way it was. Whoever came next would not know either, but it was clear the house was a beacon.

But every harbour has its dangers. The forces that called to the lost, those in need of sanctuary would call to other forces too. Dark ones.

And now they sat, waiting for Claudette to find her words. Columbus had wandered in at some point to lounge by the fire. Even he sat up now. Clare was listening, the cat was listening, the house was listening.

"This place, this island they all talk about. It takes people by feeding on their loneliness. Like here, in a way. But it isn't a safe place. If this is a house where you can find freedom from pain, that island sends you right into the heart of it. To stare into its eyes."

"If thou gaze long into an abyss." Clare quoted, and Claudette nodded.

"Only in the later years, there are less and less mention of this happening."

"Do you think it's because we don't believe in this sort of stuff anymore?"

Claudette's necklaces rattled as she shrugged. "Perhaps. But I think it is probably down to more than just one thing." She spread her jewelled fingers across the papers. "There are some religions, old religions, where their gods only exist as long people believe in them. Maybe we're dealing with something similar. Maybe not."

Well, Clare had no better explanation. She tucked her hair behind her ear and sat forward in her seat, trying to articulate the thing that had been bothering her, floating around in her stomach, ever since she'd sat down.

"Say all this is true, and Carys got spirited away to this place because of whatever it was she was feeling." She shook her head. "It doesn't make sense for it to happen now. There were whole groups of people living here before, and it didn't happen to them for years. How does one girl have the power to make this place see her, when it didn't see the others?" She looked at Claudette pleadingly. "Could it…could it have really been so bad, and I didn't even see it?"

She can hear the desperation in her voice. Aisling had told her that Carys had been having problems – but she thought she'd been getting a little better.

Claudette reached out and took hold of Clare's thin fingers in her round ones.

"You're right. You're asking the right questions. You didn't fail her, not like that." She gripped Clare's fingers tightly, her rings digging into Clare's fingers. Clare held on even tighter as they leaned toward each other. "Thing is, I don't think your niece could have got there by herself." She says this calmly and slowly, like she's explaining something very delicate. Like she doesn't want to scare her.

"What do you mean?" Clare whispers, even though she thinks she already knows the answer.

"Now I don't know for sure. But I think it's a pretty safe bet that your girl had a – a conduit, of sorts."

"The painting." Clare nods.

Claudette looks away from her, just for a second. When she looks back at her, her mouth is shaking, though she's trying to hide it.

"Not just the painting. She had you." Clare tried to tug her hands away but Claudette slammed them back onto the table, keeping her there with her. "The island felt your pain first. You sealed yourself up in this house like you was burying yourself in a coffin. You heard it first. You made the painting. Your pain seeped into this house, and it opened a door. Your niece stepped through that door, carrying not just her pain, but yours too."

"No! You can't know that. I wouldn't do that to her." Clare shakes her head. She's writhing about in her seat, like the very information is causing her pain. Claudette doesn't let her go.

"I'm sorry Clare. But you – you are the gatekeeper. Charon,

Heimdall, Saint Peter. Someone always has to guard the gate. Someone carries the souls from one side to the other. But – now listen – listen. If you opened the gate for her to go through, it stands to reason that you can open it to bring her back."

Clare nodded numbly. "Like Michael said."

"Yeah girl, just like that."

It isn't until Claudette is gone that Clare remembers. She hadn't told her about Michael, or what he had said.

She had wanted Claudette to stay, but she didn't want to risk her getting caught in whatever came next.

And so Clare stands in front of her painting alone.

All of her loss. All of her fear. All of her pain over her man, over her parents. It had caused something to awaken. Something evil. Something invisible, but no less dangerous. Carrie had amplified what was already there.

Claudette hadn't known exactly how she would get to Carys, only that she could, and that the best place to start was the painting.

"Right then, you bastard."

She'd thrown herself at the wall repeatedly, landing flat out on the floor a few times. Nothing had happened except for the large, dark purple bruise growing on her arm.

"Tell me what to do!"

No one was here to help her. Not Claudette, not Michael. Not even Aisling, who knew nothing of this. She had to work it out herself. She could do it. She was a grown woman.

She'd shooed Columbus out of the room because she didn't want anything to happen to him. But so far nothing had happened to her either.

Clare sighed in frustration and leaned her head against the wall. Think, think.

Maybe that was the problem. Maybe she had to stop thinking so hard and it would come to her, if she really was the gatekeeper. What did she always do when she was trying not to think? She sang, she sang.

"Little girl, little girl...don't you lie to me." She sang quietly. It was a slow, old song. "Tell me where did you sleep last night?"

She spread her arms wide either side of her, stretching her fingers across the bumps of the paint.

"In the pines...in the pines..."

She thinks about her niece and how her grief had hurt them both.

"Where the sun never shines..." she breathes deeply.

She thinks about Michael, who was young, who had loved her, who she didn't remember leaving the house that day.

"I shiver the whole night through..."

Her parents had raised their girls well for as long as they could. Would they be proud of her, of what she had become?

"Little girl, little girl, where did you go?"

Their bodies were rotting in a foreign sea. They were experienced sailors. Michael had known everything about motorbikes. How had any of this happened? At two, did it become a curse?

"To the place where the cold wind blows."

She and Aisling only ever spoke on the phone a few times a year. The rest was emails. She missed her big sister. Her bossy, beautiful sister. No matter how much she loved her niece, it wasn't a replacement for the mother. She missed having someone who looked like her. Seeing how they both looked like her mother, and her mother before that.

"In the pines, in the pines, where the sun never shines."

She can't remember when she stopped being brave. Now she only ever went as far as the bottom of her garden path, to the post box. She never left the grounds of this house. She lets her tears smear onto the wall.

"I shiver the whole night through."

And then, finally, as if it felt her heart calling, the world falls away.

18

Perdita

As they trudged back through the jungle together, Carrie could not help the disappointment settling inside her.

But, she reasoned, at least this near death experience was somewhat more informative than the last one. She had started to work out a way that she could use, perhaps, to shield herself from Pan, a way to protect herself from his magic. She knew at least that it could be done. And they had managed to stop the storms, buying her more time. That was how they knew the fairy had found her way home.

They had let Tinkerbell out with very little ceremony.

She wasn't what Carrie had expected. Not like the films, buxom and bright or like those sweet Victorian imaginings. Tinkerbell had two arms and two legs, like a person in miniature. But her skin was so pale it looked lilac, with dark black veins and eyes like little droplets of oil, and sharp little claws. Her skin was covered in blue spirals and patterns that looked almost Celtic. She reminded Carrie of a Boudicca in miniature. She didn't have that flame red hair though – just fleshy spikes on top of her head. It all served to make her look fairly androgynous. Only a few clues pointed to her gender from her appearance – a scrap of green fabric covered her almost totally flat breasts and genitals. Also Carrie knew that Tinkerbell's – for it was a rank, not a name, only given to Pan's closest servant – were always female fairies. Like the native tribe and the mermaids, the fairies, amongst themselves, were a matriarchal society, despite then answering to pan. It was a shame really. This was an entirely matriarchal island, with that exception.

Tinkerbell didn't look back at them as she zoomed away, but within a few minutes the distant storms stopped and Carrie let herself be content.

Back at camp, after the others had run and tackled them, after the cheers and the hugs and hastily wiped tears, Carrie sat uselessly hacking at a stick with her knife. She'd intended to make a spear, but frustration and tiredness had got the better of her. When was she going to get off this island? She could not settle. Even now the storms had gone, the first real taste of Pan's power, and not even his worse attack – she still felt itchy and misplaced. Something else was going to come, eventually. Maybe more fighting, like the night she arrived. She couldn't just relax. She didn't know how they all did this. She couldn't stop and start, over and over.

"Sweet Jesus, will ya stop grumbling'?"

Carrie jumps as Willow snapped her fingers angrily at her. She didn't realize she'd been muttering. She flushed, though a part of her felt entitled to a bit of a moan.

"Sorry – I just – "

"No!" Willow snapped.

"Willow!" Nala hissed, but she was ignored.

Carrie, Willow and Nala had all been sat round the fire together, but now Willow jumped up and marched over to her.

"You have not stopped complaining since the moment you got here."

She was six foot and easily towered over Carrie's five foot two inches, but Carrie still jumped up in indignation, staring up at her.

"Well I'm very bloody sorry if I'm not ready to just move on in here-"

"You wouldn't be happy anywhere!" Willow snaps, and Carrie blanches in shock. She pressed her lips together tightly. "We took you in, taught you how to survive, as much as you could be taught. You'd be dead if it weren't for us. And all you can do is talk about how much you wanna leave! Like you're smarter than us cos you read all your damn books, because you're from a different time. Like you're doing us some massive favour being here, callin' us your friends-"

"You are my friends!"

"Then stop reminding us how much you don't want to be here. Like we've given up." Willow shook her head and her voice started to shake. "There ain't nothing wrong with living with what you got. Making the best of it."

She took a few deep, racking breaths. Her eyes glowed with emotion. No one spoke for a whole minute. Even Nala, steady and true, could not meet anyone's eye. Then there was a softening in Willow, a defeated slump and she opened her mouth again. Carrie could see the surprise on her face. Before she could jump in and apologize, before she could say anything, Carrie shook her head, hot embarrassed tears pricking her eyes. She ignored their calls as she walked away from them.

"Well maybe she has a point." Perdy shrugged casually when Carrie had finished telling her what had happened. Carrie hadn't given her time to speak after she'd barged into her tent. To her credit, Perdy had listened in silence until Carrie had finished.

"So you agree?" Carrie yelled, her face screwing up and Perdy rolled her eyes.

Perdy turned to her properly to glare. She threw down the cloth she had been using to take off her war paint, the heavy black stuff that covered her eyes. She always lefts bit of it on by accident, it made her look like she was wearing eyeliner.

"No." She said clearly. What she actually meant was 'Don't be an idiot'. "I just mean it's a little disheartening when you decide to tell us all that trying to be happy here is pointless. Doesn't actually make us feel all that good."

Carrie spluttered. "That is not what I'm doing. At least not how you mean."

"Oh and who exactly are you trying to convince right now?" Perdy watched simply as Carrie slumped. "Look." she said, "Willow is just annoyed she missed out on all the action. Anyway, haven't you ever found someone unbearably annoying and loved them for it anyway?"

"You find me unbearably annoying?" Carrie asked and Perdy smiled at her gently. She sighed and sat next to Perdy on the bed. She threw her hands up in defeat. "You just described me entire family."

"Even Clare? I thought you wanted to be here when you grow up."

"Shut up." Carrie laughed, nudging Perdy with her elbow. "She's just so extra about stuff. Like, all the time." Glancing at Perdy she saw a small frown of confusion. "Intense, I mean. She's unfailingly, fantastically nice to people or she's completely out of it and doing stupid stuff, like painting on the walls or not leaving a room for two days. That's what my mum always said, anyway. There's no real calm to her. I know what she means now. But I adore her for it anyway." Carrie lets herself fall back, to lie down and stare at the great dark ceiling, like a sky without stars. "I think there's something there, something we don't talk about. When I first met her I thought she was just this cool auntie I didn't know. But now I think…I don't know. There's something unnamed. Something more than grief. It didn't just start after Michael – Uncle Michael? Anyway – she did shit like that before. Quitting school and running off somewhere by herself just because she wanted too. And…And maybe I'm more like her than anyone ever thought."

They stayed quiet for a long moment. And then Carrie spoke again, into the dark, into the infinite nothing that surrounded the island, into the past.

"There was a photo, in Clare's house. I found it tucked away behind some books. I thought the house was showing it to me. It was of some girls that used to live there, a long time ago."

Perdy made a non-committal noise.

"I think the date said 1970. There was one girl – she was very pretty. I remember the I thought you looked like her, when I first saw you. I couldn't place it at first, but I've been thinking about it a lot since. And now I think I've remembered her name."

Carrie propped herself back up to sit next to Perdy again. The other girl, her girl, her face held no hint of what was going to come. It made it hard to speak.

"Who is Emmeline Scott?"

In a shot, without warning, Perdy clamped her hand hard over Carrie's mouth.

"Don't say that name here!" She hissed. For a second Carrie thought she was angry - but she saw her eyes flick all around her. What she saw in those eyes was pure undiluted fear.

When she was certain the tent wasn't going to implode on top of them, she relaxed and sat on her bed, pulling Carrie down next to her. Carrie gently reached up to remove Perdy's hand from her face. Perdy flinched and Carrie saw her hand shaking. Perdy made fist and shoved it out of sight in her furs - but Carrie had seen her unsettled she was.

"Don't say her for name. I don't want Pan to know her name."

"Who is she?" Carrie whispered, afraid suddenly to talk too loud. "Is she your sister, or your mum or something?"

Perdy shook her head closing her eyes. "She's not any of those things."

"But your last names are the same...and you look so similar!"

"No - Carrie." Perdy sucked in a breath, tears clouding in her big blue eyes. "She isn't my sister or my mother because she's..."

With one last glance toward the tent flap like she was expecting pan to burst in right then, she said in a shaking voice, "She is my daughter. My Emmeline."

"I lived in France with my family until I was eight. Then the war came and we fled our home - like criminals. Me, my mother and my father - we moved to Ireland. It was 1943. That was the year the Nazis rounded up everyone where I lived - Marseille in France. We escaped, we were lucky."

Carrie sucked in a breath of surprise Perdy stared intently at the floor of the tent.

"We lived. But I grew up remembering my home, feeling displaced. The school I went to - I found it too strict, too cruel. But we lived. Many did not. When I was eighteen, I met a boy." she smiled sadly. "His name was Marcello. His family was Italian - they had fled the war as well. He was twenty-two, so he remembered more than me. and he was Jewish - He had dark curly hair and skin the colour of peaches in summer. He looked at you like he knew something you didn't. He worked as an odd job man at my school, and I used to sneak away from class to go and meet him. it was the only time I didn't feel alone. I suppose you could say one thing led to another..."

"And you found out you were pregnant."

Perdy wiped away a stray tear from her cheek and nodded.

"It was·1953 by then - I don't know how much you know about Ireland in 1953."

"My great grandmother was Irish. I've been a few times. But even if I hadn't everybody knows there has been and still is a lot of trouble there. I'm not an expert...but you hear stories, just like any place."

"The English decimated Ireland – but that's another story. As for me and my problem, back then it felt like nobody wanted to help me. It was the same all over. To have a child out of wedlock was one thing - but to a relation with an old Jewish boy?" She shook her head. "The school fired him. I never saw him again. Nobody would answer my questions about him. So I just stopped asking them. All the while our child my child was growing inside of me. And underneath all the fear and uncertainty, I knew I loved her. She was mine the one thing in the world that was truly mine. But my parents - they loved me they let the church pressure them. They thought they were doing what was right in the eyes of God. But it was not right. What they were planning. Have you heard the stories of the mother and baby homes? They were no place to live, let alone have a child. And they took the child. They always took the child. I have never known feel like I knew it then. I wouldn't let them take my baby."

"So what did you do?"

"I ran, only this time without my family. I made it to England, managed to find work as a maid. I lived in a horrible little flat with three other girls." Perdy smiled sadly as she remembered. She had lived her whole life with women, one way or another.

"We all shared a room - it was in London, the bad parts of London. The poverty ran so deeply through the east end it seeped into every Corner. I pretended that I was married and that my husband was away working. I managed to buy a cheap wedding ring when I pawned the family silver. The other girls did not believe me, but they didn't tell, not ever. They had their secrets too. Like Angela, who brought men home for money? Like Carol, whose finger showed where a wedding ring used to live. Like Juana, who could never make herself sound English enough. Just like here, we all existed together in our own world of secrets and hurts."

Perdy looked away sharply, her eyes starting to shine. Absentmindedly she touched her belly, as if it were still round with her daughter instead of flat, taut and now scarred in places.

"As my time came closer I had to stop lying to myself. I knew I couldn't take care of the baby. I knew people would ask questions. I thought...I thought the best thing for her...was to give her up. To someone who would take care of her. I could barely afford to feed myself, let alone a child!" Perdy's voice raised in hysteria and she hiccupped it back, trying to calm herself. Carrie clenched her fists to stop herself taking Perdy's hand.

"Anyway. I gave birth early. I was meant to be making tea in the kitchens for the woman I worked for. Tried to act like it wasn't happening. But it was. She found me, the woman I worked for. She took care of me. But she wasn't going to let me stay. But she did let me name her, before she took her from me. Emmeline Louisa Scott. I didn't see her again. Didn't know where she was. I didn't have a job. Or a daughter. I didn't have anything. I was nothing, no one. And as an Irishwoman, I was one of the lowest of the low. I had nothing."
Carrie's heart pinched and she felt angry for this girl in front of her, who had never seemed as vulnerable as she did then.

"Is that when you ended up here?"

Perdy nodded. She finally looked at Carrie, who tried to smile at her, but barely could. "It was like you. Sort of. I was starving, alone. I fell asleep one night on the street. I woke up on an island. From who is here now, only Willow was here then, with other girls. They're all gone now. Pan..."

She didn't have to finish. Perdy was crying, her face crumpled in on itself, childlike. She looked like a different person. She was normally so stoic, so controlled. Not then. Carrie had gutted her. But she couldn't bring herself to regret the act of asking. She wanted, selfish though it might be, to know the girl she cared about. To understand the things that had made her. Most importantly she wanted Perdy to know that her secrets were safe with her, that she could trust her, and that there were some things Pan would never touch.

Carrie tried to think of what to say. She could only think of what she would want to hear, if it were her.

"The photo I saw. In Clare's house, in the girl's home." She rushed out breathily. "She looked happy."

"Really?" Perdy gasped, like a drowning woman seeing shore. Carrie saw it in her face. She was desperate and hungry for this. For her child. She'd gone...how long – 64 years, over half a century, without her baby. It must have been the cruellest kind of torture.

"Yes, she looked very happy. I think she had a friend, too, so she wasn't alone when she was there."

Carrie reached up to wipe at Perdy's tears that littered her cheeks still. She rested her hand on her cheek. "And she was so beautiful." She nodded looking Perdy in the eyes, unwavering in her sincerity. "She looked just like you. Her mother." Carrie added, trying to get used to saying it.

"Thank you." Perdy whispered, her voice hoarse. "Thank you, thank you." It's all she can say. She keeps repeating it in a quiet voice as Carrie pulls her into a tight hug. She smooth's Perdy's wild curly hair down, Perdy's arms coming round her, holding onto her for dear life.

Carrie smiled as she tried to move Perdy's hair over her shoulder – it had gone even curlier and wilder in the rain and humidity of their recent days. Then, without over thinking it, she kissed Perdy's shoulder. Then she kissed her cheek. Perdy was still breathing heavily, but she didn't stop her. Carrie pulled away, unsure, looking for permission. Perdy pressed their foreheads together and kissed her lightly on the lips.

It was Carrie's first real kiss, and it was a little clumsy. There was a small head bump here, a barely supressed giggle there. But it was nice.

"Sorry." She laughed.

She felt Perdy smile against her mouth. "It's ok."

"I've never really – I don't really know what I'm doing." She said in a nervous rush.

"Neither do I." Perdy cocked an eyebrow. "I've only been with one man, remember."

She leant in to kiss Carrie again, but Carrie stopped her. Perdy took her hands away in question, waiting. "Would it be alright with you if we stop at kissing?"

Perdy reached out and stroked Carrie's cheek. "Of course. I'd never make you do anything you didn't want to do yet. Never."

They smiled again. Carrie couldn't stop smiling. She thinks her cheeks are gonna hurt from it – but she is distracted quickly when she lays down next to Perdy.

Carrie stroked a hand over the soft animal furs underneath her. Perdy was asleep beside her.

She sighed and stared at the ceiling. The darkness of the tent plunged them into a deep blackness as night crept in around them. It made her feel like she was staring at an endless, starless sky. Or an abyss.

In the quiet, she begins to try and sort through the thoughts jumbled in her head.

First and foremost she began to suspect she'd been somewhat unfair on her parents.

Perdy's words had hit her like a thunderclap. She didn't know what it was like to be a parent – didn't know that she ever would. But she saw it was a language of its own, of hard decisions, of sacrifice, of not knowing all the answers even when you had to.

They weren't the most emotionally confident people. They were showers, not tellers. They had kept her with them because they wanted to share their lives and their travels with her. And, she had to admit, they had listened to her wanting to stay in one place. They just didn't know she'd meant with them.

They weren't perfect, and they'd gone about it completely the wrong way, but they had at least tried. That's why, she's beginning to realize, they sent her to stay with Clare. Not that she was a burden, they just thought they were doing what she wanted. They should have talked to her, asked her. But there were good intentions in there.

And maybe she'd needed to come here. Maybe her parents knew what she needed before she did. And maybe – this was something she was coming to suspect more and more – her mother had known Clare had needed someone too.

Carrie approached her feelings warily, like they are a wounded animal. She cannot pin point when and why she started feeling so sad and lonely all the time. But her parents must have noticed eventually more than she thought. And maybe they had been worried about Clare too. At 38, she was afraid to go past her driveway, reclusive and shy in a way she never had been. She'd been doing strange, impulsive things for years and they had left her to that encroaching madness. Maybe they saw that Carrie and Clare could help each other more than her parents could.

Maybe they saw two lonely people – suffering from an illness, perhaps for years in Clare's part – and realized two healthy minded people might not know how to fix it. Even if they wanted to. So they had brought them together in the hopes they could understand and help each other. Clearly it hadn't worked as well as they'd hoped. But there was still time. Maybe, if she could get home.

Perdy's breathing is peaceful in the darkness. Carrie wants to curl around her, pull the furs over them and hibernate until this is over. But she knows they cannot.

Especially since at that moment the tent is flooded in the blue of the night as the tent flap is lifted in a sudden rush.

Perdy jolts awake to glare at Willow. After a hesitant look at both of them, Willow seems to remember why she's there.

"You'd better get out here now. Someone is here."

Carrie's stomach drops. "What do you mean? Is it him?" her heart thunders in her ears. She'd been so lucky up to this point not to have to fight him face to face. Maybe her luck was up.

"No, but it looks like one of his boys. Peaches caught him in the trees just outside camp. We got him tied up like a prize hog. Just waiting on you now chief."

Perdy needs no more information. She and Carrie jump from the bed, all traces of sleepiness gone.

19

Kill or be killed

The boy looks about sixteen, but no older. With light brown hair and wide eyes, he might have grown into a good looking man one day, if only he wasn't so scarred and so hungry looking.

Carrie had had no direct experience with the boys since almost being impaled by one of their arrows the night she got here. She didn't really want experience with any boys, if she was honest, but especially not these ones. In her mind Pan and his boys had taken on almost mythic proportions. unseen but always there, watching all the time, dangerous and feral. Looking down at the boy in front of them, his skinny wrists tied behind his back, she was almost surprised to see her was a kid just like her.

Carrie stood with Nala, who had her arms wrapped around herself in worry. Peaches hopped about and Carrie didn't know if she was nervous or excited. Willow stood behind Perdy as her second.

Perdy paced.

All traces of the vulnerable teenager from earlier was gone. This was Perdy the tribe leader, the warrior, the girl she'd met all those weeks ago with a cruel stare to chill your bones. This was the girl forged by the island, forged by a war Carrie had not truly seen until now.

Perdy had her knives in her hands. She showed off with them twirling them over her fingers expertly. When the silence gets unbearable she stops pacing finally and stares directly down at their captive.

"We got your damned fairy back." She hisses. Carrie can tell she's trying to keep her voice steady. "So tell me what one of Pan's boys is doing skulking around our camp at night, when there has been no more summons?"

The boys just smiled. A feral animal smile. It was twisted, and it scared Carrie. His eyes danced like he knew something they didn't. that was how Carrie always felt nowadays.

"Someone new arrives on his island for the first time in two decades and you think you can just carry on like before?" He sneered. "How dumb are you bitches?"

"You've had weeks to investigate."

The boy blanched, his eyes cutting to Carrie just for a second. But it was enough. She saw the surprise. Pan hadn't told them how long she'd been there. He hadn't sensed her for so long, but he couldn't admit that weakness to his boys. Carrie seizes her thoughts as they fly through her head. He was afraid – Pan was afraid! Of her! She was living proof that he wasn't as powerful as he pretended to be.

"You think you can keep her from Pan? You can't. This is his island."

No, Carrie thinks. It was never his. It belonged to its native people, who's real tribe name had been lost because of them, the white invaders that turned their land into a battle ground and forced them onto a reservation. And Pan - He'd brainwashed all the other children to think only he could use the powers of this island. But not her. She knew she had something, she'd been hidden from him. Perdy had hidden her lavender from him. He couldn't touch the Native people. They all used something that lived here even without knowing.

"So he sent you to spy on us. To find out how a normal girl could hide from him?" Perdy cocked her head. "Is he that desperate?" she leant forward and Carrie was surprised the boy didn't shrink back. Perdy speaks through gritted teeth. "That afraid?"

"Afraid?" the boy laughed – but even to Carrie he sounded

unsure. She saw Willow and Peaches stiffen, and she stepped closer to Nala, who leaned into her gratefully. They all watched Perdy carefully.

"We aren't afraid of girls." The boy said petulantly. It made him seem even more pathetic. "Girls crying over their babies?"

Perdy had turned away from him, but now she whipped back round, rage overtaking her.

"What did you just say?" the grabbed the boy by his hair and held a knife to his bobbing throat before any of them could think. Willow drew her own weapon. But he didn't stop. The stupid little boy didn't stop. Carrie willed him too, but he didn't. Couldn't.

"Yeah! That's right!" the boy laughed again, but it was a panic, high pitched sound. It made Carrie feel sick. He was scared. So was she. "I had to listen to all your whiney gashes all night!" He spat the foul words out. "You're all pathetic, but you worst of all!" his looked at Perdy, goading her. "Whinging about your long lost baby. I'm sure Pan would love to hear all about that."

Carrie's hands fly up to her mouth. She could tell from the other girls faces they had no idea what he was talking about. She felt something inside her fracture for Perdy.

She wanted to step forward, grab Perdy and remind her that even if Pan knew about Emmeline, there was nothing he could do about it. Nothing. He wasn't strong enough anymore. She had kept her daughter safe. But she could see that in her rage Perdy wasn't thinking all this. All she was feeling was anger and fear.

"And I'm sure he'd be even more interested to know about you and your little girlfriend." Then the boy looked at Carrie, who scowled back. She wasn't embarrassed though, just angry. She'd been ashamed about a lot of things, but never that. She wouldn't let him do that to her. She wouldn't.

Perdy pressed the knife harder against his throat.

"Perdy." Carrie warned, moving forward. "It's alright." She raised her hand, trying to still Perdy.

"That's right. Let her tell you what to do. That's why you girls can't be warriors. Too emotional."

And then, with no ceremony and no hesitation, Perdy stabbed the boy in the chest.

Carrie let out a groan and covered her eyes. She heard the boy let out a gargled little noise before a thud on the ground. His body. She'd killed him.

Slowly, very slowly, she lowered her hands. Perdy stood looking at them all, her hands covered in blood.

"Why..." Carrie shook her head. She felt cold all over. She couldn't think. She felt tears fall unchecked, burning down her cheeks. They hurt. Everything was sharp.

"You didn't...have to do that." She felt dizzy and her hands shook as she reached to wipe away her tears. Her vision blurred and for a second Perdy was nothing but a smudge she couldn't recognize.

She felt a sickening dread at the idea that maybe that's all Perdy had ever been.

"I told you before Blondie. This is a war. In a war people die."

That name snaps Carrie back to the present. She hadn't called her that since she'd first got here.

"Don't you fucking dare call me that! And he did not just die! You murdered him Perdita! You killed him!" Her voice was pitching higher and louder and she felt hysteria washing over her, hot panic and fear.

"He's not the first and he won't be the last." Perdy replied, but she had the decency to look a little deflated under Carrie's wide eyed glare. Everyone else was silent. They had seen this before.

Perdy shook her head and stomped forward without looking back at the body she was leaving. She shoved Carrie's shoulder with her own as she passed her. "You won't make me feel bad about this. We might not like it, but it's what needs to happen for us all to survive. If you don't know that maybe you really don't belong here."

Everything turned white for a second, or at least, Carrie thought it did. She understood after a second that it was anger. Burning, boiling, white hot anger, quick and bright as thunder.

"Of course I don't belong here!" she screamed, her voice a loud growl that didn't belong to her. For want of anything better, she grabbed a clump of dirt and hurled it as hard as she could at Perdy's retreating back.

Perdy stilled as it bounced off her with a dull thud, before she turned to march back up to her. Carrie wasn't scared. She was too angry to be scared, and so was Perdy.

Carrie let out an ungodly howl. The others flinched away, getting their distance from her. She felt insane. She didn't know what she was doing. It felt good to scream though. She wanted to scream until she burst, until she had nothing left inside her. She wanted to scream herself empty. Scream until she blacked out.

"Of course I don't belong here!" she panted, words not coming out right. "You god damn...you god damn, shit fuck moron!" she sounded like a banshee, wailing every hoarse breath.

She stamped over to the nearest tree and kicked it as hard as she could. Then she hit it with the palms of her hands. This caused the other girls to stir. The wanted to go to her but Perdy put a hand up to stop them. Carrie couldn't make herself stop. All the things that had happened to her, pressing and sweating out of the lines on her hands, scratched and bloody now on the tree. She kept screaming the whole time. She couldn't control herself.

Then she managed to push herself away, stumbling around, her breaths more like moans. She rounded on the others.

"Of course I don't belong here." She looked at them all. They looked scared of her. "That's what I've been saying since I got here! And newsflash-" She threw her arms out wildly. "None of you belong here! You are all lost! YOU'RE LOST! YOU DON'T EXIST! You are just lonely, miserable cowards who just stay here so you don't have to make any of your own decisions! So you can blame other people for how lonely you are! Maybe it was Pan's fault once, but it isn't anymore! None of you have helped me find a way home because you don't want to go home! You are all choosing not to live! Just like Clare –" Her heart broke round the name, the understanding. "Just like Clare never leaving her dead boyfriends house. All of you are too scared, and it's pathetic. And I was ready to just like all of you! Well I won't do it anymore! D'you hear me?"

She looks up into the sky, not knowing if Pan can hear her. "I won't let any of you control my life anymore! I am not going to wait to die here!"

And she was finally, finally done.

Everything was as silent as death.

Carrie felt her legs give way underneath her. No one caught her. She found herself kneeling, her face in the leaves and the dirt, next to the dead boy. Up close she saw he had long, almost feminine eyelashes. She didn't know his name. Even if they had hurt them, no one deserved that, did they? She didn't want to be another nameless child.

She closed her eyes and pressed her forehead into the dirt.

When she looked up she was alone with the dead boy. The others were gone.

She started crying. "Please." She said quietly. To herself, to the island, to anyone who would listen. She had nothing else she could do. "Please help. Someone. Please. Tiger lily, please help."

Then she heard a twig snap. She stops talking, stops moving.

God. Why had she stayed alone out here with a corpse, knowing Pan wanted to spy on them – on her?

Carrie forces herself to look up.

She sees a pair of tiny bare feet, covered in dirt. Tough and calloused from years of climbing trees.

"Peaches." She breathes in relief.

Peaches, of course, says nothing. But she looks less grumpy than usual. And she holds her hand out.

After hesitating for a second, Carrie puts her hand in Peaches tiny one, and lets her little friend pull her gently all the way back to their camp.

"We've been talking." Nala says.

They had all sat round the campfire, sullen faces watching each other warily. Perdy hadn't said anything but she had washed her hands. She'd put her knives down away from her when she'd seen Carrie. Willow looked torn and Peaches just watched as always. Carrie stared at the crackling flames, but Nala touched her shoulder softly. She saw that Nala was smiling gently. It made her less nervous.

"Oh?" Is all Carrie can say.

"We love you." Nala says simply.

"Oh..." Carrie says again. "Right."

"You are our sister now. We are all sisters. Well, except you and Perdita of course."

Perdy rolled her eyes and Willow shifted uncomfortably. Nala coughed awkwardly and continued. "And I would like to think there was another way to fight Pan...without becoming him. There may not be one. We have never tried to find another one."

No one else looks impressed.

"And we would like for you to be able to go home, if that is what you want. So...we've come up with an idea. Avery dangerous idea."

"Thank you." Carrie says, but she shakes her head. "At this point I'm starting to think no one knows how to get me home."

"That's just it!" Nala starts to sound excited, and even Willow's eyes soften. "Alone these factions do not know how to fight Pan, or they are too afraid to. But that might change if we find a way to work together."

"I...I don't understand." Carrie admitted with a frown, her eyes darting round the girls.

"For you." Perdy cuts in, finally looking right at her. Carrie tries to read her expression. She had thought she'd been getting better at it. Right now she wasn't sure, but she thought the fact it was Perdy speaking now was a good sign. "For you – Carys." She breathes her name like a sigh. "For you we have done something...something no one has done on this island for over two hundred years." She looks at the other girls. Carrie sees Nala nod at her. Checking the woods for listening ears, Perdy takes a deep breath before speaking again.

"We have called a council meeting. All the factions are going to come together."

"Pan is not the only one who can send summons, thanks to Peaches and her quick feet." Nala beamed.

Carrie put her hands up, shaking her head. "Wait, what are you saying exactly?"

Willow sighed. "It means, Blondie, that we're risking our hides to find a way to get you home. And so are the mermaids."

"And Wild Rose's people." Nala supplied.

"And, joy of joys, the pirates." Perdy drawled sarcastically. "Apparently Peaches has a way to walk on water too."

Carrie didn't know what to expect. She'd spent all night tossing and turning. She had a pallet of furs in the corner of her small tent, the one she had built ramshackle and compact, but with her own hands. She'd spent so much time in Perdy's tent, what with the storm and everything that had happened since, it felt strange to be back in here. But she could think and be by herself, and she needed that now more than ever. She found being around people all the time draining sometimes.

Last night she and Perdy hadn't really talked. Either about the kiss, or the murder. Pan would be sending another spy soon, when his boy didn't return. He might mark it another loss, just part of playing the game. Or he might decide to take revenge. No one ever knew how he would react. He was ever changing, as a child is.

Carrie supposed she should probably be worried about that. Or the super-secret meeting they were apparently having all for her. But in reality, she was thinking about Perdy.

She had often thought she wouldn't ever find someone to have a relationship and that she had better start being fine with that. She'd been a socially awkward teenage lesbian with no friends, and staying inside all the time wasn't exactly conducive to meeting someone you might like. But now she had met someone, on a magical island of all places, where everything wanted to kill her.

But what did she really have with Perdy? She cares about her. Maybe even loved her – though that was a word with teeth, a frightening word that she pushed out of her head as soon as she thought it. But how did Perdy feel? Things had shifted and cracked so suddenly, after the woods. Could they claw something back from the chaos? And if they could, should they? Perdy hadn't talked about leaving the island with her, not once. If it was going to end anyway, was it all worth it?

Before she could really convince herself either way the tent flap was lifted, letting in startling sunlight. She'd been thinking all the way into the morning. Carrie felt like she was having déjà vu from last night. But its Nala this time, and she's smiling. It's a weird smile, from what Carrie can see as she squints through the light. She lifts her hand to shade her eyes. Sitting up, she can see Perdy hovering around impatiently behind Nala.

"What's happening?" Carrie began reaching for her boots straight away. "Something has happened."

"Yes!" Nala cried breathlessly. She sounds like she's going to cry. She shakes her head like she can't find her words. "It's – she's – Oh Carrie, you're not going to believe who's here!"

"Who?" Carrie pulled on her second boot. "Who, Nala?" she repeated loudly.

"She was calling your name! She knew your name. How could this be?"

"Nala!" Carrie cried, finally jumping up and moving toward her friend. "Either calm down or let me past you hon."

Nala lets her through the tent opening and into the daylight. Perdy blocks her path quickly though. “Carrie.” She starts in a serious voice. She sounds nervous. “If it’s who I think it is we need to get her out of sight right now. She’s down there by the water. We didn’t bring her over here – she looks a bit scared of us.”

Then she steps back, letting Carrie see what all the fuss is about.

When she sees her against the sparkling blue of the sea, she doesn’t think before she starts running. She doesn’t even think about how impossible this is, about how dangerous it is, about anything. She can feel tears trailing into her hair as she runs.

“Clare!”

Clare clung to her bone crushing tight, howling into her hair. The waves crashed around them and neither of them cared.

Clare kept hysterically sobbing, making Carrie shake with it, saying "I'm sorry, I'm sorry." over and over. Carrie thinks maybe she is not saying it to just her. Carrie did not know what she was sorry for, she didn't much care, at least not then. All she cared about was that her family was here, right here holding her tightly. All bony shoulders and long hair, loud painful breaths of relief.

Clare pulled back to gaze at her, pushing Carrie's sea salt matted hair away from her face, her long fingers gripping her face in reverie. Carrie could not stop grinning. This was her Aunt Clare. Emotional, in her own world, and there for her.

"Do you know how worried I've been about you?" Clare cried almost angrily.

Carrie put her hands on Clare's arms, partly to reassure her and partly to steady her against the relentless buffering of the waves.

"Clare." She says, and the name means many things.

"Are you alright? You hurt? Did anyone hurt you? Hm? Carys? You ok?" Clare fires of questions without waiting for the answer, trying to assess any damage that might have befallen her niece.

Carrie shook her head with a laugh. She barely knows what to say. She only knows that she is happy. The kind of blazing happy that makes you forget everything else.

"I'm fine." She says. "Honestly, I'm alright, or as alright as I can be. But I missed you. And the cat - He isn't here too is he?"

Clare laughs too loudly in relief and starts crying again. She didn't know she had this much left in her.

She can't remember the last time she cried with happiness, free of self-consciousness and doubt. Before there had only been the sadness, the deep dark grief that lived inside her. She had spent so long shut down, aching for what she had lost, what she had missed. Somewhere along the way she had lost the person Michael had loved. She hadn't known how to start moving again.

But the answer was the thing that stopped her in the first place. She might not ever be the same person she was before, before love killed her. But now love had helped bring her back to life. This girl, who seemed to know everything and nothing. Her niece, whose life she had glimpsed in fractures for years. Who had reminded her of the life and vitality of the people she had lost. She'd brought her back.

Clare wouldn't have been able to live with herself if she hadn't tried, if she'd come to her senses too late and something dreadful had happened.

Aisling would never have forgiven her either, and the thought makes her ashamed of herself. Her sister had trusted her with the thing most precious to her in all the world, and she had almost failed her, given her up to this place.

She would never do that again. As she hugged Carrie again, she imagined she was holding Aisling too. And she promised both of them silently to try. To keep trying even when she couldn't.

She wouldn't leave them again.

20

Scurvy and an eight pack

The pirates were a motley crew.

Once the girls, as Carrie called it so several eye rolls, "screwed their courage to the sticking place", they began to explore the pirate ship. They began to see the men that inhabited the Eloise, not as the far of specks of movement on the horizon, but as the men that they were. Just like the girls, they worked in a strange harmony that only people who have known each other for a long time can understand.

Jonas was a very large, hulking dark skinned man, with a vicious scar maiming his left eye. His other was the pale blue of the ocean. The midnight black of his skin made it seem to sparkle. Willow stuck close to him, though he didn't speak very much. As it would transpire over their many low conversations over knife sharpening, they had a lot in common. They were both loyal lieutenants and fond of being angry. They also both experienced something they had never had the word for and never talked much about. They watched Perdy and Carrie slowly find their way back to one another, with small touches and smiles. This was something they understood, the romance, the beauty. But nothing past that. They didn't feel the urge to make love to anyone, they didn't want anyone like that in the way they saw Carrie looking at Perdy. On a war island, this hadn't been so much of a problem. But they still thought about the times before, in their old lives, when people did not understand. Especially for Jonas. His old crew had thought him broken. His crew now, just like Willow's, were all broken in some way.

That was something the girls were beginning to realize. It wasn't just them that had been called here, outcast from society. The pirates were too. They had the water and the girls had the land, but they lived in the same state of being pariahs from their worlds.

There was Cormac, the almost toothless old cook who's lack of teeth and heavy Irish accent made it difficult to understand – though it seemed Perdy understood him well enough. She even sounded Irish sometimes when she talked to him. But it was Nala who approached him and talked to him about cooking in her light and friendly way. Only Nala would have the patience, since he often shouted random things rather angrily.

Jean was a good looking, olive skinned French man who somehow managed to always have perfect hair. Perdy was jealous as she tried to comb through her mass of curls every day. He had become a pirate to find riches and a husband. So far he had found neither. He lounged in the crow's nest and shouted at people. Clare would jump out of her skin every time and everyone would pretend not to notice. She still wasn't used to so much noise, so many people, or so much open space – though she had managed to stop bursting out crying about it all in the five days they had been on the pirate ship.

They were all ruled over by one man.

Captain Hook was tall, lean and more than a little intimidating upon first glance. Somewhere in his mid-forties, he wore a broad brimmed leather hat that couldn't disguise his noble features. A long roman emperor nose with a dark scruff of a beard over a strong jaw line combined with a careful, watchful manner made him seem to be really what a good pirate captain should be. What completed this image was the thing that gave him his namesake. For in replacement of his left hand there was a hook, held securely with a leather wrist strap. He was constantly surveying his people, keeping an eye out. He also seemed to be always keeping a watchful eye on Clare, who he had stomped over to upon their arrival on the ship and promptly quizzed about who she was.

"She is an extra risk in what is already a plan leaning on the wrong side of suicidal." He'd told Perdy, acting like Clare wasn't there – though he'd stood so close to her she had to look up to see his face.

"Is there a right side?" Made Perdy hiss at Carrie to be quiet.

"Does he know she's here?"

"No." Perdy insisted. "Well, that's what we're assuming, since no one has tried to murder us yet. But we weren't about to risk it by leaving her on the beach."

Hook seemed to think a moment before his features softened. "Quite right." He said quietly, casting another glance at Clare. This one decidedly less hostile. She glared at him. She was a grown woman and they were talking about her like she wasn't there.

But then he turned to her and fixed a pair of bright green eyes on her, then dipped into a gentlemanly bow.

"Then you are a welcome addition, miss…?"

Of course he assumed she was a miss. Not that there was anything wrong with being one, but still. Clare squared her shoulders. "Miss Collingwood." She said primly. "Clare."

Then he gestured for them to follow him and Peaches, who had surprisingly taken a shine to Clare (Clare thinks Peaches has decided she's a clumsy adult who can't take care of herself, which seemed more and more true these days), pulled her along by the hand.

In the days since however, he seemed to get used to her. And they did have days, since the sea was not on their side. The pirates had agreed to let the girl tribe onto their ship under the banner of a truce, since the place they were to have their forbidden council gathering was only accessible by water. It was rather terrifyingly called skull rock, and only a few people knew how to get there. But they could not sail if the wind and the waves were not with them. So they were stuck waiting. In this time they decided going back to the beach would draw more unnecessary attention to their movements and cost them time should the wind pick up again. So they all stayed on the ship together, and tried to get along.

"Do you think the captain fancies you, or is he scared of you?"

The question comes from Carrie. She'd been angry at Clare for a little while, because she had explained she sort of, vaguely knew how to get home, and swore it would happen. At some point. Probably. And she had not brought any supplies, a pack of clothes, anything. Clare wasn't an organized person though, and she had been in a twisted depression cycle at the time, and she had cried over Carrie's story of her time on the island, so she'd been forgiven very quickly.

Carrie and Clare were sunbathing with their tops pulled up over their stomachs, rickety old chairs leaning precariously against the side of the ship.

"Do you fancy him?"

"Carys!" Clare spluttered. "I've known the man five days."

"Yeah but…you have eyes."

"Yes, well, *my eyes* are telling me he's a filthy pirate who probably has scurvy or something!"

"Scurvy and an eight pack." Carrie sighed and rolled her shoulders. "Sorry. It's just that he's always like, hovering around you."

This was true, though Carrie made it sound a lot stranger than it was.

He hadn't just been staring at her like some weirdo on the bus. Ok – so there had been some staring. But he'd started talking to her too. He started wandering over when she was alone – mostly because she'd been crying. But then he'd brought her things. A jumper, because all she had was a loose cotton top. A pad of previously used parchment – she could draw on the clean side, he'd explained. Small little gestures in a world so foreign.

It touched her. She found that she did really like talking to him, even about simple things. He seemed articulate and well mannered, with the hint of an upper class English accent. Mostly though he was nice and gentle, and he didn't push her or scare her. He just paid attention to her when no one else was. And she could forgive the staring, since her own artist's eye was used to that kind of curiosity.

Clare lifted a hand to shield her face from the sun. She covered her whole face with her arm then and let out a little groan.

"It doesn't matter anyway. I can't like someone like that again. Fancy someone, that's such a teenager thing to say." She sighed. Dropping her arm heavily she looked over plaintively at Carrie, who furrowed her brows.

"Sorry. I was just asking. I wasn't trying to upset you." She said. "And it's not a teenager thing to say. It's not my fault you've forgotten how actual people talk." She teased and Clare rolled her eyes good-naturedly.

"I know. I know that darling." Clare reached out and patted Carrie's arm affectionately. "It's just...I'm not going to get better after knowing someone for a few days. As of right now..." she stares at the sky, trying to find her words. "As of right now, Michael Bellbrook is the last man I kissed. That is what he was supposed to be for the rest of my life. And he is, until he isn't. Until I can let go of that, until I want to let go of that, the rest is impossible to even think about." She wrinkled her brow. "Do you think I should tell him that? Captain Hook?"

Carrie shook her head, mirroring Clare and staring above to the endless blue. "No. You don't owe the guy anything even if he does have a crush on you."

"I don't think he does. He probably has bigger things to worry about – we all do."

Carrie didn't say anything. She bit her lip, shifting to sit up properly and stare at her hands. "I know." Her knuckles whitened.

Clare sat up and touched Carrie's shoulder. "This isn't your fault. Any of it. You're too young to have that on your shoulders. I'm the adult – and so is the captain. Any decisions we make from now on are our own. All you wanted was to get home, and make things better for your friends. There isn't anything wrong with that."

Carrie's gaze darted to Clare's – her big blue eyes magnified by unshed tears. "What if Pan finds out we're here before we get to skull rock? Or what if we get there and they all refuse to help. We'll be stuck here. Or we'll get killed by him or his lost boys. I'll have killed everyone because I wanted to go home."

Clare shook her head, a determined glint in her eye, and took Carrie's face in both her hands. "Listen to me Carys. You have to be brave. You have to believe this is going to work or it never will. And if that does all happen, then at least you'll know you did everything you could. It isn't selfish to want to be safe. It isn't selfish to do what you have to. Every single person on this ship chose to follow you into this. You have to respect their decision. And you have to remember that this...this is how I make up for everything. So please let me. I haven't been there for your family, but I can do this for you. I would burn this whole island down to get you home to your mother."

Carrie smiles wetly. They sit back and she pointedly looks away as Carrie wipes at her eyes.

"You're girl is strong. I can see it. She's going to stay by your side with this."

Carrie raises her eyebrows and sees where Clare's gaze has strayed. Perdy is pretending not to watch them further down the ship as Peaches tried to get her attention. At last she turned to Peaches. Carrie tore her gaze back to Clare to find she was smiling at her knowingly.

"You are being sensible, aren't you? First relationships can be... intense. I don't want you doing anything because you think you have to."

Carrie grinned. "Not being funny, but its not like im going to get pregnant."

"I'm being serious." Clare snapped, bristling. She'd never had much experience with being the adult, and it made Carrie forget sometimes. "Tell me you're being sensible."

Carrie nods. "I am. I promise."

"Right. Well then. That's alright."

They both sat back slowly to carry on sunbathing in silence.

Clare found that she couldn't stop thinking about Carrie's question.

For a normal person it was a normal question. Not for her. For her it confronted her with the possibility she could look at someone like that again. She'd thought she'd never do that, not ever, not after him. And here she was, considering it. She turned the question over in her mind. She liked him, he was nice and good looking. She decided to leave it at that. Because, she told herself firmly, she was being stupid! You couldn't just be here for five minutes and forget about Michael. Sigh, no. Not five minutes. Five years.

She's wrapped in a blanket drawing the sunset with her legs crossed at the prow of the ship. Most of the others seem to have disappeared, apart from Jonas keeping watch in the shadows at the other end of the ship. She'd given up drawing Michael because she could never get his silly smile right. Then her mind had wandered and she'd drawn Hook, been appalled at herself, destroyed the evidence and drawn a nice, simple sunset.

Michael would tell her to stop overthinking things. What she kept coming back to was this; he had been the one who sent her, and that had to mean more than the obvious. It just had to.

She didn't tell anyone...but she'd half expected him to be here somehow. She knew she had buried his body. She had picked the quote for his gravestone ("What is done in love is well done.") She had sang hymns at his funeral. But some small part of her, some spark, half expected him to be here. That maybe the same magic that had carried her here, had carried some part of his soul across the world. That that's why he had appeared to her, called to her.

It had not, of course. Now she had to wonder if Carrie was the only reason he had sent her here. She was, after all, reason enough. But maybe, just maybe...even if she wasn't ready for someone in that way, the way Carrie had found someone, she could at least try to be open to the idea, which was a challenge in itself.

She was happy for her niece. She had Perdy didn't need to explain, they just fitted around each other, the way they moved next to each other or talked without speaking. Clare missed that kind of thing.

She supposes that's why she agrees to have a drink with the captain. Or, maybe she agreed just to be polite. She was a polite person. Yes, that sounded right.

The look on his face when she had said yes suggested he didn't actually think she'd say yes. Neither had she, truth be told.

"I haven't had a guest for a long time." He explained, looking a little sheepish. A little, because he seemed quite practiced in only letting people see the emotions he wanted them to see. Clare wished she knew how to do that. He can't stop his eyes lighting up in happy surprise at her agreeing though.

So it was just a drink. People drank, she reminded herself. Before they headed off to their possible deaths had the hands of various magical beings (Clare was still having trouble adjusting to that one, even if she did live in a magic house, fairies really were another matter entirely.) Just a drink with a nice, attentive, attractive, lonely man.

In his cabin. Alone.

Oh, god.

As night stole upon them, stealing the sun once more, the waves began to rock ever so slightly. Finally, there was movement. It looked like tomorrow was to be the day the set out for skull rock.

It was just the girls in their cabin below decks, since Clare hadn't come down yet. Carrie gets the sense she feels like an intruder, as the only adult among them. She feels bad, but there isn't a lot she can do about it just then. And besides, she and these girls had been through so much together. It seemed fitting for them to huddle together alone again just this once, as the waves picked up again.

"I hope you all like hammocks." Hook had said sarcastically when showing them to their dark little cabin. It looked like it had been a store room, if the boxes at one end had been anything to go by. But they had cleared it out, making sure their guests had enough room to all stay together.

But, as it turned out, the girls definitely did not like hammocks.

The captain had smiled ever so slightly at Clare's disgusted face upon seeing them. He didn't seem to like hammocks very much either. So Carrie assumed he wouldn't mind them all being taken down and piled on the floor.

They'd made separate pallets at first, but now the girls pulled all the sheets together to make one big one for them all. Just like they had in Perdy's tent during the storm, they sardined together under their blankets. Willow wrapped one long arm round Peaches and Nala and Perdy and Carrie huddled at the other end.

Carrie had forgiven Perdy, though they hadn't talked about it much. She stares up at her face now, knowing Perdy can feel it even though she's pretending to be asleep. Her eyes flicker open when Carrie runs a gentle finger down the shape of her nose. Perdy grins and scrunches her nose up.

"I'm sorry." Carrie said. "Not for...not for saying what I said so much as how I said it. It was awful, but...you were protecting us, in your own way." She whispered.

Perdy bit her lip. "I don't know." She admitted. Her hand reached up to find Carrie's in the dark. "When he mentioned my daughter, I was just blind to everything. I could have started another war. I wasn't thinking about protecting everyone else." She looks down guiltily.

Carrie squeezed her hand. "I think...I wasn't just angry at you. I was angry at everything. I've been thinking about it a lot. And, well, I think I was angry at myself as well."

Perdy frowned at her. "Why? You didn't do anything except... expect better from me. I'm...I'm the one who let you down."

"No!" carries shook her head. "I was angry at myself because I understood what you did. Before I came here I wouldn't have ever thought killing someone was the solution. It scared me so much that I could think that, and I blamed you, and I shouldn't have."

Perdy cranes her neck and presses her face into Carrie's. They giggle as they nuzzle together like cats. They were going to go to skull rock, into the endless not knowing of what was to come. But right now, Carrie lay in the dark with her sisters and the girl she maybe loved, and that had to be enough.

21

Kindred

"You know, I really bloody hate boats."

Clare stared up at the ceiling, her old wooden chair creaking as she leant back. She saw every groove and pattern carved into the old dark wood of the ship. Bumps and ridges that someone had carved with their hands, something that probably never got noticed anymore.

"Well, I like to call her a ship." Hook said sardonically, taking a gulp from his glass.

Clare's hand tightened around her own glass. She wasn't a big whiskey drinker - she hadn't really drunk much apart from tea for years after deciding alcohol and depressive tendencies weren't a good mix - but she'd accepted it when Hook had offered to pour her some. As she'd watched the bright amber liquid slosh into the glass, she'd craved it, to her surprise. Like its sweet, painful sharpness might shock her back to life. It has sounded so loud, the sloshing of the amber liquid when he'd poured it out in silence. The creaking wood of the ship, the womb like echoing of the water outside. It all sounded deafening to her after years of quiet.

In reality the whiskey didn't jolt her – the most it did was make her cough, which had made Hook smile, even though he'd tried to hide it behind his own glass. When she looked back down, she found him studying her.

She was in a position to study him too - sat right across the desk from him. He was dark - tanned skin turned rough from endless unforgiving sun. She thinks though; from his almost black brown hair that his skin wasn't just a tan. It made him look ruddy, as if he could withstand any assault. His hair was a dark black. He was attractive, but there was something else underneath all of that. A presence around him, simmering and primal. He had the roman kind of profile made for kings, a strong nose that looked like it had been broken at least once. Long fingers, like a pianist, that contradicted the rest of him, the muscles that were solid and compact. She imagined, with her artists eye, trying to paint him. But she didn't think she would be able to capture that indefinable thing, that motion of vitality, of knowing, that rested always behind his sharp, heavy lidded green eyes.

Hook smirks again when he catches her staring at him. He'd been doing the same thing, but unlike her he had no qualms about admitting to it. Clare blushed and looked away, hoping the low candlelight hid her thoughts.

She glanced around the cabin. There were a lot of books in here all on the walls. But there was one wall where the bookshelves sandwiched a display. Against the wall there was a painting of a ship bobbing in a storm. Underneath that a table housed several antique guns, and a sword hung against the wall. It gleamed in the candlelight. Clare wondered if they were for show or if he used them all. She had never actually seen a gun before, even with all her travelling, nor an honest to god sword. It made her a little uncomfortable, actually. Even if they weren't loaded, the idea of them, the single second it would take for an accident to happen. But, she supposed, you didn't need weapons like that for an accident to happen. She knew that from experience.

"So, you don't like boats."

"No." She said, tearing her gaze from the weapons, though she felt them in the corner of her eye.

She forced herself to look steadily at him for a second to compose herself. Then she shook her head and threw caution to the wind. "You see I have this unfortunate habit of losing everyone I love, in one way or another." She smiled weakly before nodding, trying to will sudden hot tears away. People might ask about what happened, but as soon as you started crying about it they backed off, unable to handle the damage they themselves had brought up.

"My parents died in a boating accident. So, I hate boats. They were very far away from England when they died, so seeing boats - ships - makes it feel a bit more real in a way it doesn't normally. You see, for me, it feels as if one day they simply vanished into thin air, off the edge of the world. But being here...feeling the waves and smelling the sea. Well, it makes me imagine what they felt. I travelled a lot myself, but made sure I never did it by water."

She quiets then, glancing at her hands where they worried at a loose thread in her white cotton shirt. She flexed them into fists and sighed. She looked at the captain again. The whole time he had sat in silence, watching and listening to her intently. The low light cast part of his face in a dark shadow. It made his eyes look like they were glowing, almost supernaturally.

"Sorry." Clare said awkwardly, shrugging one thin shoulder. "Got a bit morbid there, didn't I?"

She didn't know why the words had come out of her like that. Unstoppable, an old demon, a hurt that had turned to scar tissue. Something about the candles reminded her of lighting the fires in the house on a stormy night. The smell of the oak and the books, combined with the steady observance of the man opposite her. It all made her feel almost sleepy with calm. Until she sees his eyes narrow like he's worked something out and it brings her back to the moment.

"Actually." He said, breaking the silence in a drawling, friendly tone. "This is the first proper adult conversation I've had for a long time, so I rather think I can forgive you your morbidity. You have fair reason for it, it seems." He takes another gulp of whiskey, wincing against it. Then he stares into it. "Actually, death is somewhat familiar territory for me as well."

Clare raises an eyebrow. "On an island where no one ages?"

Hook set his lips into a thin line. A coldness settled over them when she realises he is talking about killing people. Something cold crawls up the back of her neck, and she once more becomes hyper aware of the weapons occupying the space with them.

But Clare, awkward as she was sometimes, did know how to change a subject. Aisling had always said she was good at nudging people. She just wasn't as good at doing it for herself.

"What do you mean that it's your first adult conversation?" She asked in a lighter tone.

His face opens up briefly, the sharp crease between his eyebrows smoothing out, just for a moment.

"Ah, that. Well, it might have escaped your attention, but this island is populated by a lot of children, and even more enemies. Doesn't lend itself well to philosophical debate, or even small talk about the weather for that matter."

"Well what about your crew?"

Hook placed his now empty whiskey glass on the desk in front of him, rolling his large shoulders as he relaxed back. He folding his hands against his stomach. Now he wasn't so hunched in on himself, it made him seem more open. More vulnerable even, despite the fact she could now see through the low neck of his old fashioned shirt the hard muscles of his chest and the dark hair the covered it, and his hook gleaming in the moonlight coming in from the window. His faced took on an amused look, but not at her, more at the seeming absurdity of what she had said.

"I am their captain. Being here, this endlessness, this unceasing nothing, would drive a man mad if he had no anchor, no compass with which to give him direction."

Clare thinks about her own never-ending sameness inside her house, and decides he is right, though she says nothing as he carries on.

"That is what I am for my crew. I cannot be their friend. I have to be able to give them orders, and for them to trust that I am right. I...care for them, I take care of them but those are two very different things, and they require different men."

He says this point by point, like he's recited this many times, perhaps to convince himself of the necessity.

It causes a spark of recognition within Clare's chest. A stirring of the ashes in her heart. He has sealed himself away to make it easier, just like she had. This room, like her house, was the place he let himself exist, where he never let the rest of the world in.

Except her, right now. He had let her in here. Let her run her hands over the books, for her eyes to consume this private world. She is grateful for it. She thinks about the night Carys had gone, when she had let her into 'The room', to see its secrets. Without realizing, she had been digging her nails into her loneliness, pulling it apart and cracking it open to peer inside for the first time in years. She thinks that is what he is trying to do now. In this, they are kindred.

"But...if you're their compass, then who is yours?"

They both know the answer already. That is why she asked it.

"Even if I were to talk to my crew like this," He carries on as if she hadn't said anything, "We do not have shared histories outside of this place." He gestures upwards, outward. One word to mean a while island, to mean hundreds of years. "We are not from the same time, or even the same places. Do you know, they have never seen England covered in snow?" He shakes his head with a disbelieving chuckle. Everything he had experienced here, and that is what he thinks of. It is strange, the things we cling to.

"No man," He glances to her "Or woman, for that matter, should die without seeing that...Does it still snow in England?"

Clare nods. "Sometimes, yes. This pesky little thing called global warming sort of makes it a bit harder, depending on where you live." She waves a hand in dismissal when she sees his confused frown at 'global warming'. She was too tired to try to explain that now, that was for sure. "But it does still snow. Especially high up - Like where I live. I'm up in the country, in the north. Where there's nothing but fields and trees for miles around. And when it snows...It's like the whole world is covered. It's like... like you're living in a snow globe." She smiles, and he smiles earnestly back at her, hearing her describe what he had seen, his home, something he knew.

"My mother used to make hot chocolate when it snowed." He said quietly.

Clare's smile widens in a mouth aching smile. He catches her and then himself with a self-conscious grunt.

"Well, we are a maudlin pair, are we not Miss Collingwood?"

Clare had taken a hesitant sip of whiskey at that particular moment and promptly spat it back out into the glass in surprise. "Wow. Please do not call me that. I'm sure that it's all very proper - part of every middle aged spinsters Mr Darcy fantasy - But you can just call me Clare."

"If that is your wish, Miss Clare."

"No, I mean - Oh never mind. But what about you? Do you have a real name or do I just have to call you Hook?"

"You could call me captain if you like." He growls, his eyes narrowing rakishly.

She shoots him a glare - though in fact she does not feel entirely unaffected by that low rumble.

It was the whiskey talking, she told herself, trying to ignore the voice in her head that told her she had barely touched her glass. God, this was an old feeling - An ancient feeling. She ached. She didn't want to, but she did. It made her want to cry almost. Or do something else as equally strange. She felt as if she had been starving for something for years without knowing.

She felt...seen. There was so much of the last five years that she couldn't remember. Chunks of time that blurred together or days lost all together. She didn't know if she'd been asleep or just drifting round her house. Great yawning gaps of time had been lost to her and it frightened her. She realized in a way she hadn't before that there had been full years where she hadn't spoken out loud. It must have added up to that, anyway. Years, where she had not seen another living soul, had not voiced the thoughts in her head to another person. Just a house and an animal, and they did not talk back. And now? Now, somehow, she felt seen again. By a man she'd known for less than a week. She doesn't know if it's the darkness or the magic bringing her back into shape. She could have been invisible for the last five years, but now someone was looking at her again. She was scared of what he might see.

"Listen, I should..." She trails off, gesturing weakly to the door, her thoughts starting to make her head spin.

"By all means, if you're tired." His tone is too genial, but he's offering her a way out.

She nods but can't make herself get up. He doesn't say anything. He barely changes facial expression, waiting patiently for her to make her decision. She's trying to decide whether he'll mind either way whether she stays or goes, but he's unreadable.

When the silence she's made gets too awkward even for her, she jumps up too quickly, accidently jostling the table. She winces at her own stupidity as they both reach out to hold the various items on the table steady. "Well. Ok then." She smiles breathily. His eyes dance in amusement.

He stands up too and smiles at her gently as they begin to make their way to the door.

When they reach it she whips round to face him again. "Sorry." She sighs. "I didn't mean to make things weird. I shouldn't have asked about your name." She's leaning back against the door now, looking up at him. "Its personal to you and I should have respected that."

She hadn't realized how close he was to her. He is all whiskey and warmth. She finds herself leaning back on her hands to keep them still. He's tall and he's a lot more bulky than she thought. He was lean, not too much muscle. But there was a presence, a boldness that made him seem bigger. On the other hand, maybe it is just because he was very close to her just then.

"Hm." Is the entire acknowledgement she gets from him. It's an earth shaking rumble. Tremors to spin the world of its axis. He's staring down at her, his eyes roaming her face.

"I mean -" She's going to start rambling now, she knows because that's what she does, but she can't stop. Five years, she thinks, without a single touch. Her palms itch.

What was wrong with her? She had always thought Michael was like the sun – or like an eclipse that blocked everything else out. Especially now he was gone. But it wasn't working anymore, and she didn't know if she even wanted it to.

She felt inexplicably drawn to the man inches away from her. And not just because it had been five years. He was a vagabond, but he was a wanderer, just as she had been. She could sense it instinctively, like an animal. He was trapped in stasis, as she had been. It felt like more than just want. It was more. She had not felt more like that for a long time, had not wanted to. It scared her. A nameless, aching, itching *more.*

"I hate my middle name, I never tell anyone, so I totally get it." Words were coming out of her before she thought them, thought about why she was saying them. She just had to fill the silence.

But she also felt struck by a sudden, inexplicable desire, to tell someone small details of her life. Things she had not even thought about for years. Like by speaking them aloud again, maybe there were parts of her, of her story, that might not simply be forgotten. Like she wouldn't just fade away in that old house of hers.

"What is it?" His eyes were soft as he looked at her, like he wanted to watch her and listen to her for as long as she let him.

"Well it's just – it's – Oh, god, you meant my name. Yes, my middle name!" She laughed breathily. "Well, I suppose I did bring it on myself. So, my grandmother was Irish, - that's why my sister is Aisling Maria - And I'm Clare, like the saint." She moved her hair from her face and winced.

Well she had to bloody tell him now she'd brought it up. God, what was wrong with her? What was she talking about? All those years of silence and this is what she chose to talk about. Amazing, Clare bear, she heard in Michael's voice. Just amazing.

"My middle name is Augustine." She explains, trying to calm herself down. "Since my birthday is the same day as her feast memorial day in august. She's like, the patron saint of sewing and TV." She finishes lamely, hunching her shoulders like she can collapse in on herself and disappear.

He nods, smiling at her. "It's a nice name." Then he cocks his head ever so slightly. "What's a TV?"

Clare smiles and shakes her head at herself. "It's - alright, so basically you it's a box where you can see people doing and saying stuff. It would be like watching a play three years after it's happened, for example, because we can capture those images."

"And a catholic saint invented this?"

"No - she didn't invent it. She's the saint of it. So basically, this girl Clare, whilst she was living her nice isolated nun life, said that she could see and hear mass on her wall even when she couldn't go herself. So now we think of it like she was watching a TV."

Clare stops and inhales a breath. A world on a wall...Of course it was. How strange. Maybe her old, sharp Irish granny had been onto something when she lectured them all about the saints.

She shifts awkwardly and almost bumps into him, breaking from her reverie. Clare knows she shouldn't stay, but she feels as if she's in a separate world from the one that exists outside the door. She has to force herself to open the door and step back out into that coldness.

"Alright then! Night!" She says, too loudly, fumbling behind her for the doorknob.

Hook leans into her and reaches an arm around her. She can feel him pressed against her. Her breath hitches in her throat for a second. Hook moves away from her and she realizes he was just opening the door for her.

She moves away from him, feeling colder by the second as she does so. The light and warmth of that room seemed a stark contrast to the corridor outside.

She doesn't say anything as she walks out of the cabin, brushing against him lightly as she does so.

Before she can start down the corridor, she hears him call her name. "Just one thing."

She turns back quickly, like she'd been waiting for it without knowing it.

"My name." He says quietly. His voice is steady and sure. "Is James."

That was a good name. A strong name. Not as fearsome as Hook, she supposes. He does not seem fearsome at all to her now. Now that she had blurted so much information about herself to him and he had accepted all of it without comment or question.

"Thank you." She says sincerely, blinking in surprise. He just nods and shuts the door gently.

As she walks away, she rubs the palm of her hand against her chest, trying to steady her sputtering heart, trying to ease the swollen, tender loneliness ballooning inside her

22

The council

Clare stood at the prow of the ship, watching as they got closer and closer to the dark shape on the horizon. The wind whipped at her face, making her eyes water.

Her eyes had been doing that a lot, because she'd cried so much when she'd got here. At first, she had not even noticed. The emotion was so unrelenting, the tears so hot and burning and she had been in such a state of shock that she hadn't felt them scorching down her face.

She remembered how much she had been shaking, how shocking it was, seeing the sea like that so suddenly. One minute she was leaning against the wall in her house, and then there was nothing but horizon.

She stared out at the sea now. She could never love it, but she had determined to get used to it. Somehow, she could surely find a way to be ok with that open, eternal blueness. But to be so surrounded by the thing that killed her parents – to have to trust it to carry her safely. She did not think she could do that. To be so confronted by it, its unceasing waves, she saw it as a gaping hungry mouth. She saw it as something that would savage her and shake her in its teeth as the deep forest and blazing sun watched in silence and indifference.

She hears footsteps approach behind her, the clank of a sword against a leg. Hook rests his arms on the prow like she was doing as he stands next to her, looking out at the horizon with her. Often she didn't hear his steps, so she thinks he's making noises on purpose so he doesn't startle her. She is getting the impression that he is a cautious man, in a world without caution.

"Are you frightened?" She asks him. She scuffs her boots on the floor as he thinks.

"Yes." He says simply. "Yes I am. Are you?"

"Yes."

"Smart girl." He smiles, turning to look at her properly.

Clare stands up properly from where she'd been leaning, letting out a deep breath. "Do you think they'll listen to us? What's so different now that will make them finally turn against Pan?"

When there is silence for a long moment, she finally looks at him. He's staring at her with a bemused smile.

"What?" When he shakes his head she laughs, "What?"

"The thing that is different is you, *Augustine*."

She shoots him a glare at the use of her middle name. "Alright then, *James*. How am I going to make a difference?"

He pushes up from the railing now too, looking down at her. He's wearing a long dark red brown coat and it makes him look rather powerful. His eyes were intent as he looked into hers and she turned to him properly.

"Because...you are the first grown woman to ever arrive here. Pan takes children, and the only other women here already live here. Don't you see? You are the proof that they need! Pan's power is not all encompassing. Not now you are here." He hisses, growing more and more excited as he speaks.

He raises his arms, like he wants to grab her arms. He glances at his hook, like he'd forgotten it was there, and drops them again.

"When they see you, they will see that the impossible has become possible, and they will have to listen to us. They can't give up on this one chance. Not now you've happened. Do you see now Clare? Do you see what you are?"

His voice is intense like his eyes, wild in its near fanaticism, and she cannot speak. She shakes her head.

"You are a miracle." He whispers with an almost pained reverie.

The caves inside skull rock seem to glow blue in the crystals and lamplight.

The rocky little island gave way to a system of long unending tunnels, dark, wet, and cavernous. Carrie felt a little claustrophobic, but having Perdy stomp along next to her was comforting.

They had a lamp of their own, but followed the faint glow of Hook's somewhere in front of them where he walked with Clare.

Perdy was impatient and twitchy. Carrie knew partly she missed the others – until Carrie had arrived she'd never really had to fight without them. When they had fought the crocodile they had left Willow, Nala and Peaches behind. They had been dismayed at being left behind again. But this was different. Even if Perdy wanted them there, there were rules. Old rules that hadn't been used in the unknown years since the last council meeting, but rules all the same. Only one second could accompany the ambassador from each faction of the island. Wild Rose was coming from the native tribe, Selene from the mermaids. Hook from the pirates, and he had brought Clare as his second. Perdy from the girl tribe, and she had brought Carrie. They were doing this together.

Just like when they had been back in the house, Carrie could hear the faint sound of Clare's absent-minded humming. It's something wildly familiar in this place. It pulls her through the darkness as well as any light.

After what seems an eternity of walking into nothingness, they reach their destination.

In the heart of skull rock there is a large, cavernous cave. A dark pool glitters on the right hand side, illuminating the room in sparkling pieces of light. Everything is brighter now, so they put their lamps into brackets on the walls that look like they haven't been used for centuries. They most likely had not.

In the centre of the space toward the left, a safe space away from the pool, there is a table.

A full on table in the middle of a bloody island cave, Carrie thinks. They really were having a proper meeting. Several high chairs are places around the table and the four of them take their seats. Carrie sits next to Perdy surprised the old chairs don't snap underneath them, and Perdy sits across from Hook. Clare is doing what Carrie wants to do. Snooping around.

"As if this place just exists here still. No one comes here, but it's ready and waiting." Clare says, staring at the ceiling, her voice echoing. Hook doesn't say anything, but he looks at the ceiling too, then back at Clare, like he's trying to work out what she is seeing.

She moves to the head of the table where a large, throne like chair sits. It's off white and uncomfortable looking.

"Who sits here? Don't you want to sit at the head of the table?" She raises a teasing eyebrow at Hook.

"Not on that chair, no." He drawls, slumping back in his chair to watch her with an amused expression. Carrie and Perdy begin to relax as well, despite their surroundings and what they were all about to let themselves in for.

Clare flops down on the chair. "It isn't that bad."

Hook raises both his eyebrows and covers his mouth subtly with his hand. He stares down at the arms of the chair pointedly as Clare frowns. Carrie gasps as she realizes what he's looking at.

Clare looks down too – and lets out a loud, undignified yelp, jumping up from the chair and shaking her hands out in disgust.

"What the hell!" She cries as Hook chuckles.

The chair she had been sat on was made out of bones. The off white colour was bones. Skulls made up the whole of the base, and god knows what made up the rest. Skull rock was finally living up to its name.

Clare throws herself into the chair beside Hook, rubbing her hands on her jeans. "Gross."

Hook was still laughing beside her.

Carrie wasn't sure she wanted to know who had made that chair, or how. She was saved by asking right then though, as the surface of the water beside them began to ripple and Perdy stiffened beside her.

She would never get used to the beauty of the mermaids, even if they had tried to drown her that one time.

Glistening from the pool, colourful as always, dark skin looking bright and blue, Selene arrives at the council meeting.

Her green hair fell loosely around her bare shoulders and as climbed from the pool. She swung her tail from the water, and as she placed it carefully down onto the ground it began to change. One by one, her green scales darkened to match the deep brown of her skin. Portia, the blue mermaid had come as her second and she did the same thing. Carrie and the others watched in awe as their scales turned to human legs.

When Selene stood up with Portia, their skin still wet, small rivulets running over there now naked bodies. The women did not seem self-conscious about this however, whilst everyone else in the room tried to avert their gaze. Selene started forward, but she couldn't quite hide the clumsiness of her legs. She used the table and the chair to guide herself into the chair. Portia sat beside her and glared at them all. Then their gazes fell on Clare. Selene, the mermaid queen, opened her mouth in shock. Portia looked at Hook with wide eyes.

"Hook. You have a little friend." She says in a teasing voice. She sounds familiar with him and it makes Clare raise her eyebrows at him.

He shifts uncomfortably and Clare bites back her retort, choosing a withering scowl instead.

"Hello Blue." He says gently. "It's been a long time."

"Too long." Portia purred. She caught sight of Selene glaring at her and quieted.

"Blue?" Clare mouthed at Hook, who grimaced.

"Is this everyone?" A husky voice came from the darkness, as princess Wild Rose appeared from nowhere, like an ethereal being.

Carrie realized how much Wild Rose belonged to this island and the island belonged to her people. She could travel over it quick as wind and not be seen, not be heard. She was at one with her land in a way the others were not.

She moves forward to the table and stops short at seeing Clare who smiles awkwardly.

"Hello."

Wild Rose ignores her. Clare is getting increasingly annoyed at people doing that here. She looks instead at Carrie. "I assume this has something to do with you, Carys of the girl tribe."

"I'm her aunt." Clare supplies a little too loudly. "Feel free to actually address me any time you like. That goes for all of you." She proclaimed to the stunned faces all around her.

Wild Rose's normally sullen mouth twitched into the smallest of smiles. "I see the resemblance."

"Sit down, Princess." Hook motioned to the chairs next to him and Clare. Wild Rose doesn't look like she enjoys taking orders, especially not from a man, but she also doesn't want to sit in the creepy bone chair, so she complies, glaring at him all the while. Her second, one of the men who had bound Carrie and Perdy's arms that night in their camp, sat stoically beside her.

"Now, you all know why we are here."

"To hear about your suicidal plan." Wild Rose quipped.

"To unite against a common foe. But I know I cannot convince you alone, just as we cannot win this battle alone." Hook turns his face to Clare. "I did not ask you aboard the Eloise, how it is you came to be on this island. Because I knew I was not the one that needed to hear it, to be convinced of it. I feel I have been waiting for something to happen for as long as I have been here. I did not know that something would come in the shape of you. But it has, and now I ask you to tell us your story, so we might glean from it how we may continue to control the events your arrival has already set in motion."

And so together Clare and Carrie piece together what they know. Clare keeps back the parts that belong only to her. The parts about Michael, about her own guilt, about the in between time when she had almost given up. But she tells them what she can, about what Claudette had helped her understand, and Carrie picks the tale up, explaining about the powers Pan had, that Clare seemed to have and what the island had. That they were not all the same, but neither were they separate. As she talked she became more and more certain about their endeavour, more certain its outcome could be positive. More certain that whatever Pan held, they also held. That the power of this island was stretching and thinning between them all, and that one day the threads would snap, and the magic contained there could be unleashed. That the people trapped here could be freed. She felt this in her heart, sat in the glimmering darkness surrounded by magic. She just had to make everyone else feel it too.

When they had finished there was a heavy silence across the table.

"Just because she came here," Selene said slowly, "Does not mean she knows how to return from where she came. And it does not mean she's not still susceptible to the power that keeps you here." She glanced between Clare and Hook.

"And what can the girl hope to do, when she comes to us to ask for answers? I don't believe any of you really know how to escape from under Pan's thumb." Wild Rose agrees.

"I don't think I can do it by myself, I've never thought that and I would not assume to think that. That's why we need to all join forces." Carrie insists, trying to control her voice.

"Clare's arrival here is a signal. Once the lost boys realize the things they have been told would not happen, can and have happened? Perhaps, like me, they can be persuaded to trust in this cause." This was the first thing Perdy had said since arriving. Even though Carrie had assumed she was Perdy's second, she was beginning to suspect it might be the other way round.

Perdy was letting her do the talking. It was unusual, since Perdy was so used to being the leader. Carrie felt her trust and was emboldened by it.

"You need a sign, a symbol, to begin a rebellion. You have one now." She said, her voice growing stronger each time she talked. She felt Perdy brush her arm against hers.

"We cannot enter into a rebellion we cannot know we will win!" Portia half laughs, half shrieks. But her queen looks pensive. She's listening properly, the way that queens do. Carrie knows Selene is fair. And she knows Wild Rose is angry.

"Princess – you hate Pan. You've always hated him for taking your land. And he has always feared you. Even when you didn't fight him he feared you. Now is the time to show him he was right to be afraid."

Wild Rose considered her silently. She looked to Selene.

Selene shook her head. "We have children to think about." She said. "It is our breeding season."

"We have children to think about too." Clare said, casting a glance at Carrie, who gave her a small smile.

"And your children won't be in danger, not if we take down Pan all at once." Hook pressed his finger into the table.

Selene threw her hands up and Portia started to smile. But Selene kept staring at the table, kept trying to come to a decision and failing. Even though part of her wanted to jump back into the water and swim away, another part of her could not.

"My people have survived for a long time." Wild Rose says. "The risk is too high. We are safe where we are, but not if we cross the borders of the great oak. Then we have forfeited our peace."

"You already did that."

Carrie's voice is quiet and they all turn to look at her.

"I beg your pardon?"

She looks up from the table, resolve in her eyes for what she had to do next. "You both already forfeited whatever peace you had with Pan." She felt a sick twisting in her stomach for what she was about to do. To force, to pound with everything she had, these women into submission. She could see the course of action she could take now. "Selene saved me from drowning. Actively helped me heal my wounds."

"You never told me that." Perdy whispers, hurt, at the same time Clare gasps "You almost *drowned*?"

Carrie held up a hand to silence them. "Don't you think if Pan were to find out about that he would see it as taking my side over his? You saved one of the biggest threats to his power on this island and covered up the arrival of another. All of us did that by coming here."

"No – no, just because we came here doesn't mean we have to do anything-"

"Yes, it does Selene. I'm sorry, but it does. You either leave here and tell Pan, in which case we all die tomorrow. Or you leave here and leave us to it, in which case we all die including you because you didn't tell him. Or you leave here ready to fight with us, and stand a chance of winning safety for you and your people forever. The same goes for you, Wild Rose."

Several mouths drop open, but Carrie schools her face into a stoic mask. She is scared she might break down and take it all back if she doesn't.

"I have one question." Clare said, whilst the others glared daggers or smiled at Carrie in their turn.

"Go on." Hook nods.

"Say we all agree to do this, to create an island rebellion. How would be defeat Pan? We cannot defeat him by magic alone, or by the absence of it." She referenced to Wild Rose. "And we can't just run away back to my world anymore, because it's become bigger than that. So...what do we do?"

Hook looks away from her. Carrie bites her lip. Its Perdy who does her the courtesy of saying what everyone else already understands. "We have to fight him. We have to pick a spot and fight him. All of us together. The only way we can coexist on this island much longer is if we all learn that the magic here belongs to the land and not to Pan. Then it cannot be used against us, at least, that's the theory. But Pan won't ever allow it. Not ever. And as long as they see him as invincible, his boys won't believe it. We have to show them that he is not invincible."

Clare frowned at her. "What, you mean like, we kill him? He's a child, isn't he? They are all children. That's what we're talking about here."

"They stopped being children the day they came here and raised their weapons against us." Wild Rose sneered.

"Carrie, you're the one who said there had to be another way – other than the killing and the fighting. That's why we called this bloody council meeting in the first place! To work together to find another way!" Clare turned to Hook, panic and frustration all over her face. "You have to see that this is the way he would think. I've never even seen this Pan, but from what I've heard about him he is cruel. But does that mean we have to be cruel in return?" she looks pleadingly to the faces around the room. "Well, does it? Look, with a bit more time I could probably get myself and my niece back home the way I got here. But we aren't doing that right now because she wants to leave this place better than how she found it. Killing someone isn't going to do that. It's going to make it worse."

"How do you know?" Portia snapped. Hook glared at the blue mermaid.

"Because I know! I know that death makes everything worse, it just does."

"Sometimes you have to do hard things to make good things happen." Perdy jumped in again. "No one likes it, but some things have to be done for the greater good."

Carrie twisted her fingers together. She had a decision to make. Somehow she knew they would listen to her. Both sides were right. She had to pick which side she could live with, which side she wanted to live with.

"Maybe there is a way we don't have to kill him. It might still involve a battle. If we draw Pan and his lost boys out into the open...maybe we don't have to kill him. Maybe if we just defeat him the battle he will start, maybe that will be the catalyst. Maybe if just one of the boys sees what we see, sees that mine and Clare's presence here is beyond Pan's control, maybe the tide will shift and they will all begin to see what is possible. Sometimes all it takes is one person, right? One voice to rise above the many and see how the world really is."

"How can we risk everything on something that may not be possible?" Selene asked sadly.

"How can you not?" Carrie's voice was open and soft, the way only people telling the truth can sound. "If it doesn't work we can kill him. They'll see it then. Maybe – or maybe Clare is right and they will become deaf and blind to us in rage. Killing him will make a martyr of him. But if it does work, and we capture him and bring him low? Then they will see him helpless and humiliated, and that might be far more effective than dead. Wild Rose said to me once that faith, hope and imagination are powerful things. Powerful magic's. That's all we have to give the boys. That's all we have to give each other, and we can claw this island back from tyranny in one fell swoop. We have to give them back their magic."

She turned to Wild Rose. "You believe the island will give Tiger Lily back to you one day, but for now she lives in the wind and the earth. If that is true, maybe she brought us here to help you. Not to save you, but to help you save everyone else."

Clare smiles proudly at her niece, her eyes pricking with tears. Hook smiles at Clare, knowing her to be all he needed to convince him to do this. Perdy grasps Carrie's hands as the two rulers that really belonged here, Wild Rose and Selene consulted their seconds, and then each other.

"Then it is settled." Wild Rose became a princess once more, her tone determined. "I told you once you had an ally in my people. That will remain true."

Selene sighed loudly and levelled a steely gaze at Carrie. "And I told you once that you would answer for your trespass into my territory."

Perdy's hand still held Carrie's, but out the corner of her eye Carrie saw her reaching with the other to brush her fingers over her knife hilt.

"Perhaps…this may be your answer. Your help, and your willingness to sacrifice." She raised her chin in a unmistakably royal gesture. Portia looked like she wanted to object, but one look from her ruler silenced her.

Hook grinned and smacked his hands together loudly, making Clare jump.

The only person who hadn't said a word was Wild Rose's second. A beautiful man with long dark hair and a chest of tattoos. Now he smiled.

"Let us defeat the white boy king, and fulfil our destinies."

Hook smiled devilishly at them all and said;

"Let's go start a god damn revolution."

23

What was, what is, and what can never be

Carrie is holding Perdy's hand back on the Eloise.

They are watching the night sky, the stars Carrie didn't recognize, huddling together for warmth.

Carrie feels calmer than she has in a long time.

She'd been thinking all the way back here about what they were about to do. Somewhere along the way it really had stopped being just about her. Clare had been right. If she was going to leave this place, she wasn't going to leave it the same way she found it. The people here had become frightened, and this was their land. She wanted to help them get it back, in any small way she could.

She's thinking also that Nala might have been right to call her the bard of their group, to have them listen to her recite poetry and stories. It made her understand how to speak, how to weave her words together to incite what feelings she wished. That's what she had done that day. And it had worked. She had been a bard, and her story had started a rebellion. Clare was the face of it, the others the soldiers, the hands of it. But she was the voice of it, carried on the wind. She could only hope now that they won and that it wasn't for nothing. She had to hope also that Clare actually did know how to get them home, when the time was right. It was all tied up in emotions – Carrie didn't understand it totally, but she knew Clare had to feel her way through it. She had to trust that she could do that. It was a hard thing to do. She liked to know what she was doing. She liked to know, step by step, what would happen. She'd spent a long time not feeling in control of anything, even herself. Now she had claimed back some control she was having to trust it to other people again. She sighed heavily.

One thing she didn't know how to trust was the thing she and Perdy still had not talked about. If they did defeat Pan, if Clare could get them home, what was Perdy going to do? She'd told her once that she could come home with her. Carrie still wished she would. She made Carrie feel safe, sure of something. She couldn't really explain it. She knew she wanted her in her life though.

Perdita was very beautiful, but it wasn't just that. It was hard to pin point exactly. It was just that she seemed more real than most things. More solid, more present. She had a permanence about her in a whirlwind of dreams and chaos. She was due north. She was to Carrie a world unconquerable that she wanted to know all about. She was her second star.

Carrie stares where the shore meets the sea, and into the shadow of the trees. The inky blackness of shadows in which their invisible tormentor had lurked for so long. She'd been afraid of Pan since she'd got here and she had never even see him. She'd seen his damage though, In Perdy's eyes, on Wild Rose's scarred face, on the weariness and wariness resting inside the captain of this ship. And why? They were scared of a shadow that was going to disappear in the light of the morning. That was what she had to tell herself, anyway.

"You know, it's sort of hard to believe that all the time, we've basically just been scared of a load of boys running around, howling at the moon and wanking off in the bushes."

Perdy lets out a snort of laughter. She shrugs. "Who says I'm afraid?" She sings out in a fake bold voice, like an over dramatic actor. "The day I'm afraid is the day they put me in the ground!"

"Yeah, well, that day might not be too far away thanks to me." Carrie mutters.

Perdy nudges her as if to say 'don't be stupid'. She sighs, leaning a little closer to Carrie.

"The offer is still open you know. For you to come with me. When all this is done." Carrie says, looking up at her.

"I know." Perdita said. She turned from her star gazing to look at Carrie with a gentle smile. "I promise I'm thinking about it."

"Well you're gonna have to think a bit quicker, my sweet. We're having a war tomorrow."

Perdy craned her head to look across the deck. Nala, Willow and Peaches were crouched round a stove with Cormac, Jonas and Jean. They were all laughing and talking together, despite their ages and everything else that had once separated them.

"I hope they understand." Perdy said sadly.

Carrie nudged her in the ribs. "They do."

She turned too and rested her head against Perdy's shoulder as they watched Hook and Clare slowly start to approach the group by the stove.

"Come on." Carrie said, nodding toward them. "Let's go mingle with the riff raff."

She steps forward but Perdy takes hold of her wrist to stop her.

"One minute Carrie." She steps closer and presses a hand to Carrie's cheek, feeling the smile spreading there. "I'm not hesitating about coming with you because of you. Does that make sense? It's because of me, and them. But not because of us."

Carrie nods. "I think I get it. No, no I do get it. Honestly I do. You've been here with them longer than you've been with me. But they can come too, if they want. We can all stay together maybe."

"I've told them to think about what they want. The problem is you know what kind of world you're going back to. No one else does."

Carrie nods. That was all she could ask for, for them to consider her offer. She was already asking so much of them all. She couldn't keep doing that to them, at least not for tonight. Tonight she just wanted to be with her sisters and the girl she now knew she loved, and her auntie, and their friends, and the stars.

Hook and Clare slowly walked the length of the Eloise and back again. It had mostly been in a comfortable silence. Mostly, because Clare was humming.

"Do you know you sing a lot?"

Clare broke off mid note and found heat gathering in her cheeks. "Oh god, I do don't I? Sorry."

Hook chuckled. "It's alright. It's quite nice actually. We haven't had anyone singing round here for a long time. Except Cormac when he gets too drunk, but I'd more call that atrocious wailing, rather than singing."

"If my sister were here she'd probably say something pretentious about it. Like it's my subconscious filling the silence so I don't go mad from it, or something. She'd probably be right."

"She sounds very smart. Aisling, isn't it? Carrie's mother."

"She is smart. Smarter than me. Like mother like daughter, I suppose." Clare shoved her hands in her back pockets, shrugging her shoulders.

Hook looks across the deck at Carrie where she is huddled deep in conversation with Perdy. "Yes, she did do rather well today, didn't she?"

Clare stared at her too, her expression hardening. "Will you promise me something, James?" she asked suddenly.

He looked down at her for a long moment, their eyes connecting, ducking his head close to hers. "If I can, Augustine."

She blinks up at him uncertainly. "I'd like you to promise me you'll protect Carys tomorrow. I am all for liberating the masses, but not at her expense. Not if it costs me her. Do I make myself clear?"

He nods, pursing his lips. "I promise… I will do everything in my power to keep your niece safe. And to keep you safe, for what it's worth."

She nods in acceptance relaxing her shoulders, goose bumps

brushing over her arms. “And stop calling me Augustine.”

“Ooh, I can’t promise that! I like the name too much!”

He laughs and jumps away from her as she tries to swat his arm.

“Speaking of names – I have something I wanna know.”

“I already told you my name. My biggest secret – the key to unlocking-“

“Not *your* name – I want to know why your boat is called Eloise.”

“Would you stop calling her a bloody boat? She’s a ship. A pirate ship. She does ship like things. She has sails. She’s a big…big ship.” He trails off, seeing Clare staring at him unimpressed. He sighed deeply, walking to the railing to stare of into the distance of the night.

“Right…if I tell you my good woman, I might as well tell everyone else. You know, if we’re all going to die horribly at the hands of a bunch of twelve year olds tomorrow.”

“But I’m the one who asked-“

“Yes, and I’m telling you – come on.” He grabbed her arm and pulled her toward his crew just as Carrie and Perdy sat down with them too.

And so there they all were, misfits and pirates and silent sad girls, clinging together in the dark, trying to find something to hold onto in the darkness that was coming with the morning.

Hook looked like he was regretting his decision. He’d been gripped by the idea of sharing something of himself. He’d been thinking more and more about how everyone who had ever known him before was dead. Perhaps he could rectify that now. But it was different, talking to Clare when no one could hear. Different to talking to his crew, who despite his having sailed with for hundreds of years, did not know all that much about him. He sighed deeply, wondering if he could get out of this.

Clare gestured to them all expectantly, amused challenge dancing in her eyes. Hook glowered at her and coughed grumpily.

“Eloise was a girl I knew, a long, long time ago.” The dark low thrum of Hook's voice managed to drown everything else out. The sea and the fear and the creaking of the ship. "A sweet girl with silver hair and a big, naïve heart in her chest that beat only for me. When she and I were young we dreamt of a magical island, where we would play with laugh with other children. The one who made this possible, we thought, was a boy named Peter."

The others exchanged shocked looks.

"Eloise was one of those people who couldn't bear to face the world. She was a dreamer, a romantic...and most of all she was weak. She wanted to live in that dream forever. But she couldn't. Pan wouldn't let her. Girls, at least back then, weren't allowed to stay here. He sent them away to grow up in a harsh, dull world. She couldn't cope with that. She got sickly, she screamed and cried every night. We stayed together, she and I, and over the next few years I watched her becoming more and more obsessed with finding this...this fucking island once more."

Hook looked around him like there wasn't anywhere he'd want to be less.

"So, being young and in love, I did the only thing a boy who's young and in love would do. I decided to find my fortune, then find this place. For her."

The stove spat flames. He didn't seem to notice, for he was lost somewhere in the past.

"I joined the navy straight out of boarding school worked my way up...then, well, things happen to us all. I won't bore you with the details of how and why piracy became my only option. A war decimates even after it finishes. Sufficed to say, once you turn to that world of criminality, of unlawfulness, there is no real way back. I did well, I didn't get killed. I didn't get rich either. I lost my hand trying to though." He stares down at his hook with disdain. "By trying to punish me, they remade me, the people who maimed me this way. By trying to unman me, they created something more terrible, more angry than man. A myth, a name. Names have power. Mine stopped being what it was before, and became Captain Hook. I found them again, in the dead of night, emerging from the sea like a ghost. Took the ship of the men that made me into a feared pirate and renamed it The Eloise. In the hopes, I suppose, that her name and therefore her wish might carry me to here, so in turn she may return to where she wanted to be. But obviously, that didn't happen. I came here in 1715, but I did not manage to return to Eloise."

They all sit in a stunned silence for a moment. Clare picks at a thread on her light blue jeans. "I lost a man." She says. And that is all she says, all she needs to say. She looks with blazing eyes at Hook, and he gives the smallest most imperceptible nod.

"I never wanted to return all that much." Willow's voice is sullen and quiet and they all turn to look at her in surprise. She doesn't look at any of them. Just stares at the heat of the fire in front of her like none of them are there.

"In 1849 my papa dragged me across the desert in our old farming cart to try and find gold. When he didn't find gold, tried to find it through sellin' commodities. I was a commodity to him. First man he tried to gimme too..." she dragged her finger across her neck. "And that's when I came here, when I seen what I done. Even though he deserved it. I didn't deserve it. Sometimes think maybe I did, because everyone else seemed to want to...to rut like animals when I didn't...but now I know I didn't deserve it none."

Nala reached over and grasped her hand tightly. "My father was a good man, but his brother was not. When my father died in 1985, my uncle tried to marry me off. I may be a good cook, a good sewer, with good hips, but I would not be a good wife. I ran too."

One by one they tell what stories the others didn't know, until it becomes a confessional, until they all unburden themselves for the first time in an age. All except Peaches, who's gift and curse was that she remembered nothing from where she came from. She touched the other girls gently on their hands though, to show them her support. For such a tiny young girl, she understood more than the rest of them put together.

This was their cry into the void, into history, to each other. They could go to their graves knowing someone at least remembered who they had been, who they could have been, and who they were now.

"You know what I'd always do, before I was about to go into an impossible fight?"

Jean had passed round a bottle of wine. Clare had snatched it from Peaches and Carrie as it went round the circle and gave them a tough luck glare when they grumbled about it. Nala passed it to Perdy without drinking. So the others were left to get melancholy and pensive.

"Run away?" Jonas laughed. It was a strange noise, guttural and joyous as it was rare.

Jean threw two fingers up at him as the others giggled. "No. I..." He pressed his hand to his heart. "Would sing a song. I was a very accomplished concertina player."

"A what?" Willow retorted.

"Well, Augus-" Hook grinned as he stopped himself. "Clare – is a singer."

"I bloody well am not." She cried. "I'm not." She threw her hands up as they all turned to look at her. "I am not singing a song just because you all drank too much and got all maudlin."

"Well...you do sing a lot." Carrie admitted.

"Thank you!" Hook cried, and they all jumped as he wildly threw his hook out to gesture to her.

Clare turned to look at him, leaning toward him without thinking. He sat comfortably letting her with a gentle, relaxed smile. Carrie is surprised to see that Clare looks relaxed about it too, whether she knows it or not.

"Well, not all of you are going to know the same songs, so if you think about it really isn't fair." Clare said primly, squaring her shoulders.

"I'm sure we'll pick it up." Nala smiled. She was trying to be encouraging, not realizing Clare was looking for a way out.

"Pan will hear us all here together."

"We want him to hear us and know we're coming for him. Or he's coming for us. Or...whatever." Perdy pointed out. They had sent one of Selene's girls out to feed information to the fairies. The information will trickle down, down, down, all the way to Tinkerbell and into Pan's ears. Pan will make the decision to retaliate thinking it was his idea, thinking he is ambushing them, and they will turn around and hopefully, somehow, destroy his ever waning power.

Clare groaned at the sky and it turned into a laugh of acceptance.

"Fine! Fine. God, alright. What song do I actually remember..." She pointed quickly as she had a light bulb moment. "Drunken sailor! Do you know that one?"

"No, I'm afraid it's a little after my time, I think." Hook replied. He was watching her, his eyes staying with her even when she swayed a little.

"It's from 17...something." She frowned at Carrie, who shrugged.

"Well, the seventeen something's did last a little while." He replied indulgently.

Peaches stomped her foot impatiently.

"Yes, darling, you're quite right." Clare patted her arm, not noticing Peaches trying to bite her (affectionately, of course.) "Let's get on with this farce."

Clare stood up too quickly and almost stumbled until Hook put a hand on her back to steady her. He looked a little transfixed by her.

"If and when you know the words, please, please, *please* join in and save me. Right." Clare cleared her throat.

And then she started to sing.

24

The confrontation

Well, Clare thinks. Michael, I'm here like you told me. Either I'll be at home by the end of the day or I'll be seeing you soon.

She tries not to think that the second option sounds comforting.

She can't think that. Not, at least, until she's seen her niece home. That's what she had to think about, that and only that.

When James had told her he'd keep them both safe, she'd wanted to snap at him. She appreciated the sentiment – she knew she was being unfair in the face of a surprising, unfailing kindness, but she'd prefer all his focus on protecting Carrie. If he really wanted to help her, then that is what he would do.

Sometimes Clare had these strange sort of feelings, like maybe all of this wasn't real, that maybe she barely existed and the world was something happening around her, not too her. She'd had these thoughts for a long time, even before Michael. But for the first time, she knew that it would be alright, as long as Carys was alright. Aisling could forgive her then, for going away, forgive her for the way she had been for all of these years.

She clenches her hands into fists at her side. She had a purpose. How she was to achieve that purpose was still unclear to her, but for the first time in years she had something to cling to, something to focus on, something important. She felt that she had failed to protect everyone in her life. Everything that had been precious to her had been lost to her, one by one, over and over. Her parents, her boyfriend, even herself – but that child would not go unprotected through this life. If she could do one thing, she'd do that. She was the only one that could. She was trying not to let that responsibility scare her. Clare had never been good at being responsible, always preferring others to take the lead, to help her. But she tried to let it bolster her conviction now. She tried to let it make her brave.

Carrie is feeling brave. It's a new sort of feeling and she doesn't entirely trust it.

She's watching Clare pace around at the bow of the ship, full of frantic energy just like usual. Carrie can't move because she's scared she'll fall apart if she does, like her stillness is a shield. Nala, Willow, Perdy and Peaches are all standing close by. She feels safer with them all clustered around her. Her friends, when she had none before, her sisters when she had been alone so long.

She was staring, waiting. She felt as if she was staring down the barrel of a gun, and when she blinked, it would go off. So she stood her ground, kept watching the horizon, until they came, the shadows and shapes and names that had dogged her steps since she came here.

Perdy steps forward. She feels their shoulders bumping together. She's watching Clare, who is distant from all of them now. She was, Carrie knew, retreating to make it easier. She'd been open, last night when they had all been together. She'd mentioned Michael in a moment of unbridled emotion. She'd let herself get close to people. Now she was stepping back, which was something she did when she was scared. It was why she'd been able to disappear from the world for so many years. Carrie lets her, for now. Hook is watching her aunt intently too, and she knows she is not unguarded.

"Remind me again why we're fighting on the ship." Carrie asks Perdy.

"Well we decided, hey! Why not make this as suicidal as humanly possible?"

Carrie glared at her and Perdy sighed. "We are fighting on the ship because it means Pan is more exposed. He doesn't have the jungle to ambush us from. He has to reveal his position to get out here. But any good war lord knows not to put all your eggs in one basket. He'll have boys in the trees, but not so many that Tiger Lily's forces can't make a significant dent in their numbers before they get out here. The boat also gives the mermaids more access to the fight."

Carrie nods a little too quickly. Perdy nudges her. "I won't let anything happen to you Blondie."

"And I won't let anything happen to you."

They smiled at each other and knew they both felt the same way. It was comforting, to entirely trust the person you were going into battle beside. Maybe that's what true love really was, in the end.

Nala looked at Peaches and Willow as she shifted uncomfortably, trying to read their thoughts. It was second nature to her usually, but panic had set in. She was trying to press it down as best she could.

"Are you ready?" She asked them. A small part of her wanted one of them to say no, to know she wasn't the only one who felt scared.

"Born ready, girl." Willow winks at her, though it feels half hearted.

In recent weeks, Peaches had become a lot more tactile than she ever had been, and it is evidenced in the way she reaches around Willow and gives Nala's wrist one quick squeeze of assurance.

"It will be alright." Nala says to them both, and to reassure herself. "We simply must trust our sisters and look out for one another. Just like always. Nothing different to any of the other battles we have faced." She crossed her arms over her chest, switching from foot to foot. "Have you two decided? Carrie's offer to let us go with them when they leave this place...have you made a decision?"

Willow and Peaches look at each other then back to her.

They nod.

When they come, they come from the distance, small spots on the horizon.

It's like something from an old black and white war movie. If it were a film, dramatic instrumental music would be playing. But there isn't any of that. There is just quiet. Silence, almost, as if the island is holding its breath. It makes it even worse.

As they approach, a formation happens on the ship with no words as they gather to face them. From far away no one can see who is coming at first. Hook curses softly under his breath behind Clare and lowers his telescope. At first, for a gut wrenching split second she thinks it hasn't worked. Then she turns her head and sees him grinning menacingly. He's staring at the boys flying toward them with murder in his eyes. It sends a shiver up her spine.

Pan circles the ship lazily in the air and his boys grin down at them. There's only two, after Pan. He's trying to say there's no way he would need more. He's wrong, though he clearly doesn't understand it yet. And he is finally in front of them. They boy who had menaced them and sent them orders. The name they had feared had taken form. It was staggering that it was really happening.

What did our heroes expect, from a child killer? From a child king, a child tyrant, an orphan with no home, no civilization?

Whatever it was, it was not the boy floating above them.

His face is still rounded with puppy fat. He has light blonde hair, and red round cheeks. It makes him look angelic. He's a floating cherub in swathes of matted green layers. That such beauty could hide such cruelty serves to make him even more frightening. Even though he was a child, no more than thirteen, he had a lazy malevolence, an arrogance that intimidated even grown men like the pirates for years.

His eyes were the biggest surprise. They weren't blue, like one would expect. They were dark brown, almost black. As if there was one part of his face that didn't match the rest, one part that truly could not disguise the darkness they knew rested inside of him. His eyes revealed the night of his soul. And if they did not, perhaps the gleaming knife at his worn leather belt did. Perhaps the feral smile that spread across his lips did, too.

He circled closer to them, still not saying a word. All that could be heard was the sloshing of the waved against the wood, the creaking of the ship and the cries of birds in the distance. It might have been paradise once. The warmth of the sun crowded the group on the boat, the sticky warmth that choked you with sweat. Nala tugged at her hijab slightly, being careful not to dislodge it or draw attention to herself and Clare wanted to pick her hair up from her neck, but she didn't dare move. None of them did. Like animals, they watched and waited.

Pan surveyed them all. He knew about the girls and the pirates had fought them for years. And he'd tested Carrie by sending out the summons for her to retrieve Tinkerbell. But it is obvious he hadn't seen her in the flesh before. It was hard to tell what he knew about her, how far his powers really reached. She wondered if he could see inside her, reach in and tear at her until he found her weakness. No, she reminded herself as his gaze travelled over her. You have to remember he cannot. He cannot touch you, that is what this is about. He isn't as strong as he appears.

Pan's gaze moves on and he stops abruptly, surprise moving over his face in a flash. He stares at Clare with wide eyes, his ears turning pink.

Hook tensed behind her – he was stood so close to her she could feel it. She felt him shift, ready to move and stand in front of her but she held up her arm lightly against his chest, stilling him. She didn't need any man to stand in front of her. Not anymore. She stared up at Pan, even though she was shaking, even though her eyes probably betrayed her fear. She stared up at him and did not look away.

"What is this?" Pan whispered. His voice was a child's, high pitched voice. Not broken yet. The boys who had flown with him fly closer to him, daring to risk a confused glance at one another. This was obviously new.

"I think you mean *who* is this." Hook called. "Didn't your mother teach you anything, boy?" He's either trying to distract attention from Clare, or he's trying to goad the boy. Or both – he was certainly succeeding at both. "Oh wait, that's right. You have no mother."

"I don't need one. I don't need some old woman telling me what to do."

"But your boys need someone telling them what to do?" Hook frowned.

The boys on either side of Pan hissed and jabbed their knifes at them threateningly.

Pan looked at Clare in a panic. He was concealing it well, but she saw it dancing in his eyes. Uncertainty. He couldn't admit he didn't know how she got here, because he was supposed to control the island. But he also could not dismiss the reality in which he found himself. So he did what all children do – he threw a tantrum.

He flew at Clare in a rush, her teeth banged together painfully as Hook tugged her out the way, raising his sword at Pan. Everyone else lifted their weapons too, and it became a standoff in a matter of seconds, eyes jumping everywhere frantically.

"Stop!"

It was Carrie who stepped forward first. "We aren't here to fight you, not like that."

She held up a placating hand. Pan scoffed, moving toward her. "I don't believe you. I'm usually the one who begins these games, but I won't back down from a dare. Fight me, all of you, if you think you can win. Surely that is why you lured me out here, letting that information of your betrayal reach me."

He was smart, but not smart enough. He still, quite literally, thought in terms of fight or flight.

"We want to talk."

"Hah!" Pan laughed loudly. The boys around him seemed to relax, letting themselves laugh too.

Pan whistled then, believing his enemies were weak. Several more of his lost boys flew over quickly, surrounding the boat.

"What would we possibly have to talk about? On my island we don't talk, we fight. And I always win. And you want to talk to me..." Pan laughed again, sneering nastily.

"No." Carrie grinned. "Not to you. I want to talk to them." Pan's face fell as she glanced at the boys the flew around the Eloise.

Everyone on the boat stepped back, turning to the starboard side. With a sudden whoosh of noise, sea water slapped onto the deck, making Pan jump, and Carrie ran to retrieve what Portia had just thrown to her.

The shell looked like any other conch shell, and as Carrie raised it to her lips, she just prayed the mermaids were right about it.

"All of you...listen to me." She said into the shell. Her voice echoed as if she were using a microphone. She allowed herself a small, relieved smile.

"The mermaids...the native people whose land you have taken... the fairies, who are forced to serve you...the boys in the trees, and in the air." She took a deep breath, circling as she spoke to look at the boys. "We aren't here for a fight. It's true...that that's what has happened in the past. It's true that lives have been lost many times over, and that anger is what bonds you, and divides you to and from us. And we are angry. But we're angry with Pan. And if you listen to me, do nothing but listen, then I hope you can see why."

Pan scoffed. "Just kill them and have done with this!" he whined. "This is no fun."

Carrie swallowed against the painful pounding of her chest, but to her surprise, none of the boys moved toward her. They kept looking from her to Clare in confusion. Carrie looked at Clare too, who nodded at her. She wanted to look at Perdy, but Perdy was behind her, guarding her.

"Ask yourselves why you fight...is it because you hate us? Or because he tells you that's the way it is? Why? Why does it have to be like this? It's for Pan's amusement. He watches us fight and die and he does nothing but laugh. He doesn't care about you, or this island!"

"He gave us a home." One of the lost boys calls, and there are a few murmurs of agreement. She can't see who it was.

"No, he took you from your homes. I'm sure that a lot of you have things you were running from – we all do. But ask yourselves – is this really better? Fighting and dying for Pan? For no reason other than that's what you've been told to do?"

Everyone is held by tension, the silence deafening them. One false move, one wrong word, and it would snap.

"Before I came here, no one had come for more than two decades, at least. No one else is coming. This is it. These are the people you're going to live and die with. After you all go, after we all go, there won't be anything left. It won't have been for anything, and no one will remember you. Don't you want the chance to live in peace, in this beautiful place?"

"She's lying!" Pan barked hysterically as the boys turned to glower at him. They were beginning to see her point. She just needed to press her advantage. "I'll bring more people whenever I want! Look –" He pointed a pudgy finger at Clare. He looks steadily at Hook just once before he speaks. "I even brought you a mother."

"No!" Hook growls. He moves in front of Clare as some of the boys advance on her. "She isn't your mother. She's a way out; don't any of you stupid children see that?"

That made them angrier, the grumbles rising and the boys inching closer, readying to fight. They were quick to anger; it had always been their default. Carrie scrambled to bring the attention back to her, to control what she'd set in motion. She hoped that if she couldn't, the other tribes were in place to do their part.

"No! Wait, listen! That's Clare, and she came here by herself! Pan had nothing to do with it. The island felt her and she came here for me."

"That's impossible! No one comes here without Pan knowing!"

"Well he didn't know about me!" Carrie snapped back. "Even if he didn't admit it, some of you must have seen it. And you heard him." She nods to the two boys he had brought with him when he'd first approached. "He didn't even know who she was!" Her voice rose, she felt like screaming at them, shaking them. Anger seeped into her, despite the boys nodding at the truth of her words. "She is how we can get out of this place. Pan has no power to match hers. He doesn't control the native people, how hard is it to imagine he cannot, in fact, control a grown woman?" She spat. "He doesn't rule this island! Not if you don't let him. It's that simple!"

She let her arm drop for a second. She took a step back and nearly collided with Perdy. Nala, Peaches and Willow left their posts slowly, drifting towards her. The pirates guarded them in turn. She smiled at them. She hoped they would be ok.

"All you have to do is know in your heart, in your bones and in your guts, that he doesn't own you. That he's just a pathetic little boy. You have the power – you have the magic. It's yours. All you have to do is take it. Feel it and take it back."

Some of the boys lowered themselves further to the ship. They didn't touch their weapons. When Pan saw them his face contorted in rage.

"Don't listen to her! She's just some silly girl! Don't take orders from a girl who can't even hold a sword."

"That's true. I don't know how to fight. But that doesn't make me weak. And it doesn't mean what I'm saying isn't true. Don't any of you feel it, even a little bit? That's all it takes. Just one spark. You can all come with us. My aunt is going to take us all home. But if you want to stay, you have to get rid of *him*."

The boys gazes flew angrily to Pan. She'd tapped into something. Something she had said had been wrong. It had sent them the wrong way.

Her stomach turned to ice as she realized. She'd wanted to get through this without bloodshed. She had invited them to get rid of their leader, told them they could do it.

That was when the chaos started.

The clang and ringing of swords, knives, spears and clubs all filled the air as slowly weapons were drawn across the ship. The boys began to shoot around, some to guard Pan and some to kill him. The same went for the group on the ship. Carrie and Nala hurried away to the edge by Perdy and Jonas, Peaches and Willow advancing further onto the ship as battle lines were drawn. Some of the boys touched their feet to the wood of the ship, a physical choice to join the rebels there. But they didn't have the same goal. They looked at Pan like they had been waiting for this, the way Hook had been waiting for it.

Carrie couldn't see Clare in the sudden rush of movement and it turned her stomach to ice.

"Where is Clare?" She asked, but no one heard her. She was hemmed in by bodies.

"Give me a sword!"

Clare was backing up, thanks to the insistence of the captain, who's sword was drawn. Cormac and Jean were close by, probably at his insistence. Jean keeps looking at their progress, tracking where they were. Clare thinks Hook must have told him to keep an eye on her. Any other time she would have appreciated it, but it made her feel a little helpless, in the face of a lot of boys wanting to kill her. They were zooming around in the air up there and she felt helpless. Things had descended in a split second.

"What?" Hook calls over his shoulder.

"James, give me a sword!" Clare repeated. He turned to look at her finally, his eyes dancing with light.

"I was junior fencing champion when I was thirteen." She shrugs. "Well its better than nothing." She hissed as his expression twisted. Then he grinned and nodded, pulling a spare sword from his belt and thrusting it at her.

She took it with two shaking hands. "What now?"

"Now you stay close to me and hope you don't need to bloody use it!"

She did hope that. She also hoped that a bit of fencing in the school gym 24 years ago was still in her brain somewhere. Mostly she hoped that she could get to Carrie in time. Even if the boys killed Pan, she could still get them home. She had to find a way across the ship however, which had descended quickly into a battleground.

Factions seemed to dissolve and it was hard to tell which boys were on their side as swords started clanging together. The thing they had feared was here, and they would have to fight.

Out of the corner of her eye she saw Pan starting to retreat, only to be accosted by two lost boys pushing him back into the fray. The coward had tried to run. She had to believe he was digging his own grave.

"Get me to Carrie will you?" She yelled over the noise at Hook, who nodded.

"Go, I'll cover you. Come on."

But before they could move he lifted his sword as it collided with another. A taller boy, he looked about sixteen, advanced on them. Clare stumbled back, holding her sword uselessly in front of her. She span round to try and find Jean only to find him fending off two lost boys.

Hook blocked another blow, using the momentary pause to yank the boy closer to him by grabbing his tattered clothes. Then he kicked the boy in his chest, sending him sprawling onto the deck. He deflected yet another blow to his left, sparring with another boy. Clare started forward.

When Hook shoved the boy back again Clare thrust her leg out, tripping the boy. She jumped over his prone body and carried on as far as she could. She ducked below something that shot past her, feeling it move the air above her. She turned in shock to see that it was a large piece of wood – it looked like a door. The Eloise was getting destroyed. That's what half the noise was. They were going to run out of time very quickly.

Then they hear a welcome sound, over the screams of being hurt, boys fighting boys, Pan shouting orders like a general. They hear a princess.

Wild Rose lets out a howl from the trees, emerging onto the shore. As her people run past her, into the shallows, some of the boys advance on them. the ship begins to rock too, the boys tumbling where everyone else had been prepared to grab onto something. The mermaids had arrived. Whilst some of them rocked the ship from beneath, others began to climb with the nets they had thrown over the side last night.

Naked women, dark skin shining with the sea and the sun, emerged from the water. They didn't hold weapons. They fought hand to hand, not flinching when the lost boys still loyal to Pan swung their weapons and the ship stopped shaking.

Portia snapped a spear over her knee and winked across at Clare with a grin before moving on.

"Blue." She whispered, shaking her head before pushing forward.

Carrie had managed to move around her guards enough to see what was happening. She had a knife in her hand, held up in front of her. Perdy was hacking and grunting at anyone who came near them, but they had been backed up against the side of the ship and they couldn't move. If Carrie wanted to get anyone out of here she had to get to Clare. But could she leave before the battle was over? Perdy was fighting for her, but she had no idea who was going to win. It seemed like even though they now had more numbers, Pan's boys still held their own. She looked around, to see what had become of Pan. They could kill him, and it might still work. But she wanted to do this the way she had planned.

She sees him out the corner of her eye. They had all gotten distracted trying to defend themselves. She shoves her knife into Nala's hands. "Hold this for me will you?"

Nala let out a spluttering protest as Carrie darted away from her.

"Jesus, Mary and Joseph!" She hears Perdy shout as she follows her.

Leaning over the side of the ship to get a better look, Carrie bats Perdy's hands away.

"What are you doing? Do you want to die you insane –"

Carrie pointed, and dashed off again.

Seeing what she'd pointed at, Perdy swore softly.

Clare clashed her sword against one belonging to a lost boy. He had long greasy hair and he cackled loudly, covered in blood. She made a disgusted face. He lashed out at her. She ducked, raising her arms to shield herself. She let out a cry as his blade nicked her arm, wet blood seeping into the white cotton of her shirt.

She flung her blade out as he came at her again, the pain of the clash jolting through her arm. He came at her again and she dropped her sword. It skidded away from her and she froze. He grinned a grin that was nothing but teeth before raising his sword.

The boy coughed.

Dark red blood spluttered out of his mouth and he dropped to his knees. Hook stood behind him, his sword bloody.

"Are you ok?"

She nodded, unable to speak. He put his arm out for her. She looked down at his hook. He motioned for her to come to him. The normally shining silver of the hook was covered in blood. Her hands started shaking. She looked around her in a daze, as if seeing the destruction of the Eloise for the first time.

Everything was covered in blood. It made the floor slippery. Rigging had been torn down, she had no idea how. Chunks of doors and wood lay strewn about as people fought one on one. The native people were still in the water, making their way back to the beach as the fairies joined the fight. The mermaids were backing them up though. Most of the mermaids had retreated into the sea. She could see some of their moves moving, and she watched as boys threw themselves into the sea, toward a song that couldn't reach her here. Peaches was up in the crow's nest by now, using a bow and arrow to take down lost boys. Willow fought like a warrior, her red hair flying everywhere. She looked like a Valkyrie. The pirates were fighting too – Cormac was clubbing boys round the head with what looked like a ladle. Nala crouched behind Jonas, though Clare saw her swiping at anyone who came near her. She wished it would all stop. She didn't see Carrie anywhere, and the panic and fear she had been fighting began to seep into her. She saw Wild Rose climb onto the ship, wanted to tell her to turn back, but she couldn't speak.

"Augustine. Come on, love."

Hook advanced toward her. He put his arm round her, resting his hook lightly on the small of her back and moving her forward, past the boy he had killed for her.

She moved in front of him, trying to look for Carrie. It was when her back was to him that she heard it. The weight of his hook dropped from her. She heard a small wheeze of surprise. Something wet sounding.

When she turned, she saw what had happened.

Hook fell to his knees, clutching his side. A lost boy grinned down at him before advancing on her. In a split second Clare's instincts took over. She saw the blade she had dropped earlier and dove for it. The boy just missed her with his. In another second, she swung her sword up, by sheer luck managing to slice it fatally across his stomach. The boy dropped to the deck. Hook slumped forward, using his only hand to prop himself up.

Clare was shaking. She wanted to be sick. But she couldn't. Her body at least knew she couldn't, and it took over in that moment.

She dove forward and caught Hook before he fell completely. Dark red blood was seeping from a wound in his side and he had gone pale. No, no, no she thinks. This can't be happening. They were so close. Michael's words echo back to her. This is it. This is the thing she got to control. This was the thing she got to keep.

Hook collapsed under her. She let out a groan, and with strength reserved only for the desperate, she grabbed his dark red coat and began dragging him across the deck. He was heavy and injured and she was so much smaller than him, but somehow she did it. The battle they had started was still raging on around her, but she dragged him through it to lean him against the side of the ship.

"I'm going to get you home. Don't worry, James." She whispered, though she didn't believe it. He didn't seem to hear her, and his eyes had drifted closed. She could still feel a faint pulse though. That would have to be enough. "Stay here." She said to his unconscious form. He, of course, obeyed.

She jumped up, trying to see her own people through the mess and blood.

As she moved forward, that's when Clare finally caught sight of her niece in the chaos. As everyone was too busy trying to kill each other, Pan had tried once more to sneak away. Flying close to the ship, he was slowly making his way to being safe once more. If he was flying – the mermaids and Wild Rose's people wouldn't be able to catch him from the ground. Carys had evidently had this same thought, as she was climbing the rigging, Perdy right behind her, trying to reach him.

Clare watched with her heart in her throat as Carrie and Perdy both reached out, wobbling perilously for just a moment before regaining balance. Together they grabbed Pan's ankles, small as bird bones in their hands, and threw him back down onto the deck of the ship with an awful, bloody thud.

All around them people seemed to feel a shift, one by one coming to a still as they saw Carrie and Perdy advancing on Pan where he knelt on the ground. Clare and Hook rushed over too then, her heart hammering with panic.

Eerie silence fell for a moment, but in the split second it took for people to realise something was about to happen, Pan pressed his advantage. Perdy looked away for just a moment to find her people, and Pan struck. Leaping up again he kicked her in the stomach as he came to float once more. Carrie had to duck away, leaving Pan free to circle around Perdy. In what seemed like one fluid motion he kicked a knife up that had been hidden in his boot and held it to her Perdy's throat. She was breathing hard, the knife pressing in on her pale skin.

"Don't!" Carrie pleaded, trying to heave in breaths. Clare reached her, bumping into her, holding her back.

"Or what? You didn't want to kill me, remember. Unfortunately I don't have the same sense of sentimentality as girls." Pan sneered.

Perdy stilled. Her eyes found Carrie's. Clare saw something shift even if no one else did. Something in Perdy's eyes, the small smile on her face. She stared at Carrie and nowhere else whilst Pan continued.

"I will forgive you all this insubordination, if you drop your weapons!" He shouted to the people on the ship, the people that spread out through the sea and onto the shore like a wave.

"He's lying." Carrie shook her head.

She caught the eye of Portia, who was looking unsure. Selene was overseeing the evacuation and hiding of her people, the ones not fit for fighting, and had sent Portia in her place. She had always backed away from this fight. Would she surrender now?

"You can't win, Pan." Perdy rasped, gasping a little as Pan pressed the knife a little deeper to her throat.

"She's right!" Carrie interrupted. "Too many people are seeing you for what you really are. You're outnumbered. You're weak, weaker than you ever have been. Soon magic will spread through the island again, to everyone here and you won't be able to stop it. You might as well surrender now before you lose even more people."

"No." He shook his head, his cheeks going pink. "This is my island! It's always going to be mine! All your stupid fighting will have been for nothing!" He spat. He sounded desperate.

Perdy let out a harsh little laugh. She was still looking at Carrie with a determined glint in her eye. Then she looked at Clare. Clare didn't know how, but somehow she knew she was telling her something. She started to pull Carrie toward the place she had left Hook. Carrie tried to fight her off, but Perdy looked away and Clare knew she had done the right thing.

"You stupid boy. Only a child like you could think fighting for love is worth nothing." Perdy hissed to Pan.

Then, quick as lightening, she rose on one knee and rammed her head back, into his face.

Carrie jumped and Clare pulled her down to crouch by Hook. Perdy fought Pan one on one, elbowing him in the face. He fell back onto the deck, cradling his bloody nose. Wild Rose advanced then too, glowering down at him.

Then they heard a small whimper. A whimper that got louder and louder until they realized the sound was coming from Pan - the boy tyrant, bringer of storms, the war leader, the shadow in the night. He was crying. Loud, undignified sobbing under the gaze of two women he had hurt.

Look around then, even the fairies, his most faithful disciples, looked faintly disgusted. He truly was pathetic. Clare tried to separate the fact that he had a child's body still. He was a killer. This strange mixture of sympathy and brutality did not fit comfortably inside her head.

She looked down at Hook. They had to go, now. They had to leave. She didn't know how. She felt it though. She concentrated on that feeling, putting all her fear and sadness and hope into it. Pulling it and nurturing it, hoping it was right.

"Please..." Pan cried, wiping his nose on the back of his hand.

"Please don't kill me. I've always been fair to you princess."

He looked plaintively at Wild Rose, who scowled at him. She looked at him as if he was nothing more than an ant.

"Just because you didn't try to murder us doesn't mean you were fair to use. You segregated us - On our own land!"

He looked at Perdy. "Please....I saved you. You were alone, and I brought you here and I saved you! I saved all of you!"

"You imprisoned us. You used to let people go. Children used to play here in their dreams." Perdy sighed, as if having to even explain this was exhausting. It was hard to tell if Pan meant what he was saying. Did he really see himself as some kind of saviour? Was that the child's logic in him winning out over the king's? "Now look what you have made of us. Killers, factions that fight for no reason. We all had to protect ourselves by killing other people. You made us selfish. You put blood on our hands. You are no leader. You are just a child, playing with other people's lives. You don't get to do that anymore. We let you because we were afraid. That's on us - But not anymore."

All around them, weapons were lowered as Perdy spoke. It was as if the fairies and the lost boys were being awakened from a sleeping curse after a hundred years. In that moment, though the future of the island was uncertain, one thing was clear: Pan would rule no longer. This was not and had never been his island.

Then Wild Rose stepped up to Pan with a knife in her had. It still had blood on it. He tries to crawl away, but he isn't quick enough.

Before anyone can let out a single protest, Wild Rose stabs him. Its silent, cold, and fatal. Pan drops to the ground as his blood pools out beneath him, staining the deck of the Eloise.

Carrie gasps, looking away, slamming her eyes shut for a second, trying not to heave up her guts.

No one else says a word.

"You said you wouldn't...we said we weren't going to kill him." Carrie moaned, a hot kind of panic washing over her. She closed her eyes tightly again. "Oh my god. All that talk about not letting him do this to us and you just..."

Wild rose wipes her blade on Pan's green tunic. "You all agreed that. And you did not kill him. I did not agree. Sometimes, the only way to have peace is to spill blood. This is the only way for Tiger Lily's spirit to be reborn once more. I told you that when we first met. My people have sought vengeance for her death for a thousand years. It is done." Wild Rose looked out to the shore, her bright eyes roaming the island hungrily, her land, she drank in its beauty and it was clear she was filled with a fire of righteousness no one could put out now.

Perdy bit her lip and turned away, but did not condemn Wild Rose. No one did. There was a dull kind of silence, nothingness. Everything was quiet. They were done.

Carrie looked at Clare with no emotion. It was like she'd been gutted. When she spoke, her voice was leaden. "I want to go home."

25

AISLING

No one had seen Portia disappear quietly from the ship, but Clare is momentarily distracted by dripping water as bare feet appear in front of her. She and Carrie had crowded around Hook, trying to stop the bleeding from the gash in his side.

"Here." Portia moved her wet tangle of blue hair over her shoulder and crouched over him, pressing something grainy into Clare's hands. "Take him with you. Save him." Portia hissed at her.

Clare looked down at what she'd given her. It looked like a crystalized paste that shined slightly in her hands.

"They'll help." Carrie nodded at Clare. "If we want to save him we have to get our people and go."

Carrie whipped her head round to look at Perdy. Perdy nodded in understanding and started toward her.

"We're going to leave this place." Carrie called out. "If you want to come we have to go now. Hook's life depends on it."

"You're leaving just like that?" One of the lost boys called out.

Carrie nodded and looked at Clare. "We have to." She said quietly. Clare nodded with a lot more confidence than she felt.

Nala ran across the deck to them, smiling breathlessly. She span to look at Willow, and Peaches crawling down from the crow's nest. At the look on their faces, her smile died.

"You aren't coming?" She asked, her voice breaking. The other girls shook their head. "But...you have to! We have to all be together!" Nala's voice raised as she started to cry.

Perdy stepped toward her and put a hand on her arm. Nala

wrenched it away.

Several of the lost boys looked at one another and slipped away quietly over the side of the ship, as if they didn't want to witness the drama. Some of them stood still on the beach with Wild Rose's people. In solidarity, it seemed, though they must not have known what was being said aboard the ship. The fairies disappeared, back to their woodland home and away from the affairs of humans. With Pan finally dead, shown to be mortal, his magic did not keep them enthralled, nor did his power or his orders.

"It's ok, girlie." Willow smiled gently at Nala. "We don't know that world. This is our world. And that's ok now. We'll take care of one another."

Peaches nodded when Willow looked at her. Nala shook her head and Perdy started to steer her to Clare and Carrie.

"My sisters." Nala whimpered. "Our sisters. I love you."

Willow nodded and Peaches thumped her heart. That was code for 'I love you too'.

"So how does this work?" Carrie asked.

Clare didn't have an answer, but she thought as best she could. She thinks about when she had come here, about the things Claudette had said about her emotions spiriting them here. About how Michael had used her love for her family to spur her into action.

"I think you have to feel it." She whispered, her voice became sharper as she gathered momentum. "You have to really want to go home. You have to feel that pull, feel the love of whoever you want to go back to. You have to want to go home. That's the best way I can explain it. Think about home. Think about nothing else but home."

She held her hand out for Carrie. Their hands squelched with all the blood that was covering them. Carrie reached out and Nala took her other hand, Perdy hers.

"James." Clare whispered. She put her hand on his cheek, lifting her face, trying to wake him up. "James, can you hear me?"

Hook groaned and seemed to blink awake. His green eyes were glassy, holding none of their usual knowing spark.

"Listen – no, don't fall asleep again, listen, listen, listen. I need you to think about home. Remember how we talked about it in the cabin? Think about that for me, alright? Think about England. Think about England covered in snow."

Hook smiled as if he didn't have a care in the world, and his eyes closed once more.

"Come on then." Carrie smiles. She looks at Perdy as if that were all the reassurance she needed.

And nothing happened.

Clare closed her eyes, trying to do as she had told them all. Wild Rose, Portia, Pan and all the remaining fighters on the ship watch them expectantly. Clare thinks she can feel something, some stirring in her heart, but it isn't enough.

"Why isn't it working?" Perdy frowned. They were all looking at Clare and she didn't know what to do. She hadn't ever really known for certain.

"I don't know. Maybe it just takes a minute."

"Well unless you want your pirate to bleed out all over his ship, then you don't have a minute." Perdy pressed, trying not to get angry.

"Clare, just tell us what you need us to do." Carrie interceded, but even she couldn't keep the worry from her voice.

Clare shook her head. She took a deep breath to try and calm down. "You know it won't all get better, don't you Carys?"

Carrie frowned. "What do you mean?"

Clare shook her head again, trying to find the right words that were going to get them through this moment and into the next. "The way you felt when you came to live with me isn't just going to go away. It's going to be with you maybe for a really long time."

Carrie nodded mutely.

"But I think...I think if you're willing to at least try and face it, then I think that will help. If we're going to go home you have to know it isn't all going to change overnight. You have to know what you're going back to. Alright? Same goes for all of you." She looked at Nala and Perdy. "You girls have to be ready now."

"Ready to do what?" Nala asked.

"Ready to know that you're going to have to wake up every morning, even when you don't want to."

They watched Clare as she started to frown. Perdy raised her eyebrows at Nala who gave an almost imperceptible shrug.

"Do you feel that?" Clare whispered.

Carrie squeezed her hand. "Feel what? What are you doing? Is it working? Clare!"

"You don't have to shout at her, Carrie." Perdy drawled. "She's right next to you."

"I can feel something. I think..." Clare looked at them, a small hopeful smile spreading across her face. "I think it's my sister."

Now the reader might bless me with their patience for a brief interlude. After all, we've come this far together. And all in all, our next new player turned out to be more important to the story than anyone realised. Her fate was always tied up with the fates of those on board the Eloise.

So now we head through worlds, over oceans, atop spires and very old temporary towers, to where, just a day or so ago, Aisling Fairchild was feeling very tired.

And it wasn't just feeling tired from the lectures she had given that day (even though she loved her job, it was hard enough to talk about Beowulf to a class of students who probably had not read the text. It was harder to do it in French.)

No, she had to admit. She had been feeling tired for weeks. She just had not been able to stop thinking about her daughter. And her sister, for that matter. She felt that somewhere along the way she had made the wrong choice. Aisling was not good with wrong choices. Clare had always been able to laugh them off – she was carefree to the point of recklessness, sometimes. But for Aisling, her mistakes though well intentioned, always sat hot and itchy within her until she found a way to fix them.

She had not stopped thinking about Carrie and Clare since she and Jude had arrived in France. The weather was beginning to turn as spring approached, and she could feel the shift in the air. In the last few days that sense of impending change, that indefinable note had crept into the spacious flat they were renting, blown in on the breeze through the French windows. Like a siren growing louder with each passing day, Aisling's thoughts strayed, and she thought she sensed a feeling of wrongness about the world.

She was never normally like this. She told herself that Carys was on a little holiday with her aunt Clare, and that it might help clear her head and cheer her up. Clare was always going on about how she never saw her niece, and it was sobering to think of her in that dreadful house all by herself. It was a holiday for both of them to get to know one another. She trusted Clare with Carrie, even if she did not trust her sister to take care of herself – despite the time she had given her to learn how to do this.

But still the little thoughts crept in. It was even making her forgetful, scatter-brained. That was such a Clare thing.

She would have gone with Carrie, if she'd had the time – if she'd thought it was have done them good. But as far as she could tell, Carrie wanted a break not just from the travelling but from always being with her parents. She knew this day would come eventually, when Carrie was a teenager, and didn't want to always spend time with her fussy, scholarly parents. But it still stung a little. But she was willing to listen to her child, and try and give her what she wanted. She'd thought that was what she wanted.

And besides, it was only for a little while. She wasn't abandoning Carrie to the whims of Clare forever. No one could survive that. It was for a month or two, at the most. So why, why did she feel like she should go and bring her home?

Aisling sighed and shoved the papers she had been trying and failing to grade away from her across the table, slumping back in her chair and taking a swig of red wine from the glass in front of her.

This happened to occur just as Jude walked in, rubbing his hands together to rid them of the chill from the night air.

"Did you get the wrong train again?" She raised an eyebrow.

He grinned sheepishly. "I just can't work the damn things out. Every time I think I do, I realize I'm on the wrong one again. I need you to be my guide at all times I think darling."

She huffed a small laugh. "We should have put that in the vows. I will promise to always help you navigate French railway systems."

He came into the open plan room, placing a kiss on her cheek. His hand gripped her shoulder gently and she held it with her own.

"Ah, Beowulf." He picked up a paper from the table. "Fate will unwind as it must." He quoted.

Yes, Aisling thinks, as Jude moves to peer aimlessly into the fridge. Fate had a way of doing that.

"I've been thinking I might visit my sister." She tried, hesitating. She didn't look at her husband, since she was trying to sound nonchalant and he could always tell when she was lying.

It turned out she didn't need to look at him for him to know this. They had been married for eighteen years, after all.

"You're worried about Carys is getting on." He pulled out a chair and sat down, peering intently at her.

Aisling shrugged non committedly. "I just have a feeling, that's all."

Jude raised his eyebrows. He wore large square glasses that always magnified his eyes. He wore all of his emotions on his face, and she saw the surprise in his eyes. She hadn't seen her sister in person years. It must have going on five years now. She had been up for Michael's funeral, and had stayed with her sister for a few weeks after. But then she had returned to her life, thinking eventually Clare would manage to do the same. The thought turned her blood to ice. How had it been so long? They talked on the phone, sent pictures, emailed. But she had not been in the same room as Clare since then. It felt like a punch to the gut.

She hadn't known how to help Carys. She felt like a failure. But she had been one long before that, leaving her little sister alone so long. God – what would her parents say?

"I just keep thinking that it might be good for us all to spend some time together." Is all she can say.

Jude sat back and shrugged. "Have they told you anything is wrong? I thought Carys was having a nice time."

"No, like I said. I've just been thinking, that's all."

"A dangerous pass time, to be sure." He smiled gently.

"Do you think it was the right decision? Carrie was...well, I think maybe she was worse than we could admit to ourselves - And sending her off to be with Clare of all people." Aisling shook her head.

"Now, now. Don't give your sister a hard time. You know she was never the same after Michael's death."

Aisling put steadying hands on the table. "That's what I'm saying. She told me everything was fine and I believed her, but now I think I was being...wilfully ignorant. I didn't want to face the idea that she'd never gotten better. That I hadn't been there for her all this time. So when she told me things were normal, that she was moving on, I accepted it. And i think I should have tried harder to make sure that really was the case. I do not want to make the same mistake with our daughter."

Jude put his hand on hers to try and calm her down. "It isn't the same thing. Clare is a grown woman. I know how responsible you feel for her, but she's an adult. You can't accept responsibility for everything she does. You have your own life and she's always known that. And as for Carys – well, maybe you're right. Maybe we are guilty of pretending she's fine." He sighed and squeezed her hands. "But once she comes back, we can start working on that. Together, as a family."

Aisling nods, but she's frowning. All of her words rang with a dreadful truth she had not acknowledged before.

Jude smiles at the conflict on her face gently. He always did everything gently. Sometimes she thought he was entirely too good for the world. That one day it would eat him up and she wouldn't be able to stop it. Carys had inherited his eyes. Those big blue eyes stared at her now. In Carys they seemed sad, mysterious. In Jude they were open and as honest as a baby.

"This isn't like you, love. Are you sure you're feeling well?" He asked her.

"I know it isn't like me, Jude. That's why you have to trust me on it. Now, you know I'm not given to sentimentality, or flights of fancy. So if I have raving about these feelings, if I'm admitting something is wrong then I won't be able to settle until I sort it out. That much at least is like me."

Jude nodded. "If you really think you have to go and see them, then of course you must. But at least call them first."

"Right." Aisling nodded. She always felt better when she had a plan. She liked to have a focus, instructions. She liked to always know what she was doing. It made her feel safer. "What are you going to do?"

Jude stood up. "I'm going to make us some food. Can't go off on most likely unnecessary rescue missions on an empty stomach."

Neither Carrie or Clare had answered their phones.

Clare never answered her phone, so that shouldn't have been surprising. If she were feeling her usual practical minded self, Aisling might have put Carys lack of contact down to the fact she was staying in the middle of nowhere in a house resembling the most distressing hammer horror houses.

But since she was not feeling her usual, practical minded self, she jumped on a plane. Let that fatuous Marie Therese from the department have her lecture spot. There would be others. Jude had wanted to go with her, but she'd insisted he stay behind and keep up with his work. Chances are everything was fine and that she was overreacting. The feelings inside her might be easily put down to indigestion.

It was when there was no answer at the house that Aisling really felt sure. Something had called her here. Impossible as it was, silly as it was, she couldn't stop herself thinking that.

She'd always hated Clare's house. The surrounding countryside was beautiful. But the house…it always felt as if it were watching her. It felt haunted. It made her shiver as she crept into the entrance. She could hear no sounds, at least, no sounds of humans. The house creaked eerily.

She called out and received no response.

Suddenly a yowl sounded and something soft and insistent rammed into Aisling's legs, nearly tipping her off balance.

She picked the squirming Columbus up and cradled him in her arms. "Stupid cat. Are you trying to give me a heart attack? You're supposed to be the sensible member of the house."

And she was supposed to be the sensible sister, she admonished herself. And here she was, cuddling cats and being scared of an old pile of wood.

"Where's your mummy?" She asked Columbus, placing him down slowly. "And where on earth is Carrie?"

She'd half expected him to take her straight to her sister. Half expected her sister to be lying face down in a puddle of spilt milk in the kitchen. That didn't happen, as cats cannot be relied upon to be altruistic. First he nosed around her feet for several seconds, then lead her to an empty food bowl in the kitchen.

After she'd found his food and over filled his bowl he shot back into the house somewhere. She followed where she thought she had seen his ragged grey fur disappearing, her heart hammering. She was beginning to feel a little sick, truth be told.

But she tried to keep calm down. She was quite good at that, normally. And she knew that if she let even the smallest amount of worry in, she wouldn't even make it up the stairs.

There is a door wide open, when she reaches the top of the stairs. It wasn't quite as far as the library and the bedrooms, and she knew Michael's study was up another set of stairs. So what this room was for, she didn't know.

It was light and airy when she walked in. sunlight dappled in through the wide windows. Dust motes hung in the air. But the thing that grabbed your attention immediately was the single splash of colour in the room.

Where all the other walls were white the far wall bore all the evidence Aisling needed that Clare had been there.

A beautiful mural covered the whole of the wall. It looked so real, like it was growing out of the plaster. Leaves and flowers bloomed, trees and fruit and the smallest glimpse of a beach. Rain drops glittered. The longer she stared at the painting, which she knew her sister had made, the more she felt as if it really did move, as if a breeze shifted and shivered through the room. She was scared to reach out and touch it, fearing to feel the waxiness of a real green leaf.

Somewhere, through that painting, the same shiver ran through Clare. She felt her sister wishing for her. No – not just her of course. For Carrie. They still crouched on board the ship, above an unconscious man who had trusted them enough to fight for them. Clare held onto him tightly. She held onto Carrie tightly. She saw in her minds eye, like she was in the room, Aisling. Like she was looking through a window straight at her.

All around them, the shape of the world seemed to glow and move and melt away. She let herself smile at Carrie just once, before everything was swallowed in a brilliant, blinding light.

She was taking them home.

26

JAMES

"My heart is pierced by cupid, I disdain all glittering gold, no nothing can console me, but my jolly sailor bold..."

He wakes to the sound of singing. He floats toward it, like a siren song on a distant shore. The distant shore is bright, and it smells like jasmine. There is cold white sunlight that hurts his eyes.

James groans and the singing stops. He doesn't want the singing to stop. It makes him feel safe, as if he has something to reach for. So he stays quiet.

He hears muffled voices that live in the fractures of light, the seconds between sleeping and waking, they float like the dust motes in the air.

"Is he awake yet?" "We just need to give him time. I think. Those crystals from the island seem to be helping. I thought he might wake up yesterday, but now I think I was imagining it." "He'll be alright Clare. Do you want me to get you anything?" –

"Stop telling me all this stuff! I don't want to use the mobile phone, I don't want to know who that band is, and I don't know any of this!" "Perdita! Don't walk away from me when I'm trying to argue with you!"

"I'm going to read to you now James. Thankfully, since you're still asleep, you can't comment on my choice. Trust me; it's better than Carys reciting Shakespeare at you endlessly."

And singing, always with the singing. He thinks he could sleep forever to the sound of that lullaby. The world is so still is hurts. There are no waves churning underneath him. It feels so slow it's as if time had stopped – but no. That was the other place. But what place was this?

"Where are we?"

Clare doesn't jump, but she does sit up instantly. She throws her book down on the bedside table. He doesn't look around the room; he just looks up at her. She's sitting in a chair and he's lying down on a bed, his lower half covered in a clean white cover. He thinks he's been lying down for a long time. He looks up at her.

"Yorkshire." She grinned. "God's own country and all that."

"Really?" he smiles. He's too tired to pretend anything. He lets his emotions, everything just wash over him like a ceaseless wave. "I grew up in Yorkshire. Before I was sent to boarding school. Before I joined the navy."

She puts a cool hand on his forehead and smooth's his long dark hair back. He feels unclean, sweaty, and ill, so he just thinks about her hand on his head. It feels good to concentrate on something.

"Well, now you're back in the sceptred isle. And you're getting better and better."

"Don't quote Shakespeare at a sick man. I can barely remember my own name right now."

"Well, as long as you remember mine." Clare laughed. "Then we'll get to the rest. This sounds stupid, considering where we came from, but we have time. Nothing but time."

"Remember when I told you about Saint Clare?" she said, pretending to potter around with things on the bedside table.

He's not sure how long he's been there, because he'd been asleep for so long. But it had been almost two weeks since he'd woken up. He isn't sure why it's taking him so long to get better. He's feeling useless, helpless, and more than a little embarrassed. He hears the howling wind outside at night, wants to feel it whipping at his skin. But he knows he can barely stand unaided, so he lets Clare talk at him. It's something, at least, that someone cares.

"You're holy namesake? Yes, I remember. Though I rather think that it was a little optimistic. Naming you after a saint, the way you badger me. Do leave those things alone." He drawled. Clare's head snapped up, ready to retort, until she saw him grinning up at her.

She sighed and sat down gently on the bed, his legs resting against the small of her back. She smiled down at him.

"Well, I looked her up a bit more when I got back. And I think it might have been fitting, in the end. You know what they called her followers? The poor Clare's."

Hook scoffed and she raised her eyebrows at him.

"Well that's rubbish, if you've decided to think what I think you have."

Clare frowned as she tried to catch up with what he'd just said.

"You're not anyone's poor anything." He carried on, as if it were a perfectly obvious fact.

"No? I still feel like I am. I thought everything would change, when we all got back here. Suddenly there would be sunshine again. But that's not how it goes, is it? I might be different, but I'm still the same. Stupid of me really, to think I'd become a different person overnight. You know what Saint Clare said? We become what we love, and what we love defines what we become. I think that's true, even if we don't want it to be. Michael died and I loved him, and I became that ...that death. I don't want to be that anymore. I want to love something else. To become something else."

She leans forward earnestly as she speaks, pressing her hand into the mattress right by his thigh. For a long moment that's all her can think about.

Hook sighed deeply. "You don't need to become anything other than what you are." He turned to her and looked at her seriously. He looked at her for so long in silence that she ducked her head awkwardly.

He shifted his weight and she realized he was trying to sit up. When she saw he wasn't going to be stopped from doing it, she tried to steady him. He leant on his elbow, his face suddenly close beneath hers. Her long brown hair was floating down her front, tickling his arm softly.

"You're not a Poor Clare. Nor a saint nor anything like that. You're..." He looked her up and down as if searching for the right word. Then carefully he put his free arm on her waist. He always did everything carefully, like a cat taking measurements before a leap. Especially so when it came to the arm that was on her waist, since it was the one missing a hand. He seemed to think she'd be afraid of it. She wasn't, but she didn't know how to tell him.

"You are...you. Just you. Clare." He smiled again and made a low contented noise. "Augustine." He flopped back down and rolled his eyes. "If you needed any more proof woman, that you are an entirely separate phenomenon to the dear sister, then you should know she was also the patron saint of eye conditions. Now are you so ready to align yourself with her?"

Clare burst out laughing. She couldn't help it. Soon the bed was shaking with it, and James laughed too. "You looked her up too?"

"I'm looking up everything. She just happened to come first."

Clare glanced at all the books piled up in the bookshelves against the far wall. The big encyclopaedias that no one ever touched. All the information, all the words and knowledge that were commonplace to her, but not to him. He had been gone for so long. How could one learn a whole history? But she saw the way he stared at them too, and knew he was determined.

And so that's what she starts with.

She makes sure he can reach the books, piling them all beside his bed. When he gets stronger but refuses to help himself, she inches them further and further away until he's forced to try get them himself. Soon, he's shuffling along and moaning quite nicely. Piracy is all theatrics really, and it showed.

When he's read all of those - he was a quick reader and learner, she moves on to some magazine's - about trains and wonderfully boring things like that. Clare learns to tune out his constant reciting of passages and exclamations, since she had literally no interest whatsoever in learning about who designed the decor of the trains or how windmills were made. She does like hearing the hum of his voice in the background though, so she concentrates on that. It's nice really, to see someone so excited about now ordinary things. To see him smiling to himself, to hear him laugh. It's nice that he wants to tell her all of the things he's discovering for the very first time. It makes her feel wanted, in a way. The sound of his voice makes her feel less lonely. She hadn't noticed how quiet it had been before.

Eventually she gets him to leave his room. He doesn't want to at first. He'd been complaining about being cramped up so much that by the time he was able to, he'd built himself up to it too much. But she put his arm round her shoulders and they hobbled along to the end of the hall and back. He spends a long time looking out the window. It is, she knows, the first time in an age that he's looked out and not seen the sea. She wonders if he's frightened, if he feels claustrophobic at having the land and earth coiled around him once more.

A painting hangs by the stairs at the far end of the hall. The rest is all dark wood and slightly lopsided walls, but there just as you turn to descend is one of Clare's creations. She didn't often paint landscapes anymore, but this one was from a few years ago, when she'd been travelling. It's the view from the balcony of her hotel in Spain. It's blue, red, green, and yellow, and it's warm and bright and familiar to James. He doesn't touch the glass, but his hand hovers over it reverently. She hasn't really looked at it for a long time. But there is something about seeing a thing through someone else's eyes. It's a transformative power. Something you've seen before, something ordinary can become beautiful, just because someone else thinks so. She puts the painting in his room the next day.

Therefore, they go on in their routine as James heals.

Carrie and Perdita had stayed away most of the time, since he'd flat out refused to be nursed by children ("I don't have all of my extremities, but i have my bloody dignity!" "Please tell me that by your extremities you mean your hand. I shouldn't like to think of you mentioning the other sort in front of the girls.") But once he got stronger and started to be less antagonistic, they begin to pop in and out to talk to him. Carrie takes him sweet tea that Clare insists is good for him and Perdita goes and sits by his bed in total silence. Occasionally they will talk about new inventions or discoveries that they both find strange. For a while, they were completely fascinated and appalled by the deep fat fryer, as are we all.

He argues with Clare. The confinement of weeks upon weeks begins to get to him, the helplessness. He throws of his covers feeling stifled, hot, like he can't breathe. He wants to smell the salt in the air again. He never wants to see the sea again. Different days bring different needs. He does not know where he fits now. He is no captain. He has no purpose. He gives himself to his studies, his learning, but there is something missing. Something that crouches in him, some goblin of fear that beats at the inside of his chest, some swooping emptiness that he cannot put a face to.

“I need you to do something for me.” Clare tells him one day.

He's being rude today. He's in a sulk. He's healing well but he still doesn't move around a lot.

He'd been introduced to something called a laptop several days before, and it was hurting his hand. He had to do most things delicately now which meant he had to do them one handed. It put a strain on his fingers and everything took more time than it ought to. It frustrated him. Made him feel weak. He liked the glowing box though. He could look things up on it. He was a fast learner and he enjoyed it. Just not when it took so long to type something. Carys had taken him through the basics, her fingers fast as a humming bird's wing. He felt cripplingly old in comparison.

"James. Are you hearing me?" Clare stood in the doorway staring down at him like a matron, her arms crossed.

He was staring dejectedly at a wall. "Yes, I hear you." He croaked out. "What do you want?"

"You need to take that thing off." Her voice came out quiet. James flicked his gaze at her and saw she looked worried. She was staring at his hook.

"No."

He should have known she wouldn't leave it there. She was a force that blew through him and scattered him like the wind.

"If you want to stay in this house then you'll have too." Clare sounds stronger then. She's trying to stare at his face now.

"Why?"

"Because it isn't safe. And it isn't nice and normal people don't wear hooks for hands anymore."

He rolled his eyes and went back to staring at the wall. He was not going to take it off. Why should he? He might be an invalid, a prisoner, a patient but that did not mean he couldn't make his own decisions. He was a man. He was not a child. Who was she to order him about?

"I don't care." He spits.

Clare threw her arms down and marched over to him, moving so she stood in his eye line. He forced himself to move and look up at her, lest he stare solely at her midriff.

"Well I do! This is my house! I saved you and you are going to do this for me. Because my niece lives here and I will not have a weapon like that near her, or near me for that matter. Because it makes me uncomfortable, because it scares me!" she breathes heavily when she is finished.

He stifles a groan when he sits up. "I scare you?" He frowns in confusion.

"No. Not you." She breathes gently. "That. That thing." She looks to the hook again.

He supposed it was not nice to look at. It wasn't meant to be.

He looks up at her again. Her eyes are wide. Her hair is flying all about her furiously. He doesn't want her to be afraid. He had put the hook on to remake himself. When they had taken his hand...it had almost broken him. He had been half a person, a cripple, no captain. But then he had put on that hook...he had become that. A butcher. Feared. He had become a legend. He had become a name. Captain hook. It had been his shield, not his weapon. It had kept him from becoming nothing, from becoming obsolete. Who would he be without it? Who would he be now? Himself? Who was that? Could he remake himself once more? Would she remake him now? Would he let her? He would have only one hand. He would have to learn not just the strange and new things of this world he once called home, but things about himself. What he could do and what he couldn't. The idea frightened him. He would feel naked without his hook. It had saved him once. But had the woman in front of him not saved him too?

"I don't know." He whispers. "Who am I if I am not him?"

He looks up at her pleadingly. She smiles gently at him and motions for him to put his wrist out.

She slides her hands down his arm to stop at the leather clasps that secured his hook. "You're just you. You are James. And you are my friend." She said, slowly undoing the straps. He sucked in a breath.

"Is that what I am?" He whispers, not looking at her.

She doesn't say anything. Just concentrates on her task. When she is done, she slides the hook from the end of his arm very slowly. He looks away, squeezing his eyes shut. He always hated seeing the mess of a stump that they had left him with. Pink and scarred forever. He can't bear to have this woman look at that. At the truth of him. He has to though. It will set the course of his new life here. He knows that.

So he looks. And he sees nothing but kindness. Not the pity he hated, not the revulsion. He was her friend.

"I'll keep it somewhere safe, if you don't want to get rid of it yet."

"No, get rid of it. Get rid of him. Captain Hook." He sneers the name as if it were something diseased. "Throw him out of this place."

She nods, biting her lip in worry, but she does as he says.

He keeps the leather strap round his wrist, which covers most of his scars. He feels lighter though. How had she known that was what he needed? How did this woman see a truth in him that he did not see himself? It felt as if she saw into the bones of him. No one had seen him as himself for more than a century. Now she came tumbling into his world, colour and light and change, and he felt powerless to stop it. He didn't want to stop it. He wants to be caught and carried on those winds and to be free of the things that came before.

She teaches him about music, amongst other things. But music comes most naturally as a place to start, after books. Clare drags Michael's old record player out, gently blowing the dust away. He watches her from where he sits on the bed.

He's wearing an old blue t shirt that she doesn't specifically remember as belonging to Michael. Carrie has ordered him new clothes from the internet – they had spent an enjoyable afternoon picking out clothes together. Clare worried she would end up with a shopaholic as a houseguest. Until they arrived he'd have to wear what they had. Whilst James was still strong, he was leaner than Michael, less broad. It made all his clothes look a little baggy. But still, it was nice to see what he looked like in modern clothes. Made things seem more real to her.

She's on her knees in front of the record player, trying to choose which ones to start with.

"Are you sure this is alright? There's no need to use all of his things. No need to rush. I feel bad enough that I'm wearing another man's clothes." James grumbled awkwardly.

Clare glanced over her shoulder. "It's fine. He wouldn't even care. It's not like I'm not chucking anything out. And besides, I think he'd hate to see all these nice things he loved going to waste."

"Like you, you mean?"

Clare ducked her head, pretending to be fiddling with the record player. "Yes, I suppose like me."

She stood to face him and found him looking up at her, his eyes crinkling softly. There wasn't pity or condescension there. Just understanding. He didn't say these things to make her feel awkward. He said them because he understood them in her, and thought they needed saying, at least once. He had this strange ability to articulate these things simply, things she'd always felt and never found a simple explanation for.

"Augustine, whilst you always look very beautiful when you're thinking, perhaps you should stop standing there wool gathering and put some music on."

Clare blinked, blushing slightly at being caught in a reverie. She imagined Michael giving her a wink, wink, nudge, nudge from the other side and willed him away.

"James...I..." She faltered. Clare tucked her long hair behind her ears nervously and hurried to sit beside him on the bed.

"I hope you don't take this the wrong way, or like I'm being vain though I probably am I know it's just, you know, these things should get said and whilst I understand you just got back from a 500 year trip to a magical island I –"

"Take a breath!" he interrupted widening his eyes in alarm.

Clare breathed and put a steadying hand to her chest. "Sorry. I'm just trying to say...you know I might not ever...ever want to be with anyone again. In a romantic sense. I'm not trying to assume, or anything."

"Well that's good, since I never suggested it." James drawled nonchalantly. She glared at him.

"I'm trying very hard to live without someone. That doesn't

mean living with someone else. Like that, at least. I just wanted to make sure we were clear."

"Of course." He inclined his head, not meeting her eye. He stared intently at the floor for several moments and Clare was scared she'd upset him. Then James huffed out a breath and nodded. When he looked at her again, he had his usual kind smile and no anger behind his eyes. "We are friends, aren't we?"

"Yes, of course we are."

"Then there's nothing else we need to discuss. We're friends, and friends we shall remain. I never expect anything more from you Clare. I'm sorry if I made you feel like that. Please no that I have no ulterior motive. I have no motive than the truest, deepest respect for you. You've already done so much for me. You don't need to do anything else."

Clare inhaled a shaky breath. She nodded quickly, trying not to cry. She was a very emotional sort of person, you know.

"I'm not saying never, you know." She whispered. "I'm just saying maybe never. There is a difference."

"If you say so." James laughed.

She stared at the record player again, a small frown clouding her face. "I know I just gave you a speech about our platonic relationship...but will you do something for me?"

She looked at him intently. He nodded, his face open with surprise.

"No one really touches me anymore. There's this thing that Michael used to do. He'd touch my face – but it wasn't just that. He'd hold me there, touching my face, and he'd just look at me. Like there wasn't anything else going on in the world."

James inhaled deeply and looked down. One hand was strong and callused. One hand was gone.

"It's alright. If you don't want to." Clare said sheepishly, raising one skinny shoulder awkwardly.

"No, no it isn't that. It's just..." James sighed. "Sometimes when I look down I expect to see a hook. Then other days I expect to somehow see a hand. All the magic I know exists in this world, but some things can't be fixed. I'm still not using to seeing this." He gestured to the stump of his wrist.

He turned toward her and looked at her in the eye. It was slightly strange, but they'd started now. He put his hand on one side of her face. Then, very slowly, he raised the other arm. When he faltered, she put her hand on his arm and pressed his wrist to her other cheek.

He swallowed. "Is that right? Am I doing it right?"

She laughed a little and tried not to roll her eyes however good-humouredly. "Yes, James. Thank you."

His smile was very wide and he looked rather proud of himself.

Then, finally, they danced.

27

A kept man

Things start to get less hazy. Sometimes James sticks his head out the window to feel the bracing air hitting him.

He's been there for a month. It feels like no time at all. Though he had been unconscious for half of it, and bed bound for the other.

He thinks he'll be brave enough to go outside soon. He'd been confining himself to the top floors of the house for now. A floor at a time. He's letting himself go slowly. He always liked to thinks things through before he did them.

His room, his light blue, crooked little room that he'd become very attached to, was right at the top. It was almost something of an attic, though an attic with a few bedrooms. There were two more floors underneath him, then the ground floor. He hadn't got that far yet.

It means he spends more time with Clare now, outside of her being his nurse that is. And the cat, who liked to prowl around after him and then pretend not to care when he receives attention.

Sometimes James likes to just sit on his bed and go on the computer machine. There were endless reams of information on there. Sometimes it made his head swim, but he liked it. Ever since he was a child, he'd been able to read something once or twice and then remember it forever. It meant he was very knowledgeable about this new world. But he felt that it might be time, soon, to put his knowledge into practice. For example, he knew what a microwave did, and how, and why – but he'd never actually seen one. That reminded him to ask Clare if she had a microwave for him to look at.

But for now, he was content enough existing in the upper hollows of the house. He stroked the walls the way she did when he walked behind her. The house kept quiet and warm for him. It seemed to like him once it got used to another man being there.

He helped Clare with small things, odd jobs. He stacked books – Carys was still sorting out her little library, and he helped alphabetize them for her – he held ladders, did a little bit of slow one-handed painting. It made him feel useful. Helped him build his strength back up. He and Clare talked a lot.

Sometimes he'd be distracted, seeing the small retreating figures of Carys and Perdita, walking in the rolling green fields that surrounded the house for miles. He wonders if he'll get any of that youthful energy back. For all intents and purposes, he was forty-two. Next to the young women in the house, he felt very serious and old. But Clare didn't feel that way, despite everything that she'd been through. If anyone could cheer his soul up again it was her and her unfailing brightness.

When he wakes up on this particular day however, the woman watching him from a chair at the side of the bed is not Clare.

She looks like Clare. Her face has the same high cheekbones, though this woman looks sharper. The same angles and long lines. The same long brown hair – though the woman's is immaculately styled to curl over one shoulder.

That's the main difference. This woman, not balking under his assessment, looked put together in a way Clare never did. This woman was striking though, in a wonderfully intimidating sort of way. It might have had something to do with the tailored red dress she was wearing or the steely glint in her light grey eyes as she stared boldly at him.

"I'm the sister." She explained in a clipped, no nonsense tone.

"Mrs Fairchild, mother to young Miss Carys." He inclined his head, keeping his tone just as steady. He got the impression they were two animals, measuring each other.

"It's nice to finally put a face to the name." He says, when she says nothing.

She has her legs crossed pointedly, and she's very still. If he were not of a similar disposition, he might have found it unnerving.

"Well, I would agree, though I have actually seen you before. I was here when you got here, though of course you won't remember."

"No. Bleeding to death has been known to impair mental faculties." He agreed.

"You tumbled out of a wall. Did you know that? I wouldn't have believed my sisters stories, about finding a magical island and what not. But then you all came out of the wall right in front of me. So I have to believe what I see. I've been helping my sister whilst she helps you. I had to go back and tell my husband what was going on – or some version of it, and to sort out some of my affairs. I've taken some time off work now you see. The family needed me more."

Her tone seemed to imply that this was somehow his fault. He took the blows. He didn't think it was personal, from what he'd heard about her, she was this way with everyone.

"I haven't always been there for my family. You might have been told that." She carried on, expecting him to stay quiet and listen. He obliged. The way she spoke, slowly and methodically, made it clear that she wasn't used to this. And that she had practiced.

"But I intend to be there for them now. Carrie – and I suppose Perdita – will be coming back to live with her parents sometime later in the year, and then she'll go onto to travel, or to school, or whatever she wishes. My sister will be left here. You can therefore understand certain...anxieties I may feel, about her future now."

"You're asking my intentions with your sister."

Aisling relaxed her shoulders just a little. "Yes. Now, I don't know about where you came from, but I would never assume to permit my sister to do anything. She makes her own decisions. But I would like to know I'm leaving her in good hands this time."

James grinned and held up his stump. "Pun intended?"

Aisling's eyes go wide and her mouth drops open. He lets her gape and stutter for an embarrassed moment before shaking his head.

"A tasteless joke." He said, letting her off the hook. Pun intended once more.

He puts his stump down, and she lets him think. He wouldn't say he was in love with Clare. He was probably almost there, but saying it was a wildly different matter. He could see the path though, for the first time in a long time. He liked that she brought newness, change, and laughter. He tried to put it into words. It was hard. It was like feeling the change in the air just before the sun came out.

"She saved me." He's staring at his hand very deliberately.

"I take it you don't mean from your injury?"

He breathes in deeply through his nose, taking a long moment. He's either thinking of what he wants to say, which he does a lot, or he's trying not to cry, which is something he does not do a lot. Aisling didn't know which - but I do. It's both.

"She asked me my name. No one...no one has asked me my name in over a century." He said finally. His long fingers play awkwardly with the fabric of his blankets. Then he grips them in his hand and nods, before looking back up at Aisling. She can see his eyes shining. "Stupid, is it not? That one single thing, something as simple as that can change the way you look at the world. I don't think I knew it at the time. I'm only starting to know it now."

Aisling cocks her head, waiting for him to carry on. He sees her hands twisting together.

"She asked me to take off the hook. Your sister...somehow, she reminded me that I was not one single thing. When she looks at me I do not see what I was, but what I could be."

Aisling nods and thinks over his words. "What about when you look at her? You must understand Mr...Hook - that my sister had been through a lot. More than one person should go through. If you're here, with her, because you believe she is the key to placing you once more in the world, then who is to say you won't leave her; whenever you become the thing you think you can now be?"

Hook accepts this and just like Aisling, seriously thinks about the point. She was an academic, he was careful. They both were measured and calm.

"Where would I go?" He says simply. "I've seen the world, Mrs Fairchild. I have no need to travel now. My wanderings, I think, are done. I have no desire to be anywhere but here. When I look into the endless possibilities of this world, the wonders that have been invented since I last walked here, when I think about who I want to become, I think only of this house. You might take that as you wish."

Aisling smiles a very small smile that doesn't reach her eyes. "You know, I believe you."

"Thank you." He smiles.

She sighs and looks around the room. "It will take a long time. You understand that, don't you? You may be eager to shed your former life, but my sister...it will take a long time."

"For me also." He says. "But I am practiced in the art of being patient. Besides, I have a lot more learning to do. I shall be focusing on that, first and foremost. Anything else that happens, well then it happens. If it does not, then it does not. And we shall carry on happily as we are."

"Good answer." Aisling says. This time when she smiles, she means it.

She's about to close behind her when she turns back to him. "Hook wasn't always your name, was it? If names are so important, what will yours be now?"

James hadn't given it any thought. He didn't know if he could be the person he'd been before. But he could try. Maybe that was how it was always going to start with him. With a name.

"I suppose I'll go back the name I was born with."

"So, James. What is your name?"

"Flint." He says. "My name is James Flint."

When Aisling gets back down stairs, Clare is passive aggressively ignoring her by very aggressively doing the washing up.

She's slamming the mugs into water, sloshing the suds around the sink and the worktop furiously. Aisling rolls her eyes, grabs a tea towel and joins her sister. The sink looks out of the window, over the vegetable garden, over the wall to the hills beyond. Nothing but blue sky. Bronte country, God's own country. The kind of land she read poems about but rarely ever saw for herself. She's starting to understand how someone could exist here for so long. Then, she's always understood Clare above all others.

"What's wrong?" she asks plainly.

"Nothing." Clare whimpers, trying to be casual and failing completely.

"I know you're annoyed because you've got a face on."

"I have not got a face on." Clare mutters. When she almost drops a mug by pushing it roughly into the tea towel Aisling holds out to her, she sighs heavily.

"Is this possibly because I went to go talk to your man?" Aisling nudges her.

"He isn't my man."

"Yes he is. He's your kept man."

"Please stop it. Besides, he isn't a prisoner. He can talk to whoever he likes."

Clare catches the glint in her sister's eye and they both end up laughing. Clare shakes her head.

"You forget, my dear little sister, you could never lie to me."

It was true. Ever since they were children, Aisling had read her more easily than she had anyone else. Jude, her husband, wore his heart on his sleeve, and in his eyes. He was an open book and he didn't care who knew it. Carys was still waters that ran deep, and she kept everything to herself as much as possible. Clare was the one Aisling could see clearest, even when she was trying to hide from her.

"Well then, big sister, what did you two talk about?"

"You, mostly." Aisling shrugged.

Clare looked up sharply and glanced away just as quick, trying to hide her blushes in her hair. They continued to do the washing up in silence for a few moments.

"I like him." Aisling said. She said everything in a sort of matter of fact way, which meant she always sounded sincere. There was no mincing her words or pretending with Aisling. Everything came out how she meant it. And, if she didn't know how to help or what to say, she told you that too. "He seems a steady sort of fellow. He's very calm. For a pirate."

"Yes – he is rather, isn't he?" Clare jumped in with a smile. Aisling gets the impression she'd wanted to have this chat for a while. "I like that, I think. Sometimes my brain feels like it's on fire. He seems to slow everything down for me. I don't know why." She looked up at her sister plaintively. "Does that sound silly?"

"No. I know exactly how you feel. I feel that way about Jude. He makes things...make sense." Aisling confided. She didn't often talk about her marriage. It was a good one, but it was hers. A marriage is a world shared by two, and two alone. It had its own language, its own culture, and its own wars. She found it hard to explain to other people. Clare had always been one of those people who wanted you to know just how in love she was. Aisling was not.

"He's not like Michael at all, is he?" Clare says, musing. She's been talking about Michàel a lot more now. Aisling thinks it's probably good for her. She's talking about him, acknowledging him and letting the memory of him breathe. Like taking a bandage off a wound to let it heal.

"I think he is where it counts. In terms of being a decent person, anyway. But no, he isn't like Michael. Michael was...loud. And tall."

"James is tall, Aisling, you just saw him lying down."

"I don't actually mean tall. I just mean...Michael was a force of nature. He took up space, he – well you know better than I do. He never seemed to stop. He wasn't calm. He certainly wasn't careful."

Clare stares into the murky dishwater and Aisling bites her lip. "I didn't mean, you know. The accident. I just meant..."

"No, I know what you meant, Ash. And you're right. He wasn't careful. He did things without thinking – like me. I get the impression that James doesn't do anything without thinking. He probably needs a six step program just to go to the toilet."

They burst out laughing, and Aisling sees Clare's shoulders relax. She still looks too thin, but she's getting some colour back. Some spark. It's nice.

She thinks of the man upstairs, a pirate, a man from the sea, a man of myth. She thinks of her sister, whose losses remoulded her. She thinks that perhaps they can shape each other again. Two people that looked into the eye of a storm, and did not return the same. Aisling was beginning to understand that we need different people at different times and that that was ok - just as Carys needed Clare in her seventeenth year, as she'd needed Aisling for all the ones before. Now Clare needed James when she needed gentility and softness, when before she had needed all the rough beauty of life that Michael had brought.

"It was Mary Shelley who said, "Misery had made me a fiend. Make me happy, and I shall again be virtuous."

Clare shot her a scornful look. "Now I know where Carys gets it from."

Aisling squared her shoulders, smiling proudly. "What I mean is one would expect a pirate to be raging up there. But he's not, is he? I rather think circumstance shaped him into a soldier, and now he's back in the real world he can start to live properly again. And so can you."

Clare nods, and then she can't stop nodding, then she's sniffling, and then her face crumples, and then she is crying into Aisling's shoulder. She is crying happy tears and sad tears, both.

Aisling shushes her. She had done this many times before. She smooth's down the wild tangle of Clare's hair and pats her back until Clare removes herself, stepping back with a hiccup. "I'd really like to." She said in a rushed, desperate whisper. "I'd like to do that."

"I know you would darling. And you will. You'll just be doing it with a one handed pirate alongside."

"So...he said that, did he? He's going to stay here. Or something." Clare tries not to sound too hopeful. She knew Carys wouldn't always be here. The thought of being alone again, of becoming whatever she had been before, fills her with a cold dread.

"Not in so many words. But where else is he going to go? He's from the seventeen hundreds Clare, it's not as if he has a passport." Aisling smiles knowingly, deciding to put her baby sister out of her misery. "He likes you. Really and properly likes you. I could tell. He isn't going anywhere until you tell him to. Think about it, Clare bear. You pulled him across worlds because you didn't want him to die. I think he'd do the same for you. I might be a stuffy old scholar, but I know what feelings look like."

"You're not old." Clare grinned.

"But I am a stuffy scholar?"

"You're words, not mine, dear heart!"

They turn back to the sink as Aisling throws her tea towel at Clare, who throws it straight back, getting a good face shot in.

"Besides," Aisling continues, "He's very handsome. And he's willing to accept your depressing, hermitic life style. So I'd say he's a keeper."

28

Daylight

Carrie breathed in deeply, inhaling the cool breeze, the scent of the crisp leaves and the soil of the vegetable garden she walked through.

When she reaches the end of the garden, slipping easily through the gap in the old stone wall, she turns back to look at the house.

How could she ever have hated this place?

It was so tall and wide, dark stone stretching up like it wanted to feel the clouds. It had changed her life. But here it still stood, sentinel on the hill.

She began walking, letting her feet carry her at whatever languid pace they wished. Despite all those treks up mountains and through jungles, she still loved walking, especially on sunny days like this one.

She thinks absently about everything that had happened to her over the last two or three months. She had come to this house broken, alone, and she was here now, if not whole, at least a little more hopeful.

She had felt so lost before she came here. Nothing made sense, nothing filled her with purpose. She would read books where heroes swooped in to save the day, where adventures occurred to save the characters from their boring, everyday lives. She had never dreamed it would happen to her. But what she was realizing was that the stories don't end with the last chapter. They keep going, even when the last page of the book has been read.

After all, what was the point of the adventure, if not to find a way to keep living afterwards?

Before she came here, she had been so scared of her future. She had not been able to see it. It had been a terrifying void that she couldn't imagine. Now, whilst she was still gripped occasionally by that same fear, she was at least beginning to want to see what it held for her. Beginning to form that darkness into some kind of shape. Beginning to imagine the places she wanted to go, and the people she wanted to be with. It wasn't a lot, and it may not come to pass. But it was a start, and she clung to it with a fervour.

When they had arrived – tumbling through a wall at her mothers feet – it had seemed like an impossible change. Impossible to go back, once you have glimpsed magic. But seeing Perdy, Nala and James find joy in simple things, in being back in the world once more, made it easier for her to see it too. she'd spend so long wanting to come home – in part because it was familiar to her – that she hadn't thought of what she would do once she got here. And to make it even more complicated, her mother had arrived.

She had not been fair to her mother. This thought made her stomach twist with guilt. The girls had all been given their own rooms in the house, but as they had done during Pan's storms, she, Perdy and Nala ended up having sleepovers in the same room every night at first. They had helped her, talked to her. They had helped her see things a little more clearly. Nala with her simple, unfailing support and Perdy, with her love, her big eyes and her jokes.

Perdy had reminded her about having to give up her own daughter. Sometimes, she'd told her, parents don't feel able to take care of their kids. It wasn't to the same degree, but maybe Aisling had been so afraid of doing the wrong thing that she'd sent her to someone she thought would do a better job. It was never going to be forever, though Carrie had convinced herself that it was. It might have been wrong, but it had been done out of love. When she'd said all this, Carrie knew Perdy was talking about Emmeline too. if Carrie could understand what she had done, she could try and understand her mother too. Perdy said that she would ask Emmeline's forgiveness, if she ever got the chance. Forgiveness was a gift you have to the people you loved. Carrie had to forgive herself, as well. She was trying very hard to do that.

She'd sat with her mum at the kitchen table. Clare had crept out being unsubtle as ever. Barely ten second later she'd hissed a sorry as she came back to grab the cup of tea she'd left. Carrie and her mum couldn't help but laugh. It was hard to talk at first. They weren't a very talkative family. But they managed, haltingly, and cried a little bit. And Carrie had to admit that whilst she had felt angry at first at being sent on holiday here, it had given her a lot. So she was grateful, too. She found she was grateful on Clare's behalf as well. She didn't see how much better she was already. She was never going to be completely ok. Aisling admitted she sometimes wondered if she ever had been – they were attributing Clare's ways to the loss of Michael, but in truth it reached back further. They all had a lot to face up to, in time. Had a lot to talk about. A lot of things to try and find the words for, to try and heal. It might take them all years.

The echo that had been Michael, that day by the painting, had not returned to the house. In truth it was still debatable as to its origins. It wasn't definite that Clare hadn't imagined it. But whatever it was had gone. Clare insisted it had been him – maybe not a ghost, but some part of him at least – and that he had arrived when she'd needed him most. She was tirelessly convincing herself that since he had not come back, he trusted her enough to be alright from now on. Since it was helping her, and it might very well be true, no one was talking her out of this belief.

Nala especially had listened to her. Nala was very good at that, and her absence from the house now was going to be palpable to her sisters for a long time. She had stayed with them for as long as it took to settle back into life. She had cried when she had found out what had happened to her part of the world in the twenty or so years since she had been there. She had cried too, when turning once to speak to Willow or Peaches and finding that they were not there. She decided that the best way for her to cope was to find a way to live with herself again. She had been relearning the prayers she had forgotten. She didn't have as much of the world to relearn as the others, and had made the decision to start her travels as soon as possible. She was starting small, going only around Britain. She had a mobile – they all did – and kept texting Carrie pictures of art and cats that she saw. She seemed happy.

Carrie saw Perdy in the distance, sat on the grass, staring out over the rolling hills that went on forever. A few miles off there was a village proper, with cars and tea shops and people. But right there on the hills, it was hard to imagine there was anything else in the world.

She smacked down next to Perdy, out of breath, bringing her knees up to her chest. The sun was beating down on them and she lifted her face up to it for a moment. There was a peaceful, comfortable silence.

"Do you think we'll go to the village soon? I want to know if they have bookshops." Carrie shrugged.

Perdy had been closing her eyes, and now she squinted, one eye open. "Seen as you aunt can only venture as far as her garden wall, I'm going to say it might be a solo adventure."

Carrie slumped her shoulders petulantly. "It's been a month. Don't you want to see what's out there? I bet it isn't even as different to how it was in the fifties. We still have..." she waved her hand, trying to think of things she associated with Perdy's original time. "Milkshakes. Diners. Racism."

Perdy laughed. "I promised James I would wait for him."

This at least Carrie knew to be true. Considering the fact their individual groups had been apathetic toward one another, if not enemies, for the last couple of decades at least, Perdy and Hook

– James – had found a strange kind of kinship in the time since they had come back to the house.

Clare was still not ready to venture out into the world, and neither was James. Though he was eager to learn about everything that he had missed, when it came to applying it practically he seemed to falter. As if seeing pictures and knowing what to expect was a completely different thing to being in the world itself – which it was, of course. So he was working on it. So far he'd made it to the ground floor of the house, so Carrie thought he'd be ready to go two miles down the road in about fifty years.

He'd asked Perdy to go with him, whenever that did happen, since they both were going to be experiencing the world post 2000 for the first time. She was currently using this as an excuse not to go. For now Carrie supposed she better let her.

"Mum says we're gonna talk about school." Carrie said breezily. "My dad's going to come down when his lecture post finishes in two weeks. Then we're going to see where I'm going to go. You know, soon I might be going to university. After my gap year, obviously."

"I thought you said you might not go to university." Perdy frowned at her, looking at her properly for a moment.

"I might not be. I'm just telling you that it's still an option I am considering."

Perdy stared at her legs that were stretched out in front of her. Her palms were behind her in the grass propping her up.

"So, you're giving me a time limit?" She didn't look up. She was wearing jeans and a plain pink t shirt. Carrie didn't think she'd ever see her in anything not made from black leather.

"No, and you know I'm not." Carrie nudged her, and when Perdy looked up at her she saw no vehemence in her face. She looked sad. "I'm just saying that at some point we're going to have to think about what comes next. I know it's all frightening, and that you need time, but we didn't escape from one place just to get stuck in another."

Perdy nodded. Carrie knew exactly what she was putting off, and it wasn't just going out into the world.

Carrie had retrieved the photo from Michael's study (they had all agreed to stop calling it 'the room' since it was a melodramatic reminder of what it had turned into, rather than what it had been. Calling it Michael's study meant they mentioned his name more, and it made it easier for Clare to cope with that.) The photo she had found in the library, the day al of this had been set in motion. Of Emmeline as a schoolgirl, hugging her friend outside of this very house. She'd given it to Perdy, who had put it beside her bed. They had looked through the public records, to find out what had happened to Emmeline Scott.

Emmeline Isabelle Scott was still alive. She lived in Kent, with her husband. She'd been a secretary, then she'd owned her own shop. This was all quite remarkable, considering she'd been doing this in the sixties after growing up in an orphanage. Her haberdashery shop chain had been quite successful for a number of years. Successful enough that her three children – Perdy's grandchildren – had had happy, fulfilled lives of their own. She'd had two girls and a boy. The older girl and the boy both had kids too, which made Perdy a great grandmother.

She kept the information packet tucked under her mattress. It was all public record, printed from Clare's old printer, making streaks and blots on some of the pages. But it was precious still.

Perdy had decided for now, she wasn't going to approach her daughter. She didn't know how. How did an eighteen-year-old girl turning up on your doorstep after sixty years claiming to be your long lost mother help anyone? But Carrie urged her to think about it. They didn't have to talk to Emmeline. They could just go see where she lived or something. Perdy was tempted, but she pushed it all away. After she'd been nursing all that pain over so many years, to expect her to change overnight was ridiculous. But Carrie wanted her just to know she had the option. That Carrie would go with her, if she ever decided to find her daughter.

She does think though, that there's a strong chance this won't ever happen. It definitely wouldn't happen for a long time. Emmeline seemed happy, and that was what was important. Perdy still bore the scars and shame of the things that had happened on the island. She wouldn't bring that darkness to her girls doorstep.

It was not clear if Perdy would ever truly recover from the years on the island. She was still wary, still quick to jump and tense at sudden noises. All they could do was be there for one another. Carrie still thought about the fight on the boat, at seeing Pan die, at leaving Willow and Peaches, though it had been their choice. She still thought about almost dying in the mermaid's pool.

They were going to learn how to carry those experiences, and they were going to learn to do it together. She knew that much, even if she didn't know exactly what the future held for them both.

She knew Clare was starting to open up again, to open the house, to live in it rather than wander it like a ghost. She'd hung pictures up. She'd been drawing. She knew James was slowly coming to terms with the new world in which he found himself, knew that he and Clare were going to take care of each other, and that the house in turn would take car of them both.

She knew her mother and father were coming to get her, finally, and that they didn't mind whether she went to school or not, as long as she was happy.

She knew Willow and Peaches were going to look out for each other, but hoped they wouldn't have to as much, and that peace could be restored to that island once more. That Wild Rose, Selene, the remaining girls and boys and the fairies could learn to live together.

To reassure you, readers – they did find a way. It's sad that Carrie and Perdy did not know this, did not know the harmony they brought to the island – but we may rest assured with that knowledge at least.

Carrie knew also that whilst her sad nights, her dark nights, were not entirely behind her, she was ready to look forward into the light again, with someone she loved by her side.

She and Perdy looked at each other again and smiled.

Carrie looked out across the hills once more, into the bright blue sky, and onwards, into forever, into the daylight.

There was a question posed, a story ago.

Where do they go, the lost, the searching, the children with no path?

They don't all go to the island. Some of them find their own islands, their own tribes. They are out there, everywhere, families and friends you never knew you needed until you have them.

And their stories do not end, just as this does not end. Nothing we love really ends. There would be more adventures for Carys, for Clare, for the people who love them and follow them anywhere. More stories.

This story was the first chapter – It has travelled a long way to find you. Through time and memory, through wishes and dreams. Stories can do that, you know. I hope they keep doing it. I hope your story gets howled into the wind, and carried to the hearts that need to hear it. I hope you always keep looking into the daylight, and to the next awfully big adventure.

Printed in Great Britain
by Amazon

81198177R00159